WITHDRAWN

ELSEWHERE

CREATED BY
JAY FAERBER & SUMEYYE KESGIN

IMAGE COMICS, INC.

Robert Kirkman—Chief Operating Officer
Erik Larsen—Chief Financial Officer
Todd McFarlane—President
Marc Silvestri—Chief Executive Officer
Jim Valentino—Vice President
Eric Stephenson—Publisher /
           Chief Creative Officer
Corey Hart—Director of Sales
Jeff Boison—Director of Publishing Planning
           & Book Trade Sales
Chris Ross—Director of Digital Sales
Jeff Stang—Director of Specialty Sales
Kat Salazar—Director of PR & Marketing
Drew Gill—Art Director
Heather Doornink—Production Director
Nicole Lapalme—Controller

www.imagecomics.com

ELSEWHERE, VOL. 2
ISBN: 978-1-5343-0689-9
First Printing. September 2018.

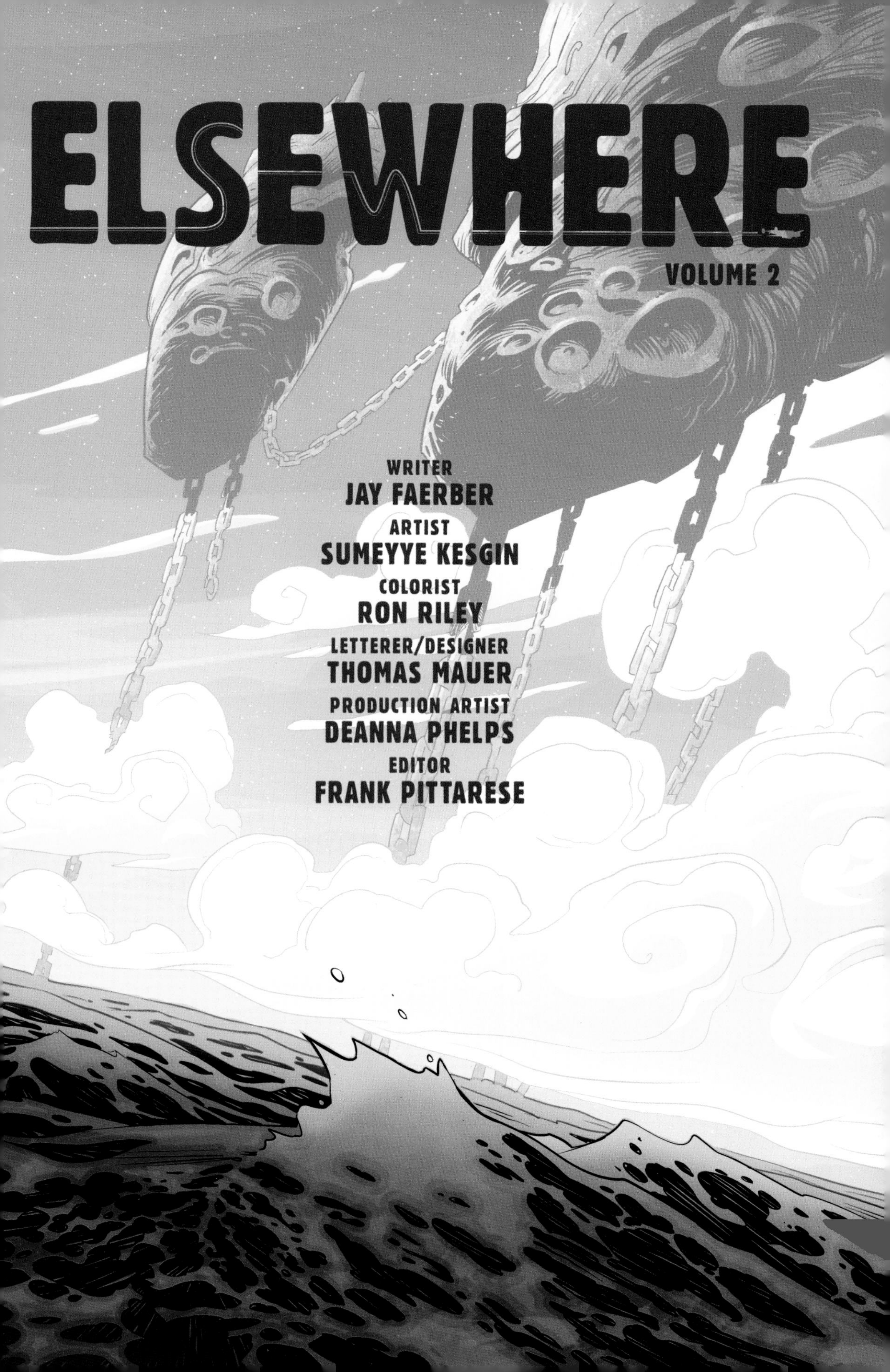

ELSEWHERE

VOLUME 2

WRITER
JAY FAERBER

ARTIST
SUMEYYE KESGIN

COLORIST
RON RILEY

LETTERER/DESIGNER
THOMAS MAUER

PRODUCTION ARTIST
DEANNA PHELPS

EDITOR
FRANK PITTARESE

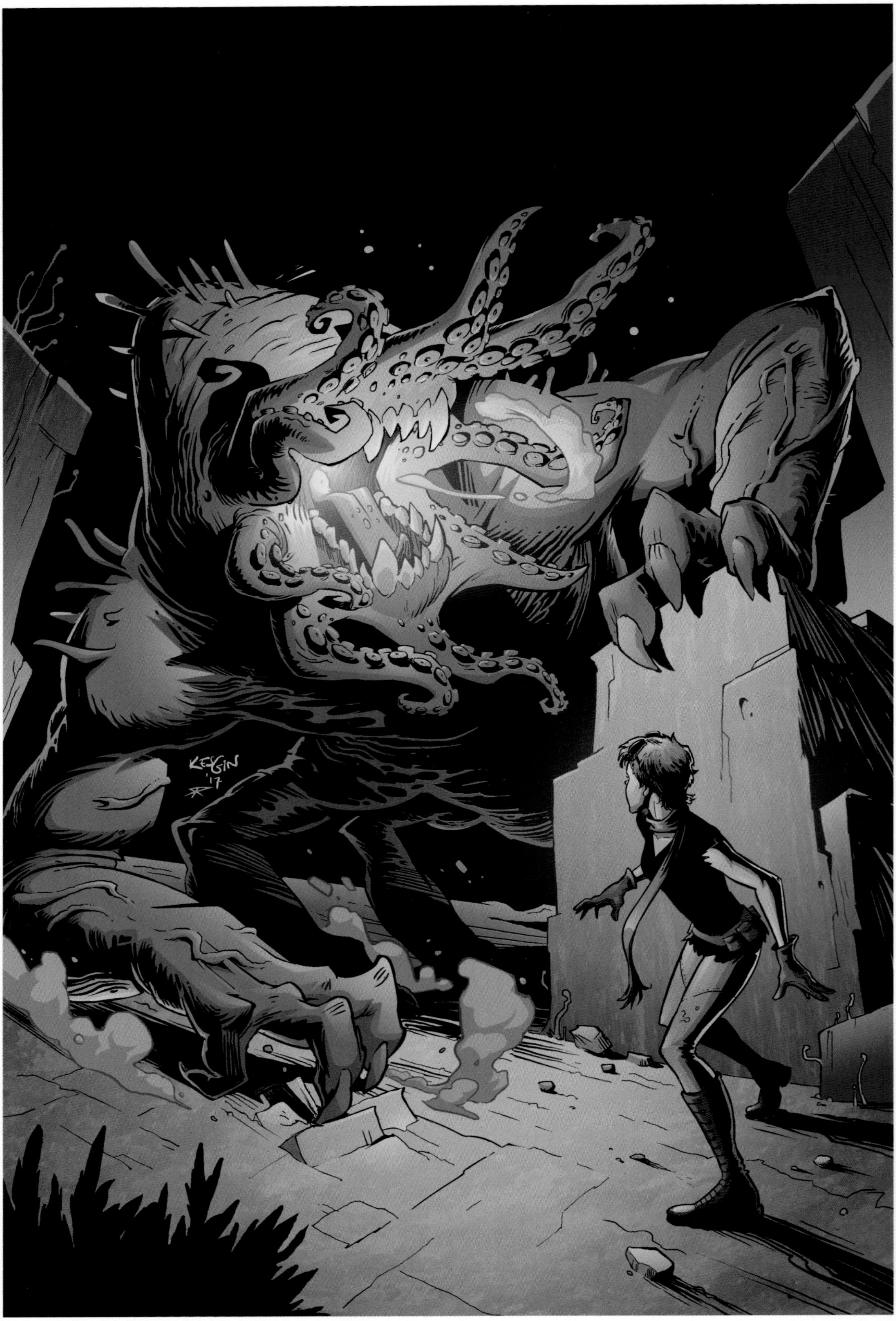

CHAPTER 1

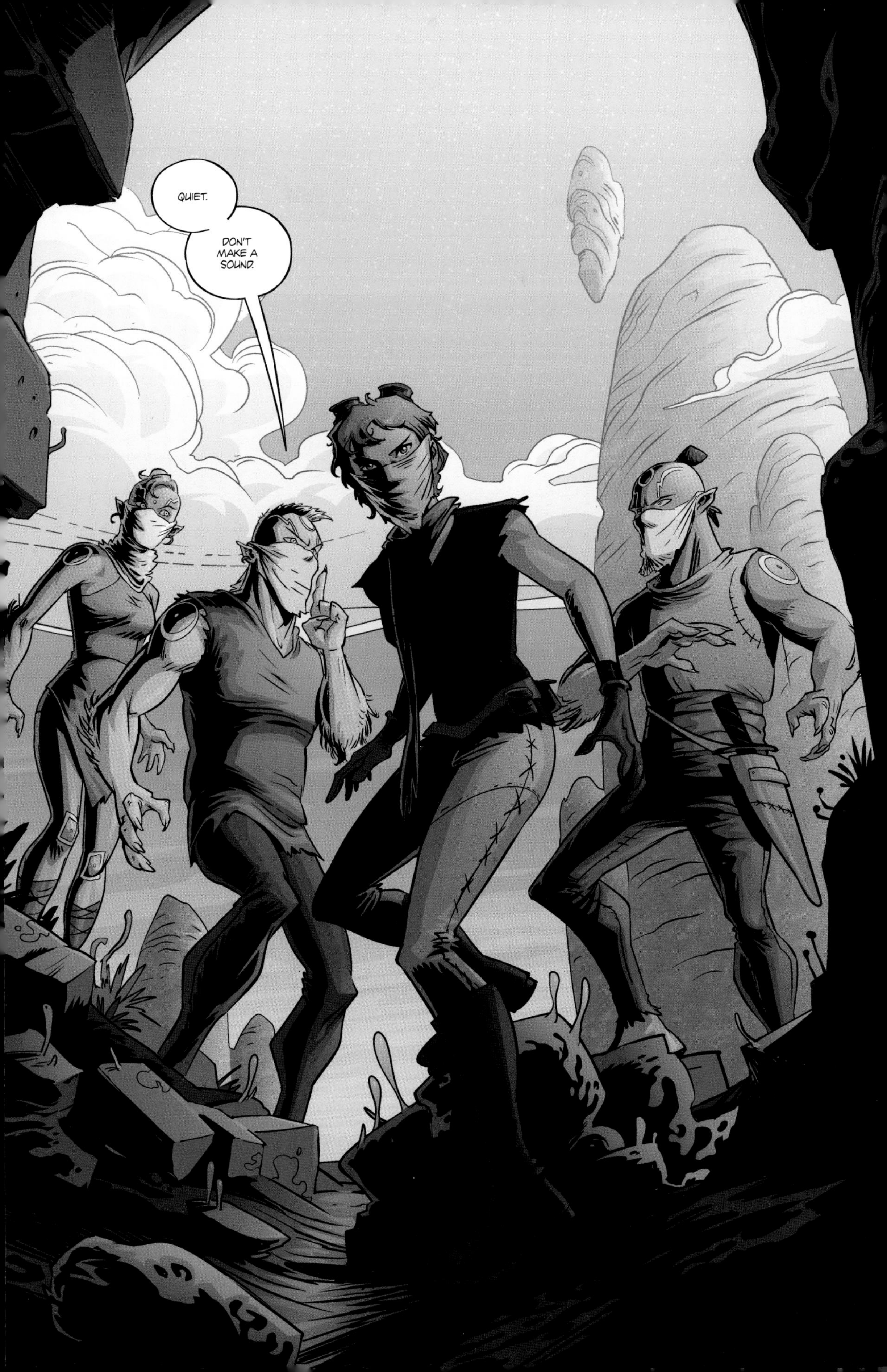
QUIET.
DON'T MAKE A SOUND.

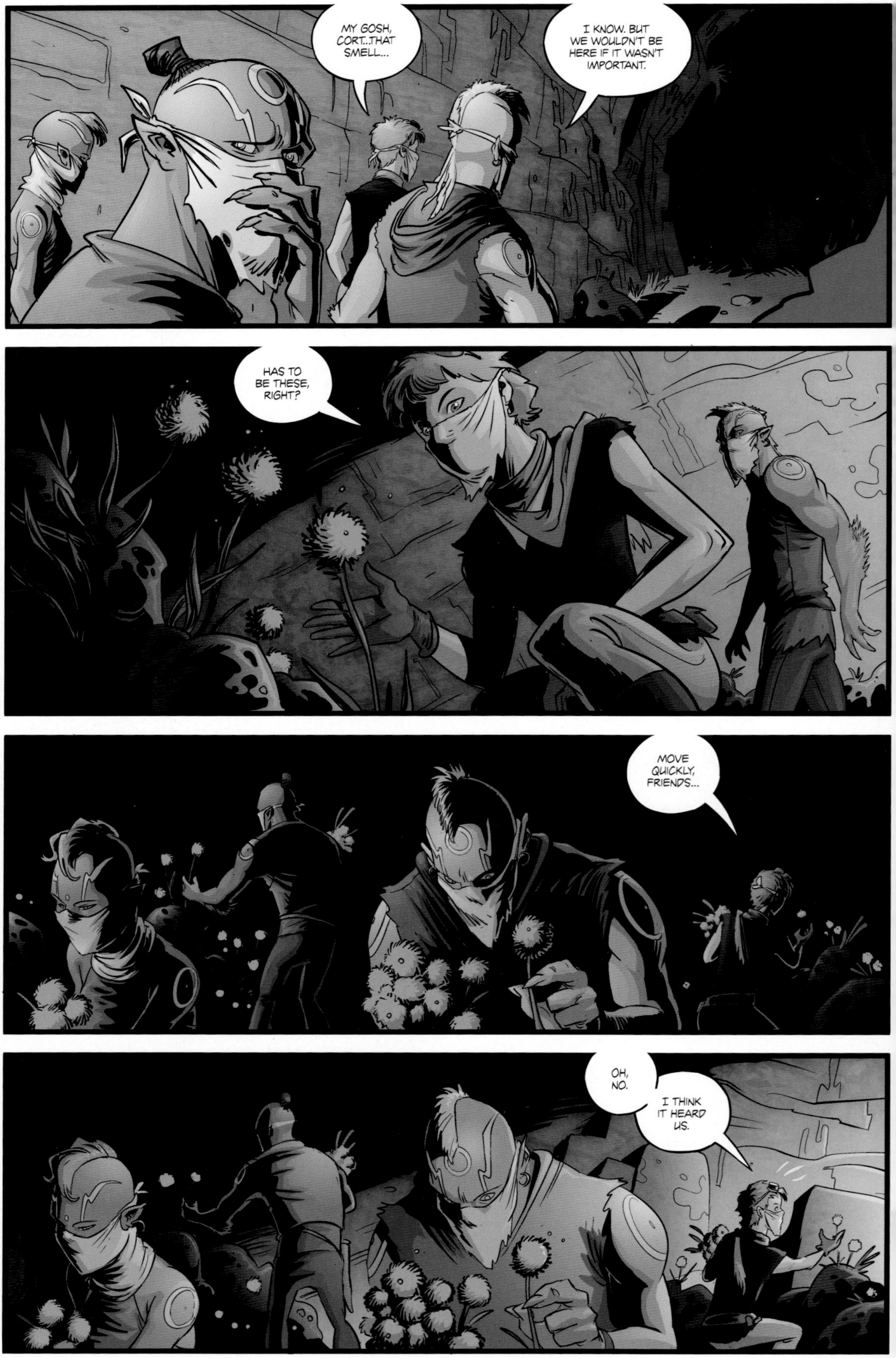
MY GOSH, CORT...THAT SMELL...
I KNOW. BUT WE WOULDN'T BE HERE IF IT WASN'T IMPORTANT.
HAS TO BE THESE, RIGHT?
MOVE QUICKLY, FRIENDS...
OH, NO.
I THINK IT HEARD US.

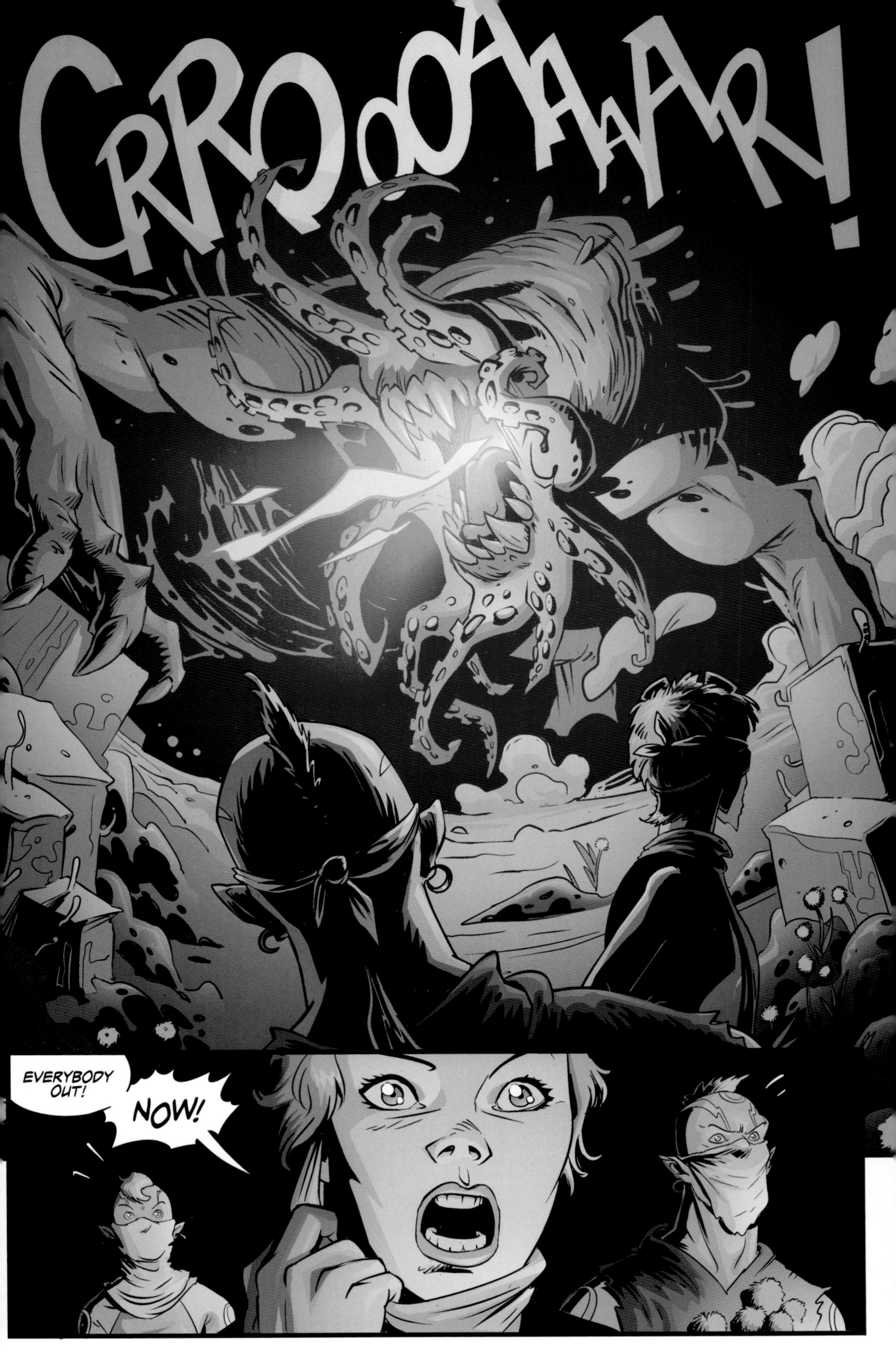
CRROOOAAAAR!
EVERYBODY OUT!
NOW!

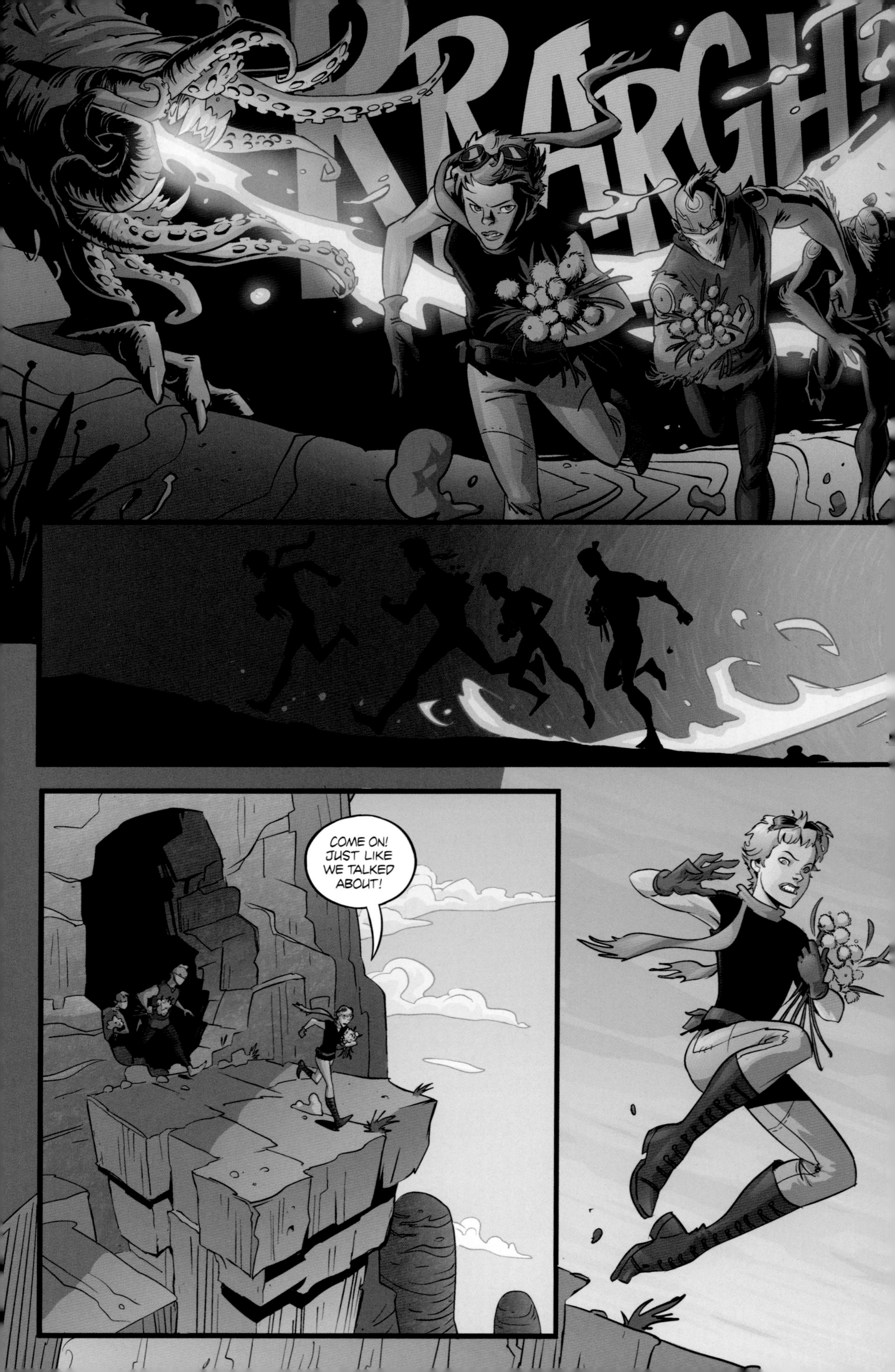
WRARGH!
COME ON! JUST LIKE WE TALKED ABOUT!

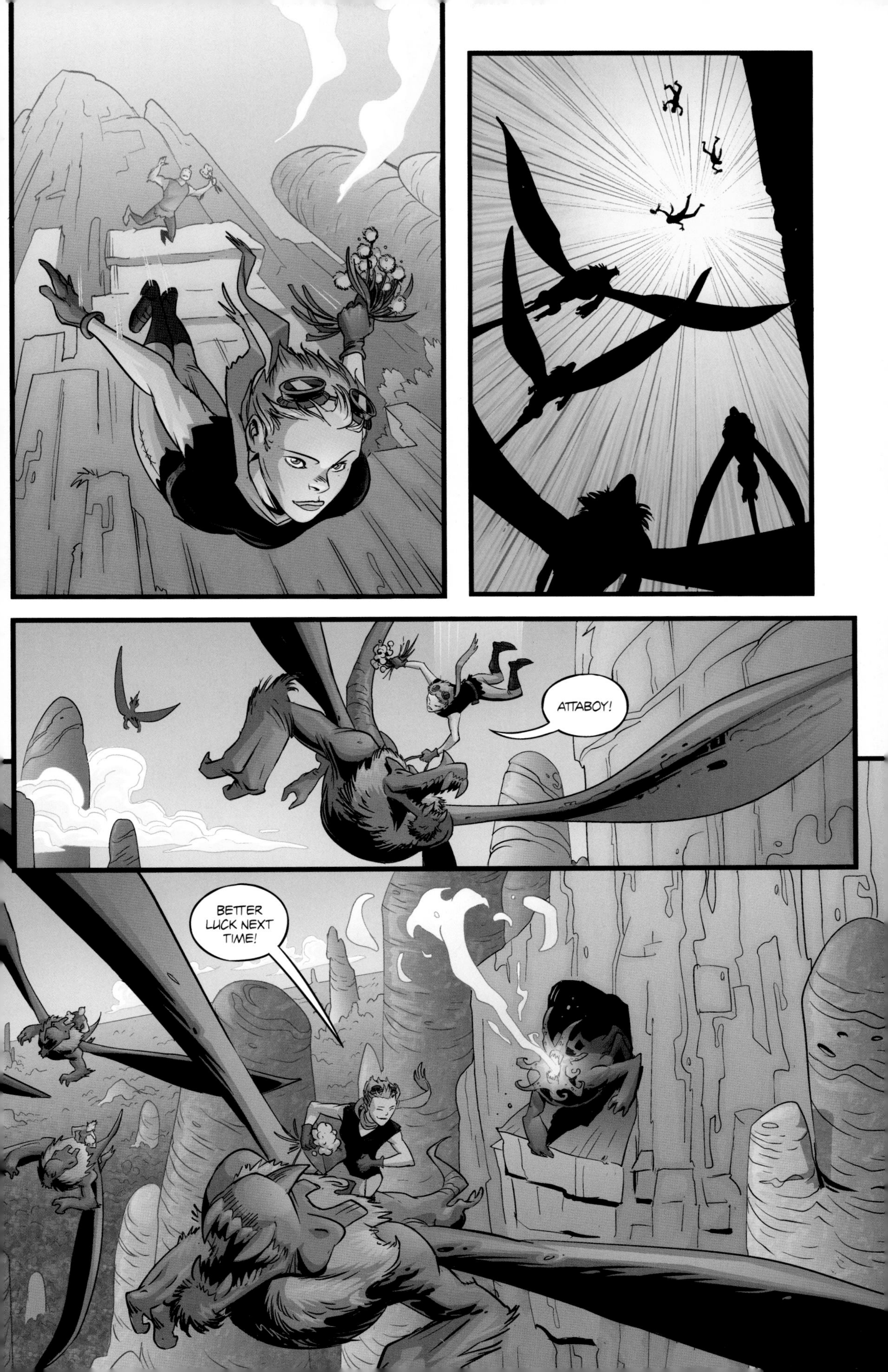
ATTABOY!
BETTER LUCK NEXT TIME!

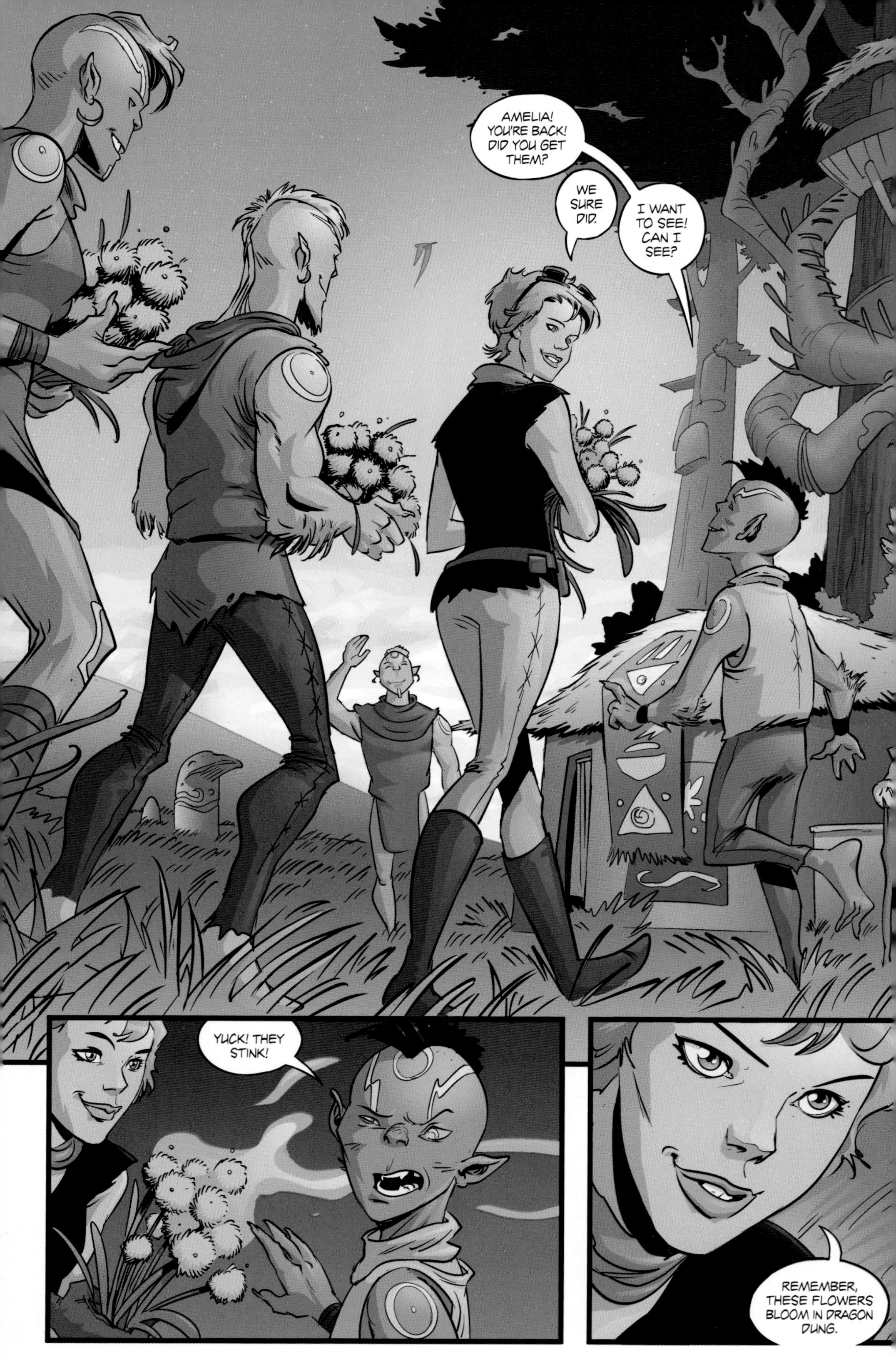
AMELIA! YOU'RE BACK! DID YOU GET THEM?
WE SURE DID.
I WANT TO SEE! CAN I SEE?
YUCK! THEY STINK!
REMEMBER, THESE FLOWERS BLOOM IN DRAGON DUNG.

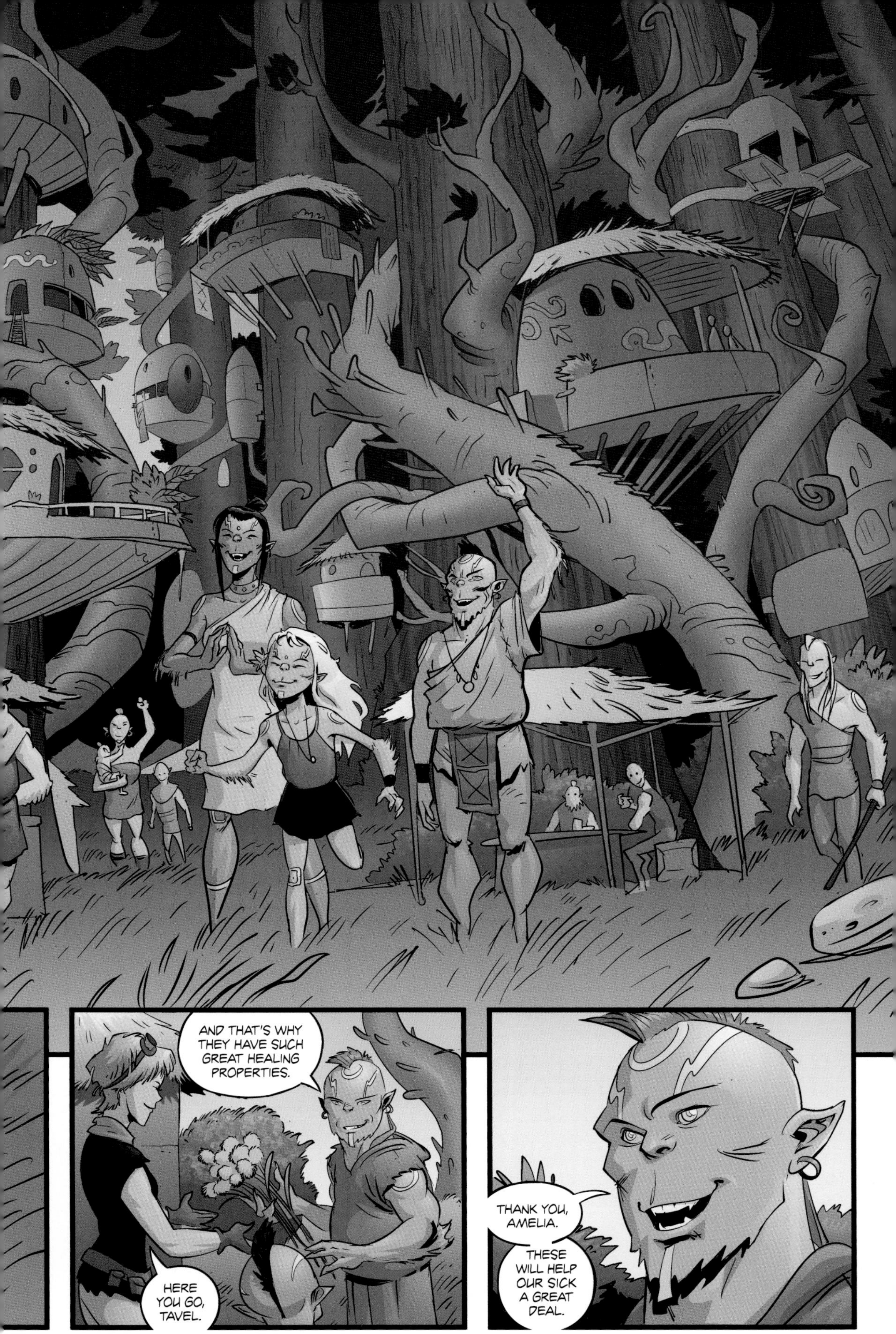
AND THAT'S WHY THEY HAVE SUCH GREAT HEALING PROPERTIES.
HERE YOU GO, TAVEL.
THANK YOU, AMELIA.
THESE WILL HELP OUR SICK A GREAT DEAL.

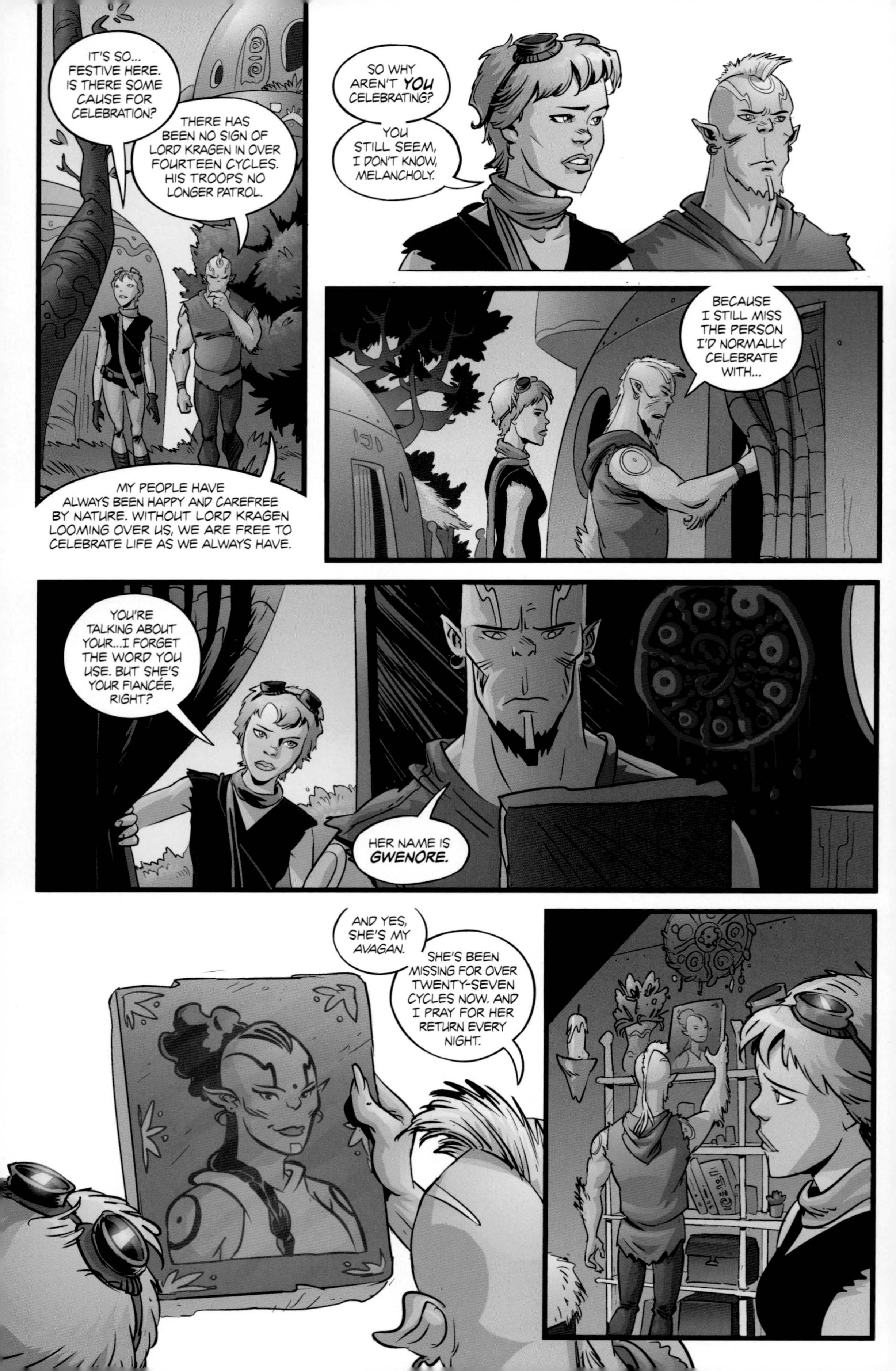
IT'S SO... FESTIVE HERE. IS THERE SOME CAUSE FOR CELEBRATION?
THERE HAS BEEN NO SIGN OF LORD KRAGEN IN OVER FOURTEEN CYCLES. HIS TROOPS NO LONGER PATROL.
MY PEOPLE HAVE ALWAYS BEEN HAPPY AND CAREFREE BY NATURE. WITHOUT LORD KRAGEN LOOMING OVER US, WE ARE FREE TO CELEBRATE LIFE AS WE ALWAYS HAVE.
SO WHY AREN'T **YOU** CELEBRATING?
YOU STILL SEEM, I DON'T KNOW, MELANCHOLY.
BECAUSE I STILL MISS THE PERSON I'D NORMALLY CELEBRATE WITH...
YOU'RE TALKING ABOUT YOUR...I FORGET THE WORD YOU USE. BUT SHE'S YOUR FIANCÉE, RIGHT?
HER NAME IS **GWENORE.**
AND YES, SHE'S MY AVAGAN.
SHE'S BEEN MISSING FOR OVER TWENTY-SEVEN CYCLES NOW. AND I PRAY FOR HER RETURN EVERY NIGHT.

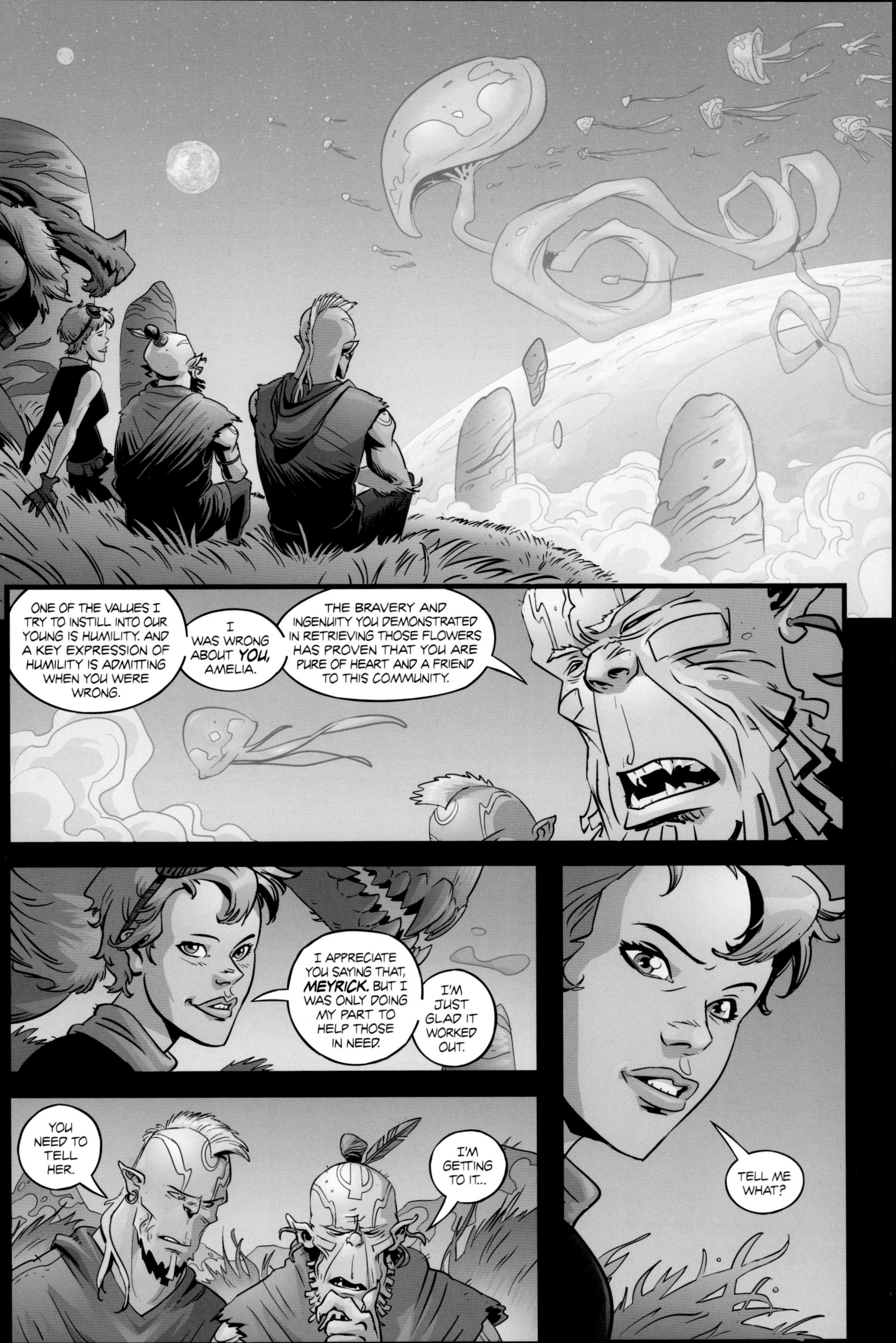
ONE OF THE VALUES I TRY TO INSTILL INTO OUR YOUNG IS HUMILITY. AND A KEY EXPRESSION OF HUMILITY IS ADMITTING WHEN YOU WERE WRONG.
I WAS WRONG ABOUT **YOU,** AMELIA.
THE BRAVERY AND INGENUITY YOU DEMONSTRATED IN RETRIEVING THOSE FLOWERS HAS PROVEN THAT YOU ARE PURE OF HEART AND A FRIEND TO THIS COMMUNITY.
I APPRECIATE YOU SAYING THAT, **MEYRICK.** BUT I WAS ONLY DOING MY PART TO HELP THOSE IN NEED.
I'M JUST GLAD IT WORKED OUT.
YOU NEED TO TELL HER.
I'M GETTING TO IT...
TELL ME WHAT?

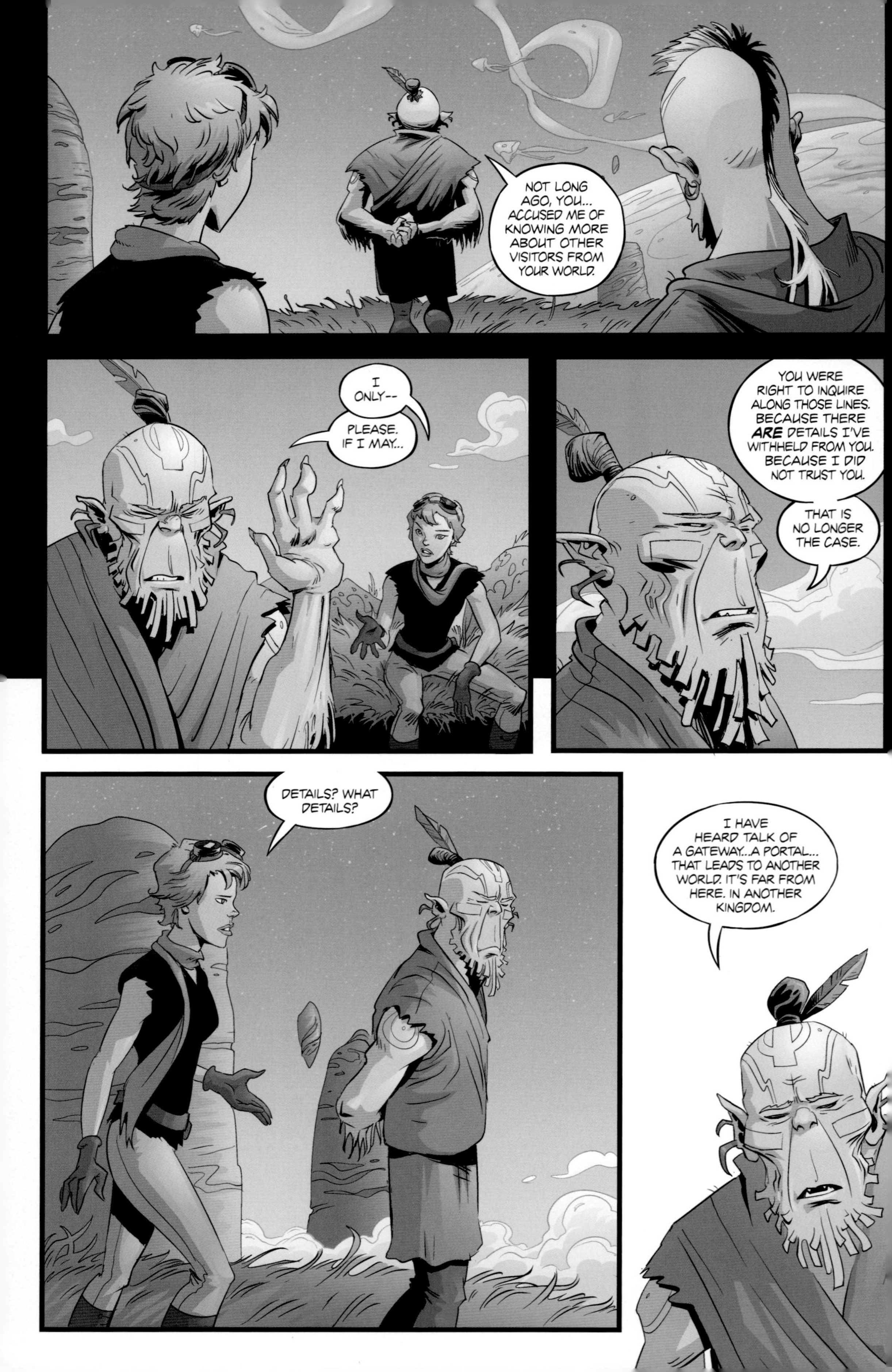
NOT LONG AGO, YOU... ACCUSED ME OF KNOWING MORE ABOUT OTHER VISITORS FROM YOUR WORLD.
I ONLY--
PLEASE. IF I MAY...
YOU WERE RIGHT TO INQUIRE ALONG THOSE LINES. BECAUSE THERE ARE DETAILS I'VE WITHHELD FROM YOU. BECAUSE I DID NOT TRUST YOU.
THAT IS NO LONGER THE CASE.
DETAILS? WHAT DETAILS?
I HAVE HEARD TALK OF A GATEWAY...A PORTAL... THAT LEADS TO ANOTHER WORLD. IT'S FAR FROM HERE. IN ANOTHER KINGDOM.

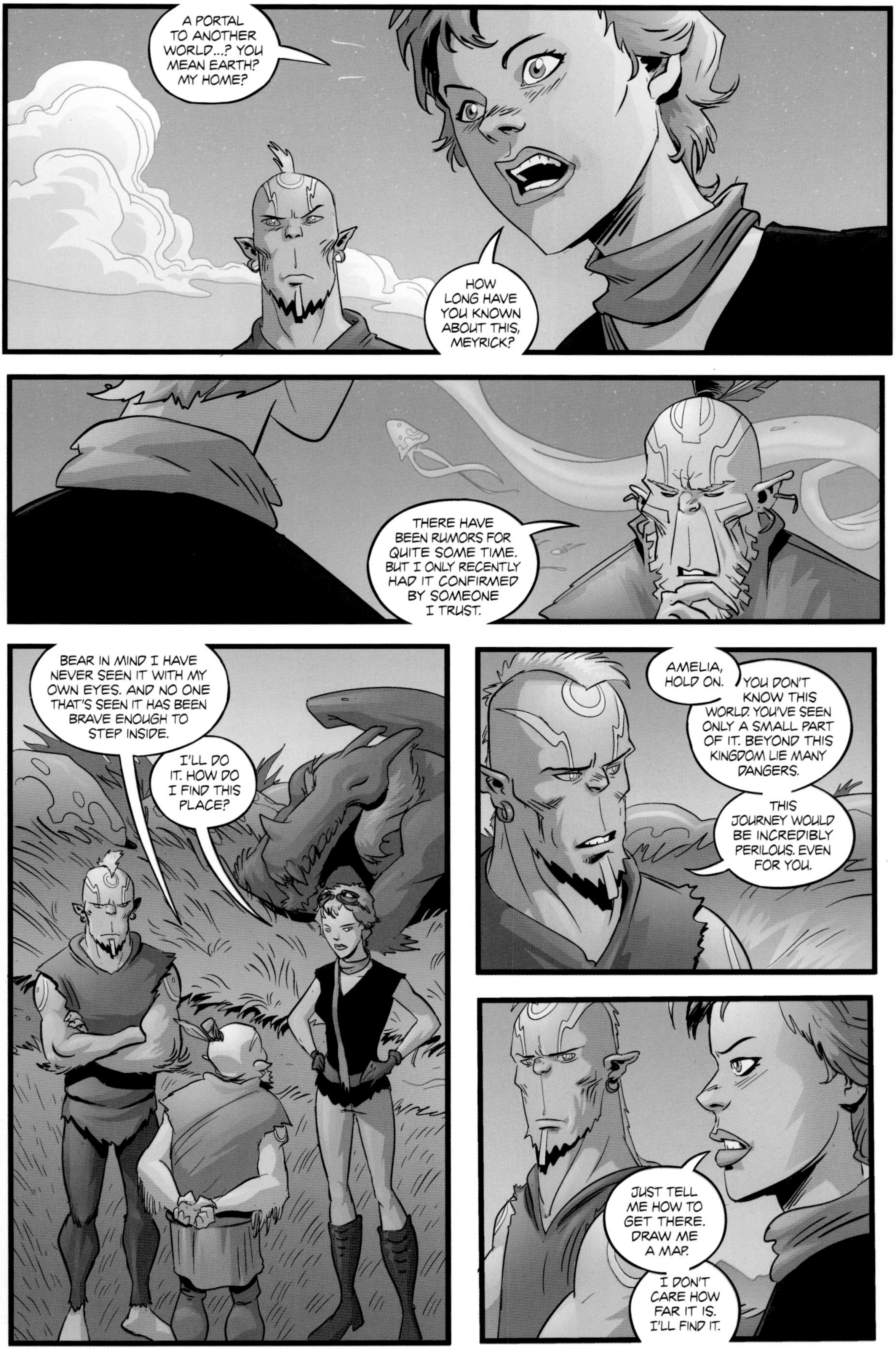
A PORTAL TO ANOTHER WORLD...? YOU MEAN EARTH? MY HOME?
HOW LONG HAVE YOU KNOWN ABOUT THIS, MEYRICK?
THERE HAVE BEEN RUMORS FOR QUITE SOME TIME. BUT I ONLY RECENTLY HAD IT CONFIRMED BY SOMEONE I TRUST.
BEAR IN MIND I HAVE NEVER SEEN IT WITH MY OWN EYES. AND NO ONE THAT'S SEEN IT HAS BEEN BRAVE ENOUGH TO STEP INSIDE.
I'LL DO IT. HOW DO I FIND THIS PLACE?
AMELIA, HOLD ON.
YOU DON'T KNOW THIS WORLD. YOU'VE SEEN ONLY A SMALL PART OF IT. BEYOND THIS KINGDOM LIE MANY DANGERS.
THIS JOURNEY WOULD BE INCREDIBLY PERILOUS. EVEN FOR YOU.
JUST TELL ME HOW TO GET THERE. DRAW ME A MAP.
I DON'T CARE HOW FAR IT IS. I'LL FIND IT.

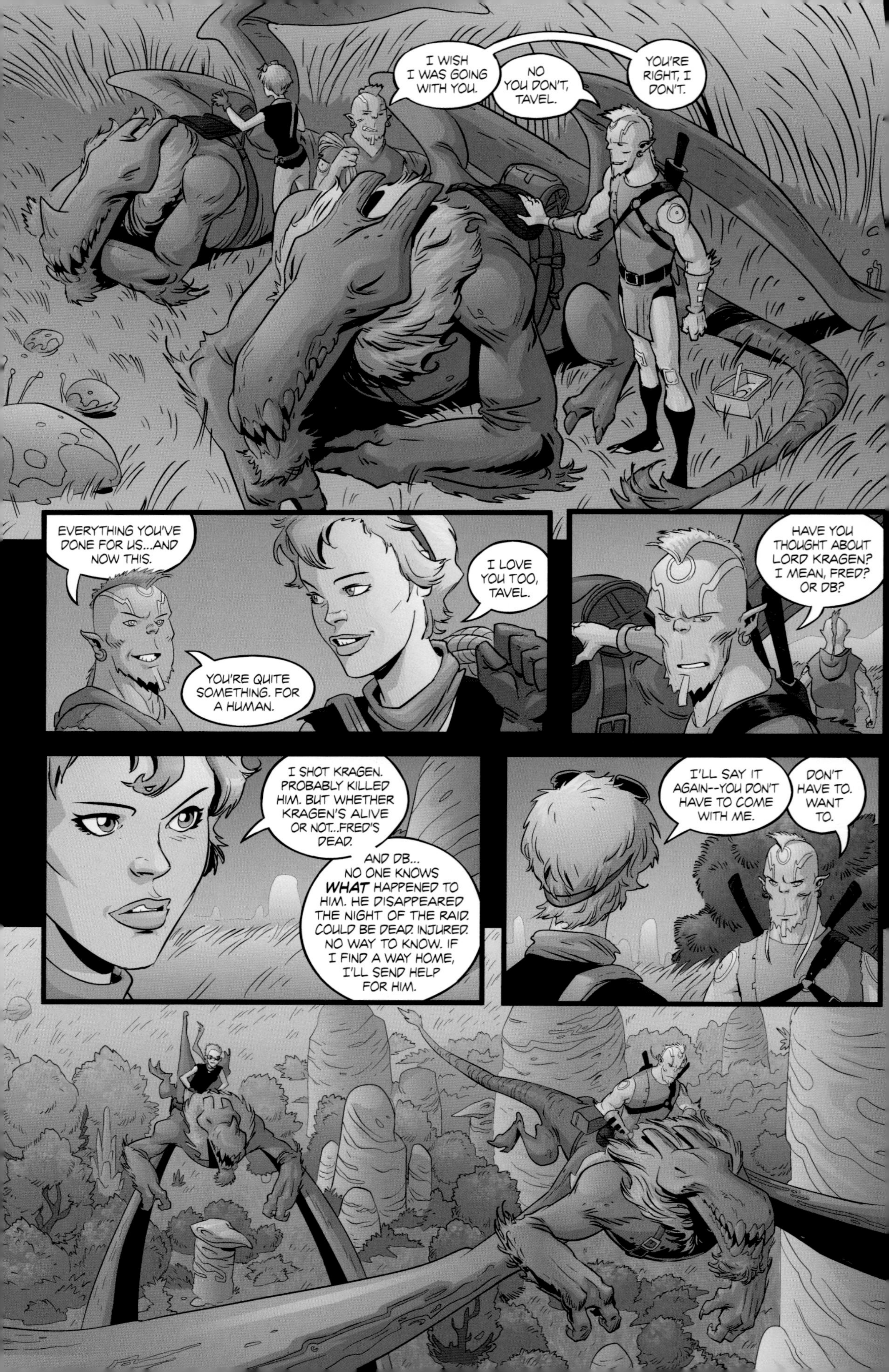
I WISH I WAS GOING WITH YOU.
NO YOU DON'T, TAVEL.
YOU'RE RIGHT, I DON'T.
EVERYTHING YOU'VE DONE FOR US...AND NOW THIS.
I LOVE YOU TOO, TAVEL.
YOU'RE QUITE SOMETHING. FOR A HUMAN.
HAVE YOU THOUGHT ABOUT LORD KRAGEN? I MEAN, FRED? OR DB?
I SHOT KRAGEN. PROBABLY KILLED HIM. BUT WHETHER KRAGEN'S ALIVE OR NOT...FRED'S DEAD.
AND DB... NO ONE KNOWS WHAT HAPPENED TO HIM. HE DISAPPEARED THE NIGHT OF THE RAID. COULD BE DEAD. INJURED. NO WAY TO KNOW. IF I FIND A WAY HOME, I'LL SEND HELP FOR HIM.
I'LL SAY IT AGAIN--YOU DON'T HAVE TO COME WITH ME.
DON'T HAVE TO. WANT TO.

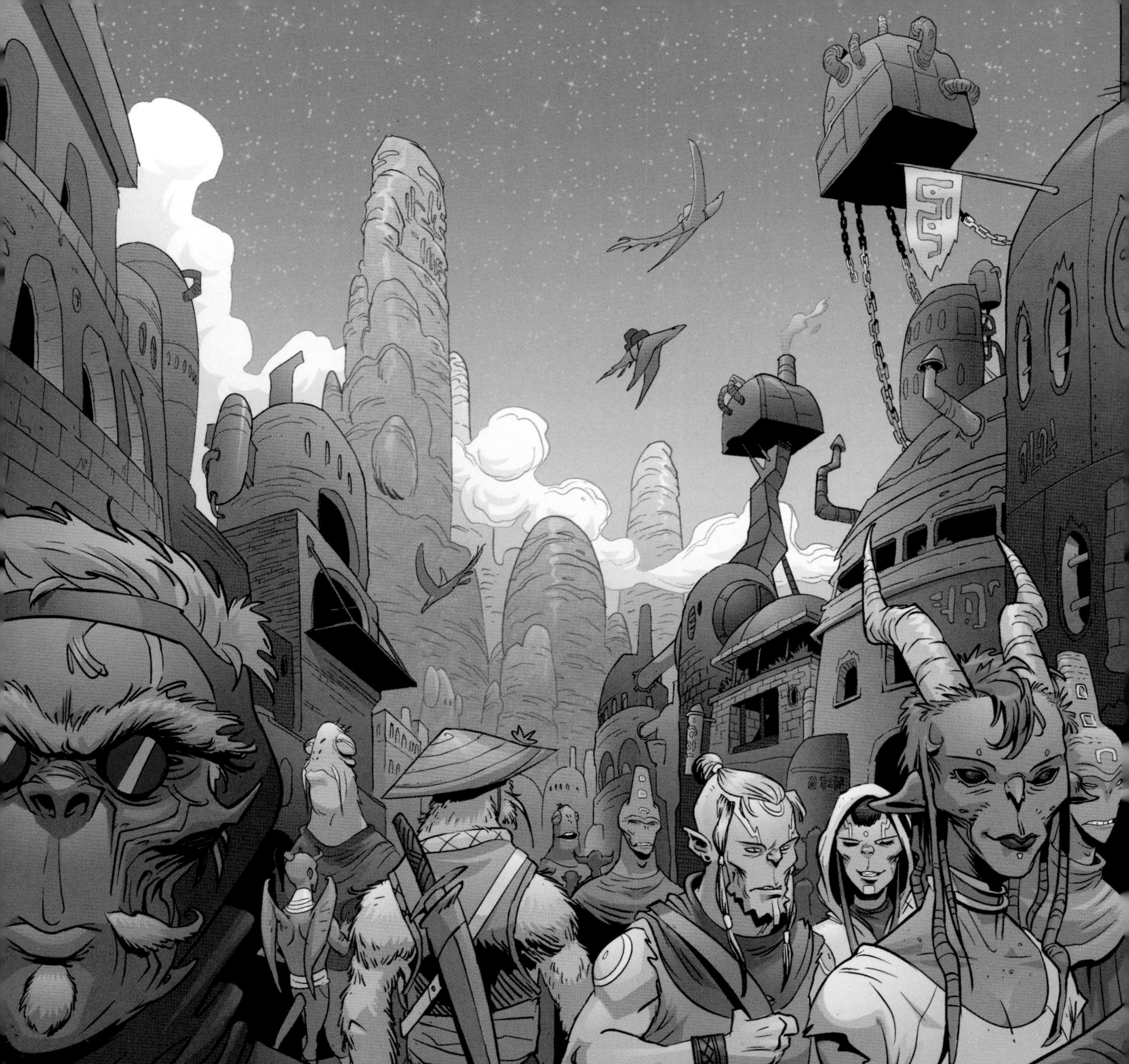

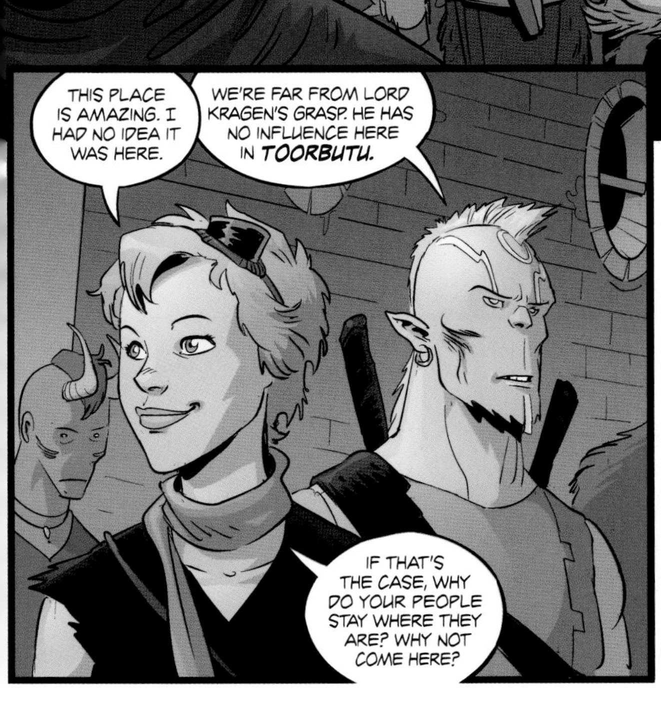

THIS PLACE IS AMAZING. I HAD NO IDEA IT WAS HERE.
WE'RE FAR FROM LORD KRAGEN'S GRASP. HE HAS NO INFLUENCE HERE IN **TOORBUTU.**
IF THAT'S THE CASE, WHY DO YOUR PEOPLE STAY WHERE THEY ARE? WHY NOT COME HERE?

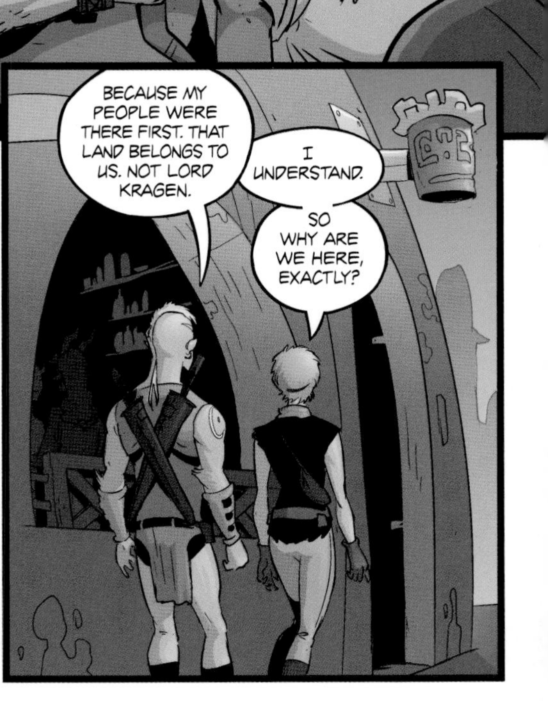

BECAUSE MY PEOPLE WERE THERE FIRST. THAT LAND BELONGS TO US. NOT LORD KRAGEN.
I UNDERSTAND.
SO WHY ARE WE HERE, EXACTLY?

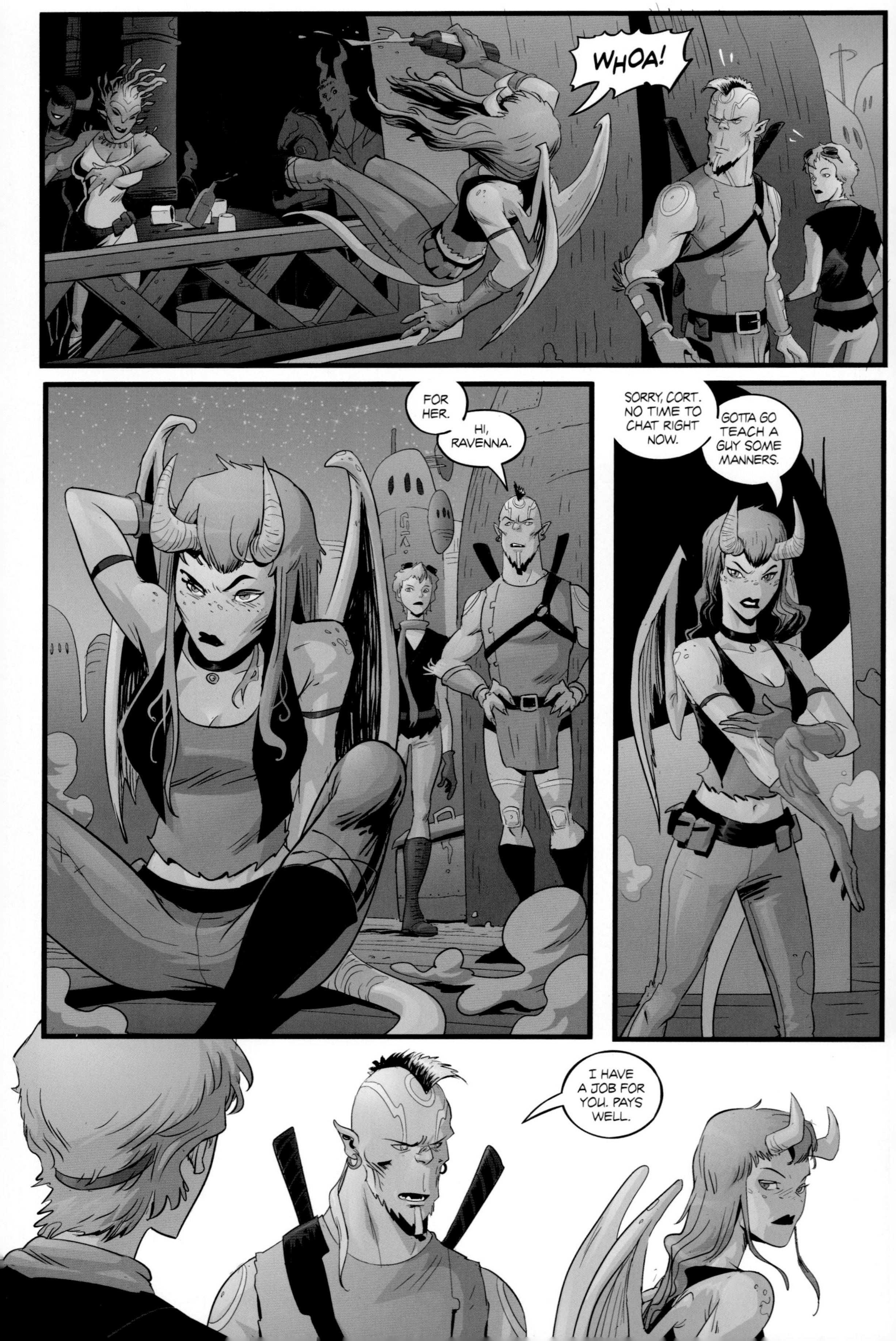
WHOA!
FOR HER.
HI, RAVENNA.
SORRY, CORT. NO TIME TO CHAT RIGHT NOW.
GOTTA GO TEACH A GUY SOME MANNERS.
I HAVE A JOB FOR YOU. PAYS WELL.

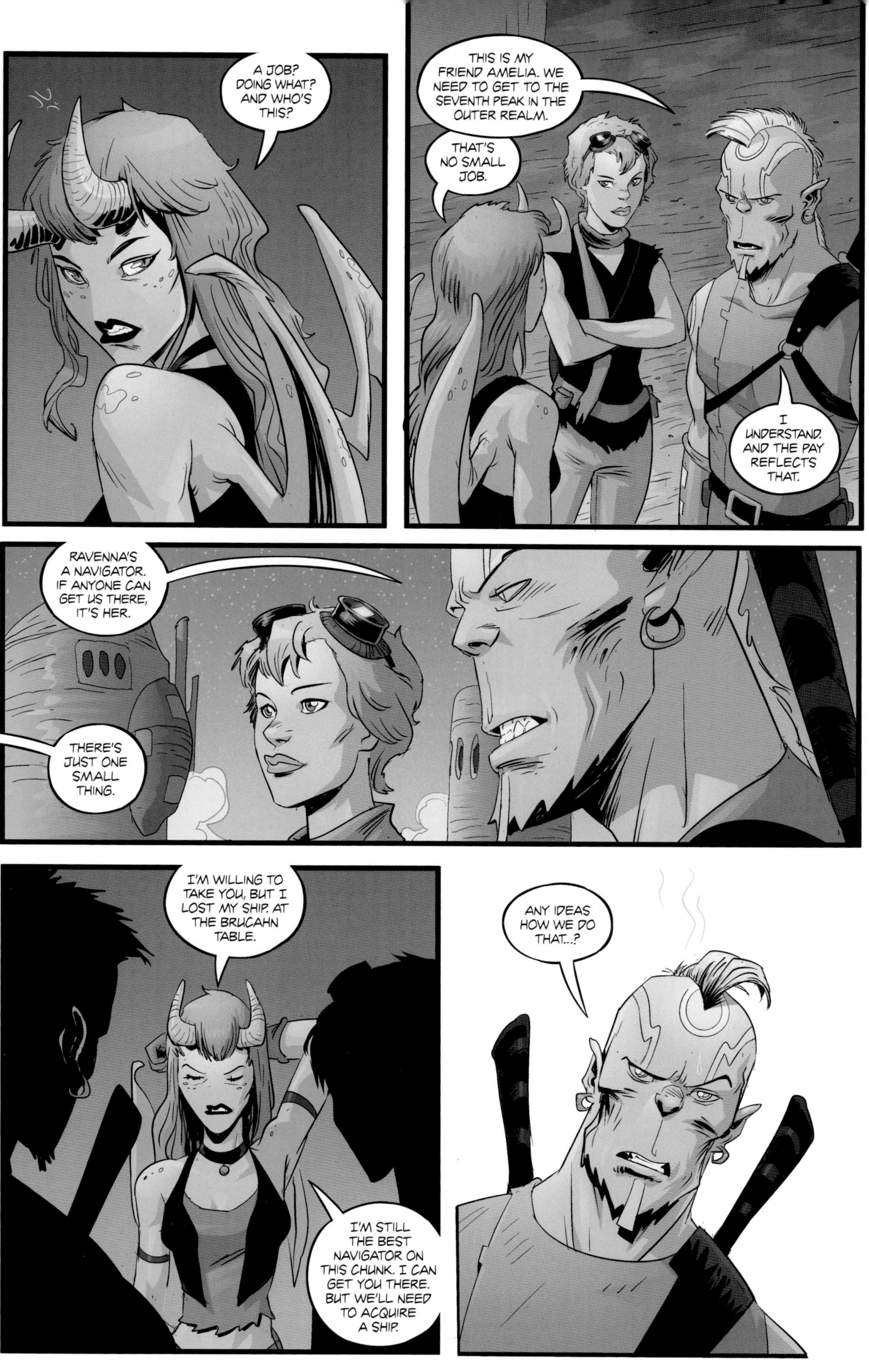
A JOB? DOING WHAT? AND WHO'S THIS?
THIS IS MY FRIEND AMELIA. WE NEED TO GET TO THE SEVENTH PEAK IN THE OUTER REALM.
THAT'S NO SMALL JOB.
I UNDERSTAND. AND THE PAY REFLECTS THAT.
RAVENNA'S A NAVIGATOR. IF ANYONE CAN GET US THERE, IT'S HER.
THERE'S JUST ONE SMALL THING.
I'M WILLING TO TAKE YOU, BUT I LOST MY SHIP. AT THE BRUCAHN TABLE.
I'M STILL THE BEST NAVIGATOR ON THIS CHUNK. I CAN GET YOU THERE. BUT WE'LL NEED TO ACQUIRE A SHIP.
ANY IDEAS HOW WE DO THAT...?

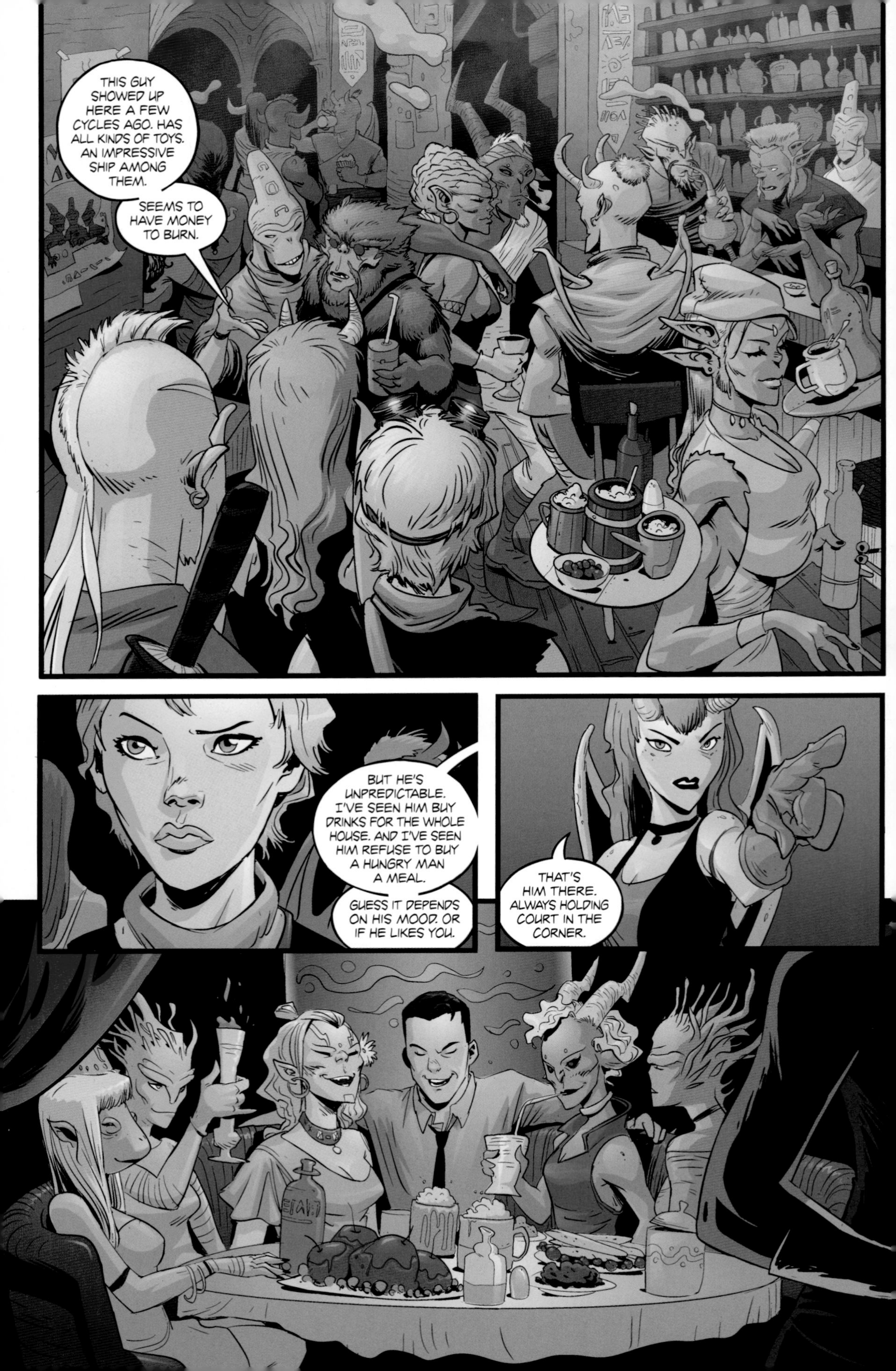
THIS GUY SHOWED UP HERE A FEW CYCLES AGO. HAS ALL KINDS OF TOYS. AN IMPRESSIVE SHIP AMONG THEM.
SEEMS TO HAVE MONEY TO BURN.
BUT HE'S UNPREDICTABLE. I'VE SEEN HIM BUY DRINKS FOR THE WHOLE HOUSE. AND I'VE SEEN HIM REFUSE TO BUY A HUNGRY MAN A MEAL.
GUESS IT DEPENDS ON HIS MOOD. OR IF HE LIKES YOU.
THAT'S HIM THERE. ALWAYS HOLDING COURT IN THE CORNER.

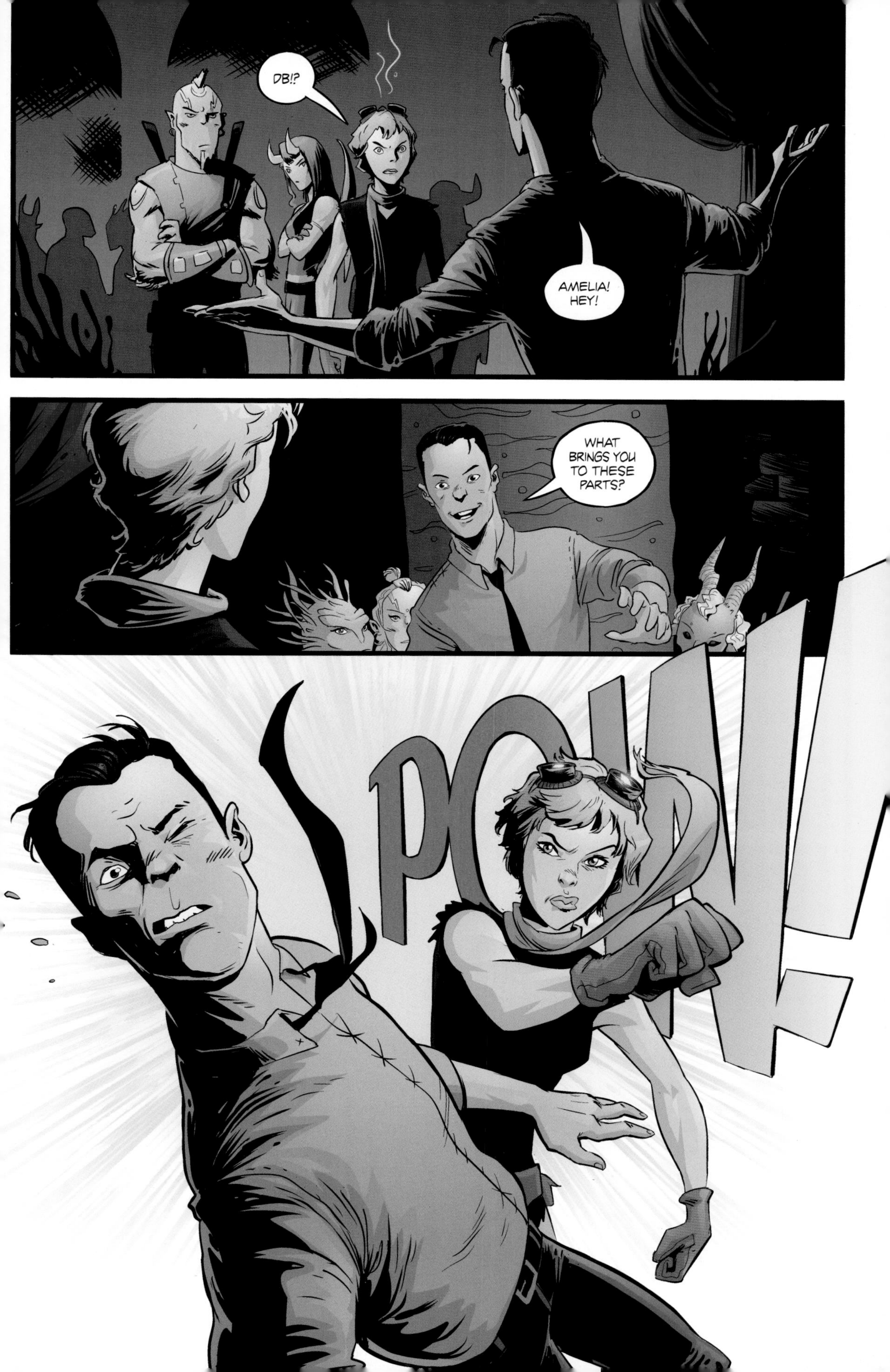
DB!?
AMELIA! HEY!
WHAT BRINGS YOU TO THESE PARTS?
POW!

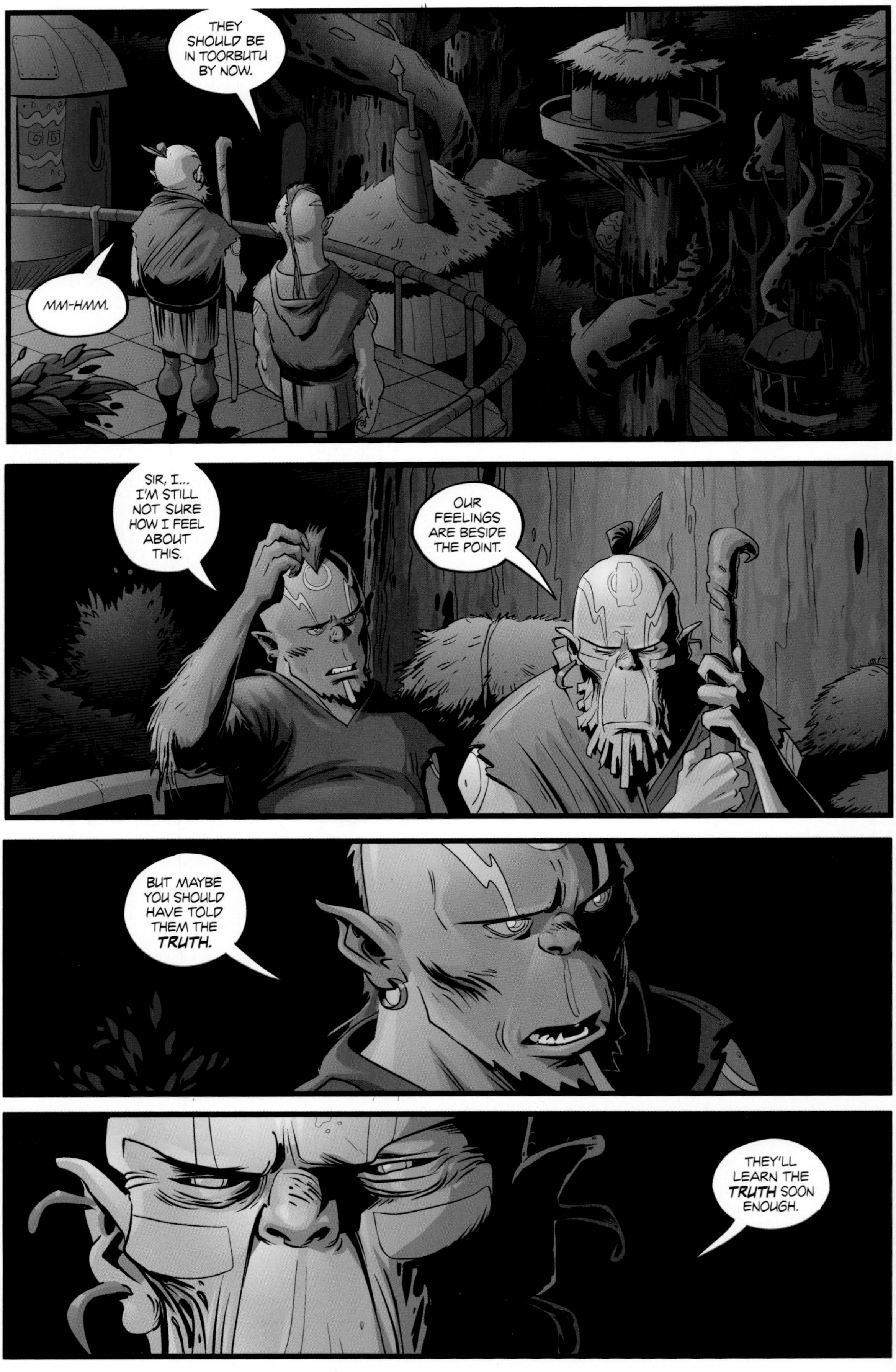
THEY SHOULD BE IN TOORBUTU BY NOW.
MM-HMM.
SIR, I... I'M STILL NOT SURE HOW I FEEL ABOUT THIS.
OUR FEELINGS ARE BESIDE THE POINT.
BUT MAYBE YOU SHOULD HAVE TOLD THEM THE TRUTH.
THEY'LL LEARN THE TRUTH SOON ENOUGH.

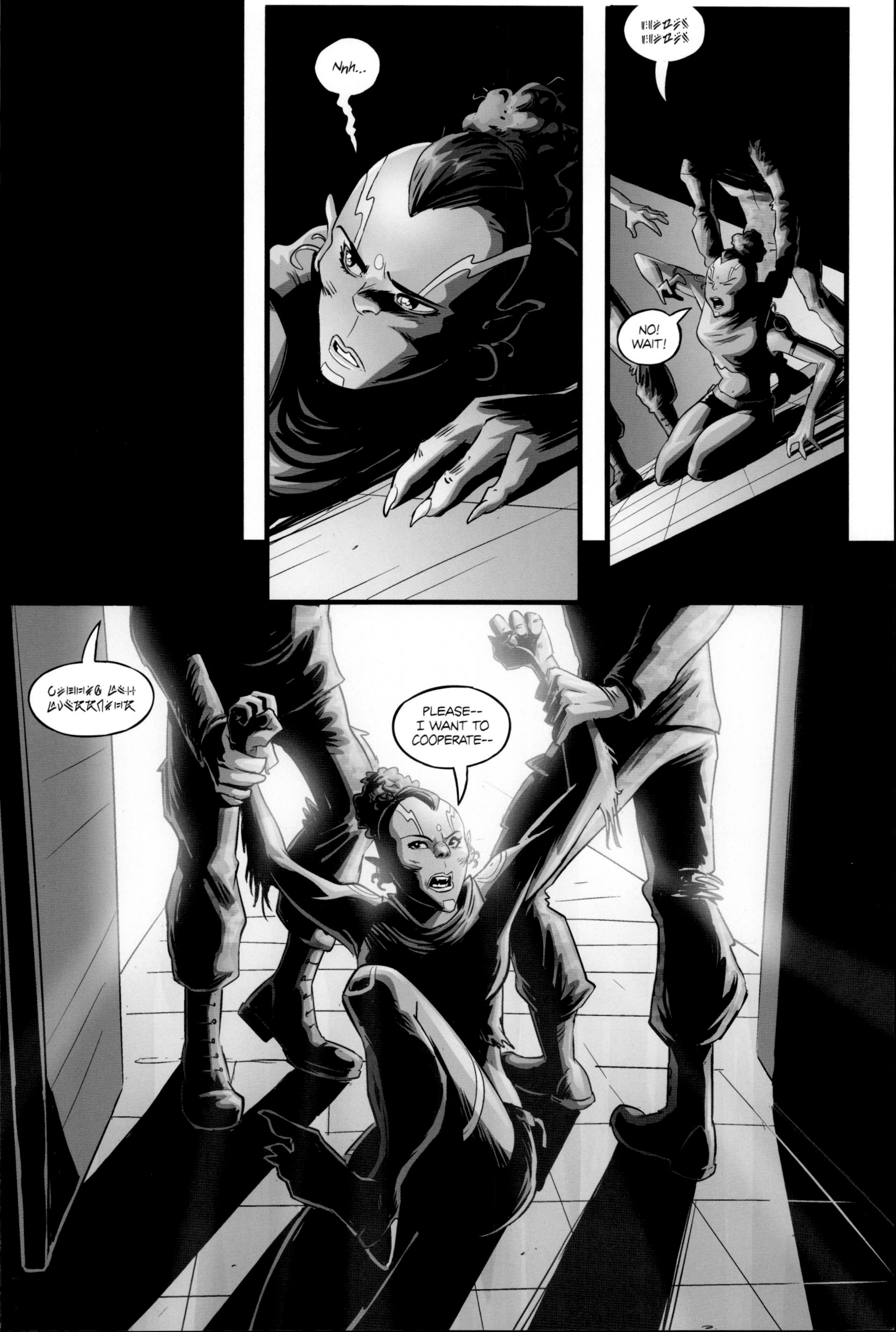
Nnh...
NO! WAIT!
PLEASE-- I WANT TO COOPERATE--

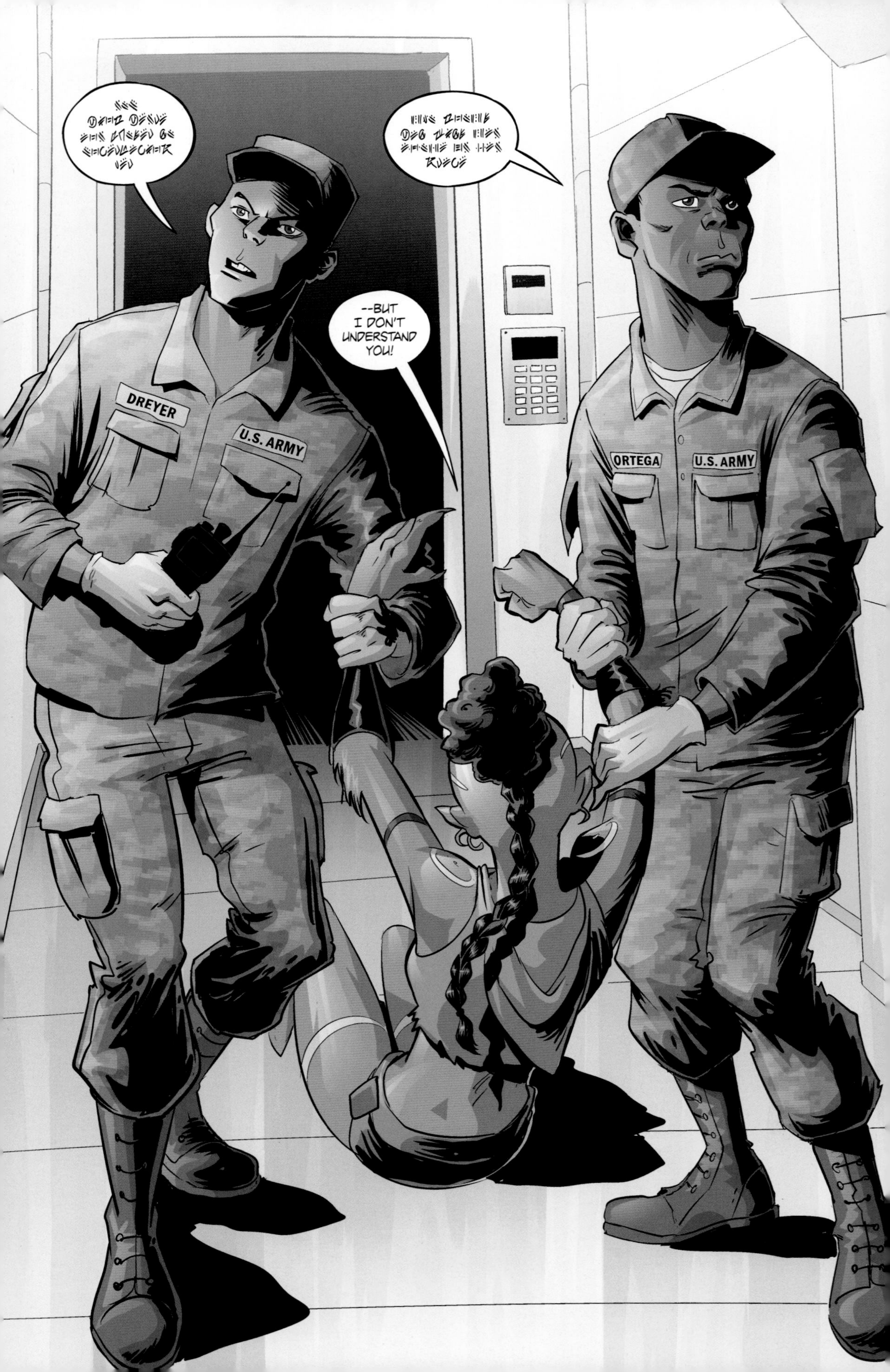
--BUT I DON'T UNDERSTAND YOU!
DREYER
U.S. ARMY
ORTEGA
U.S. ARMY

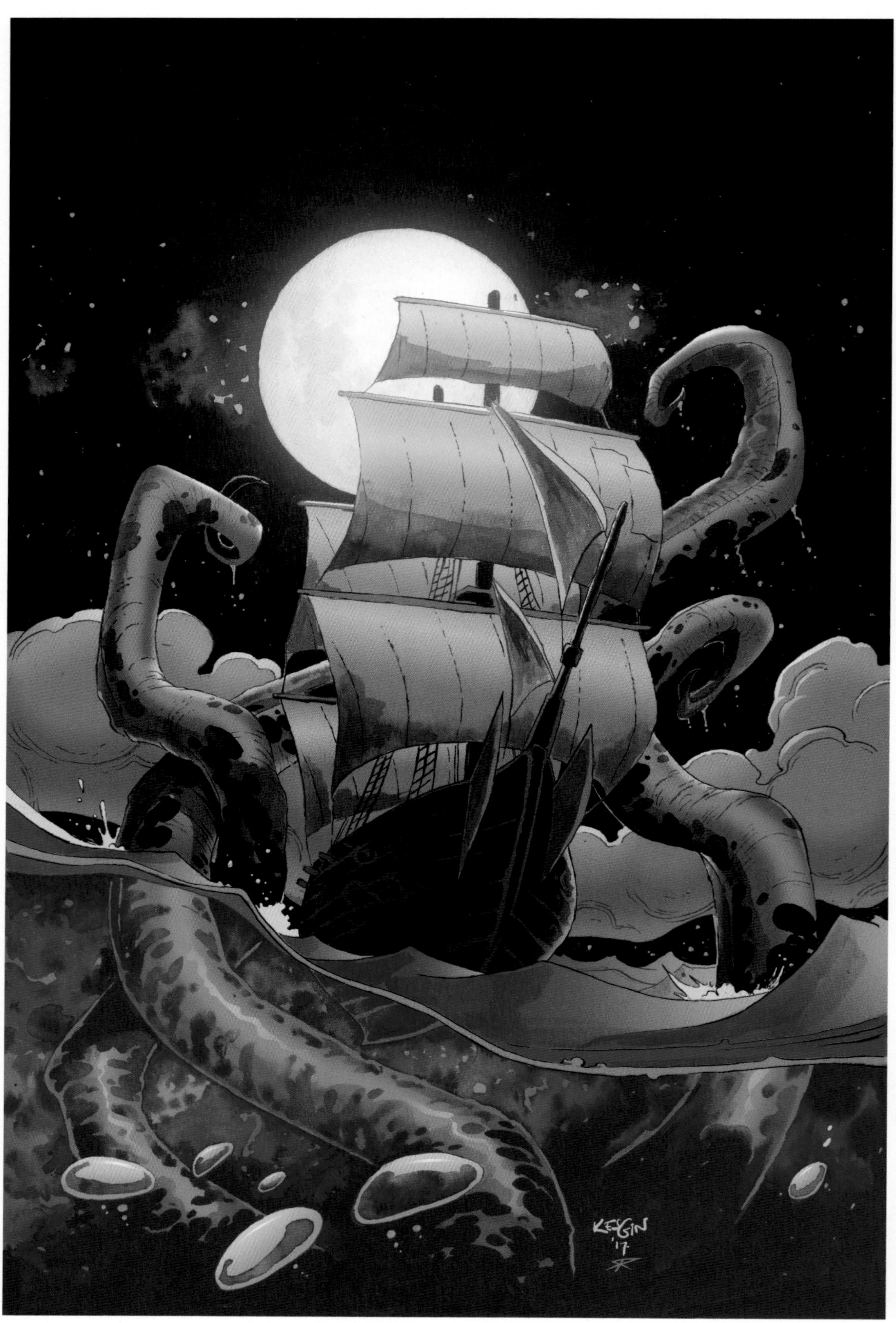
KESGIN '17

CHAPTER 2

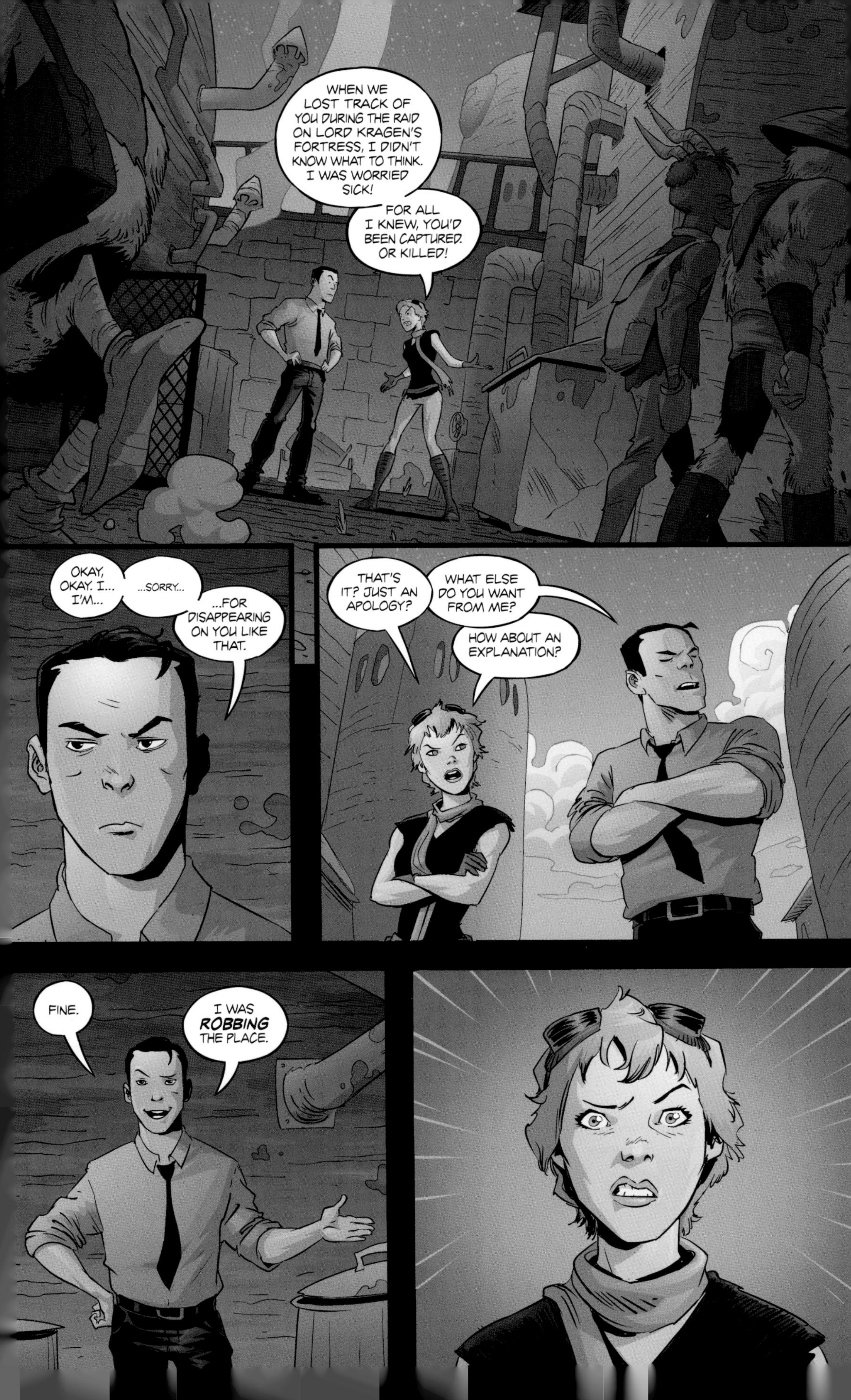
WHEN WE LOST TRACK OF YOU DURING THE RAID ON LORD KRAGEN'S FORTRESS, I DIDN'T KNOW WHAT TO THINK. I WAS WORRIED SICK!
FOR ALL I KNEW, YOU'D BEEN CAPTURED. OR KILLED!
OKAY, OKAY. I... I'M...
...SORRY...
...FOR DISAPPEARING ON YOU LIKE THAT.
THAT'S IT? JUST AN APOLOGY?
WHAT ELSE DO YOU WANT FROM ME?
HOW ABOUT AN EXPLANATION?
FINE.
I WAS **ROBBING** THE PLACE.

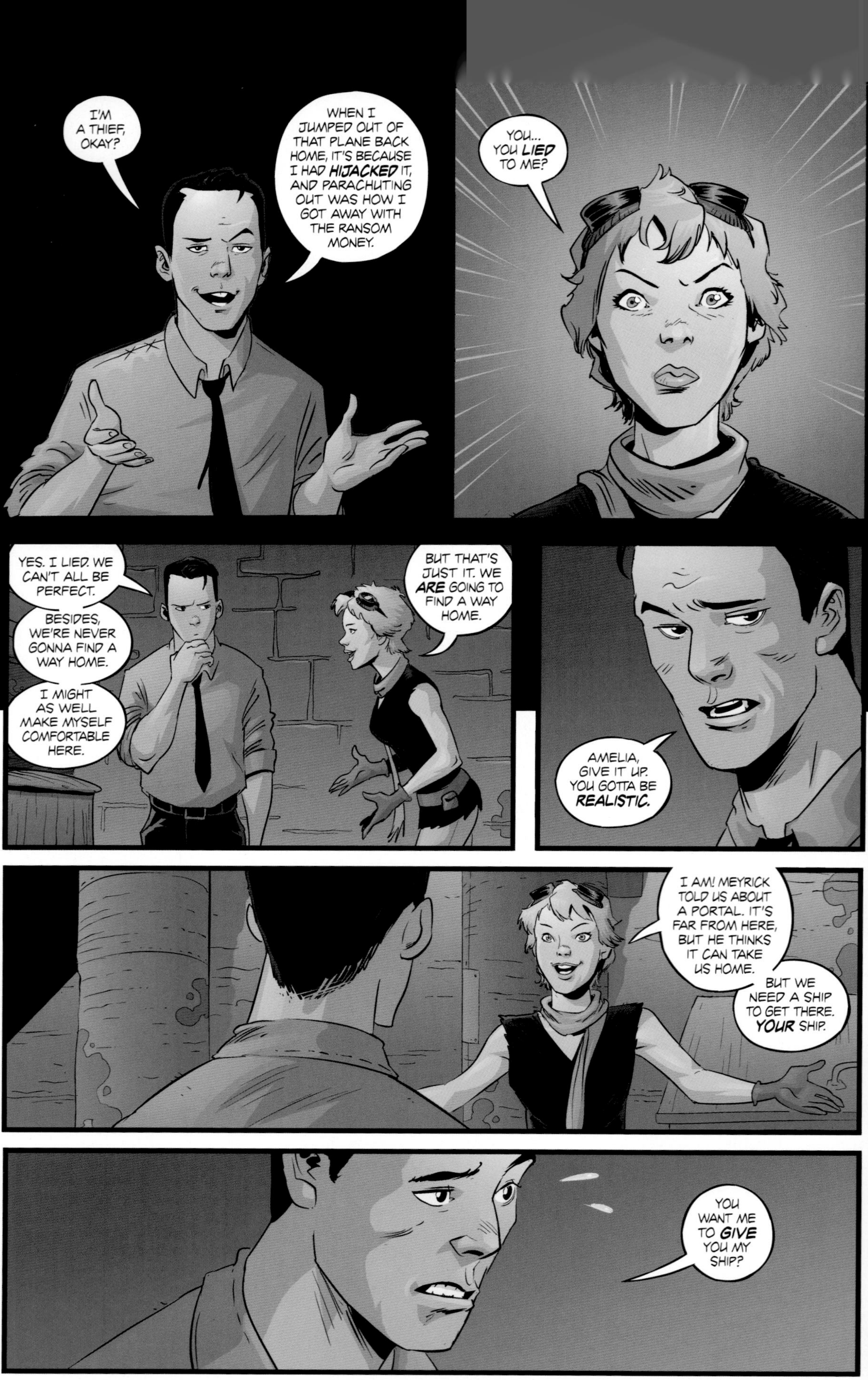
I'M A THIEF, OKAY?
WHEN I JUMPED OUT OF THAT PLANE BACK HOME, IT'S BECAUSE I HAD HIJACKED IT, AND PARACHUTING OUT WAS HOW I GOT AWAY WITH THE RANSOM MONEY.
YOU... YOU LIED TO ME?
YES. I LIED. WE CAN'T ALL BE PERFECT.
BESIDES, WE'RE NEVER GONNA FIND A WAY HOME.
I MIGHT AS WELL MAKE MYSELF COMFORTABLE HERE.
BUT THAT'S JUST IT. WE ARE GOING TO FIND A WAY HOME.
AMELIA, GIVE IT UP. YOU GOTTA BE REALISTIC.
I AM! MEYRICK TOLD US ABOUT A PORTAL. IT'S FAR FROM HERE, BUT HE THINKS IT CAN TAKE US HOME.
BUT WE NEED A SHIP TO GET THERE. YOUR SHIP.
YOU WANT ME TO GIVE YOU MY SHIP?

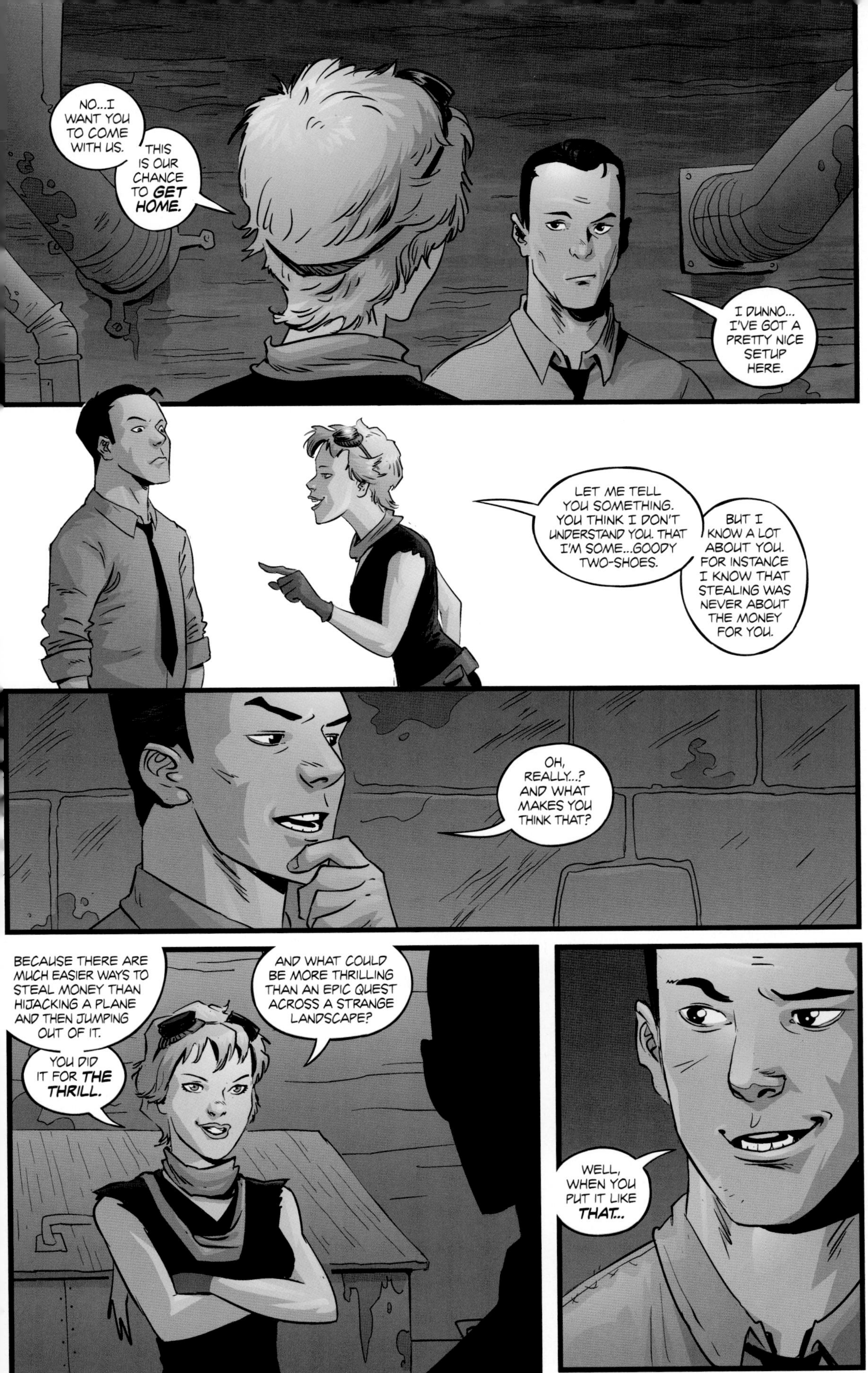
NO...I WANT YOU TO COME WITH US.
THIS IS OUR CHANCE TO **GET HOME.**
I DUNNO... I'VE GOT A PRETTY NICE SETUP HERE.
LET ME TELL YOU SOMETHING. YOU THINK I DON'T UNDERSTAND YOU. THAT I'M SOME...GOODY TWO-SHOES.
BUT I KNOW A LOT ABOUT YOU. FOR INSTANCE I KNOW THAT STEALING WAS NEVER ABOUT THE MONEY FOR YOU.
OH, REALLY...? AND WHAT MAKES YOU THINK THAT?
BECAUSE THERE ARE MUCH EASIER WAYS TO STEAL MONEY THAN HIJACKING A PLANE AND THEN JUMPING OUT OF IT.
YOU DID IT FOR **THE THRILL.**
AND WHAT COULD BE MORE THRILLING THAN AN EPIC QUEST ACROSS A STRANGE LANDSCAPE?
WELL, WHEN YOU PUT IT LIKE **THAT...**

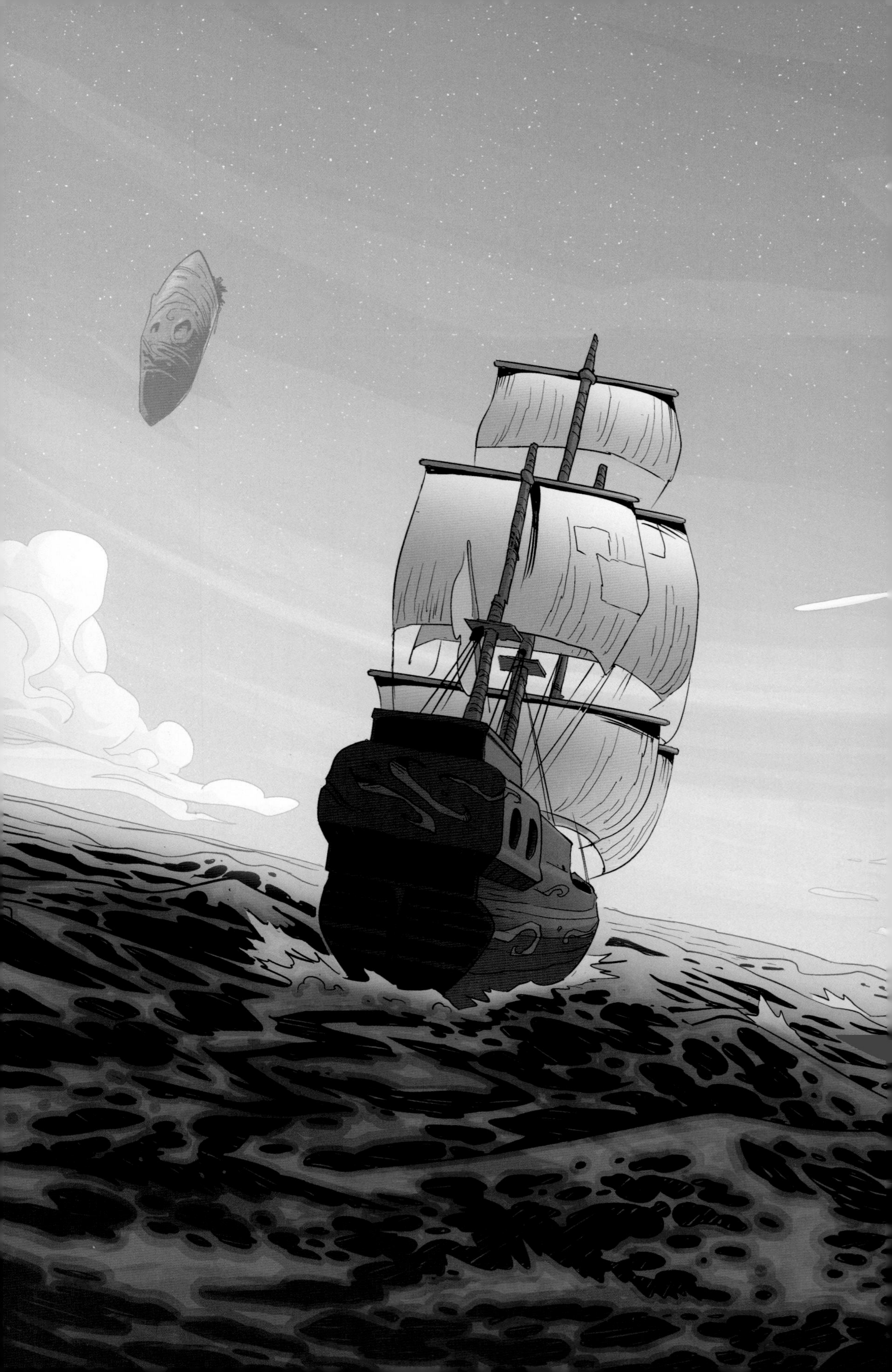

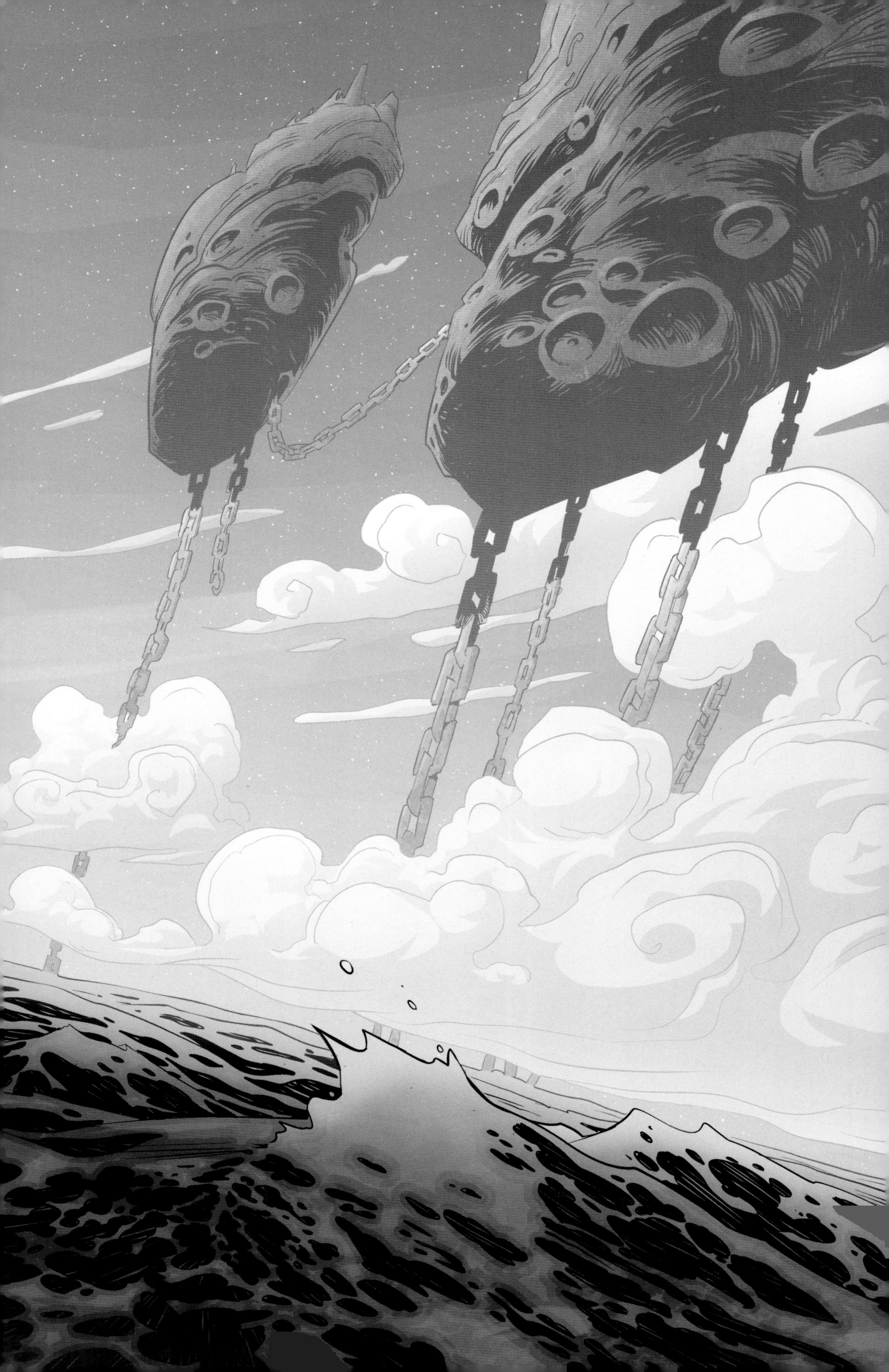

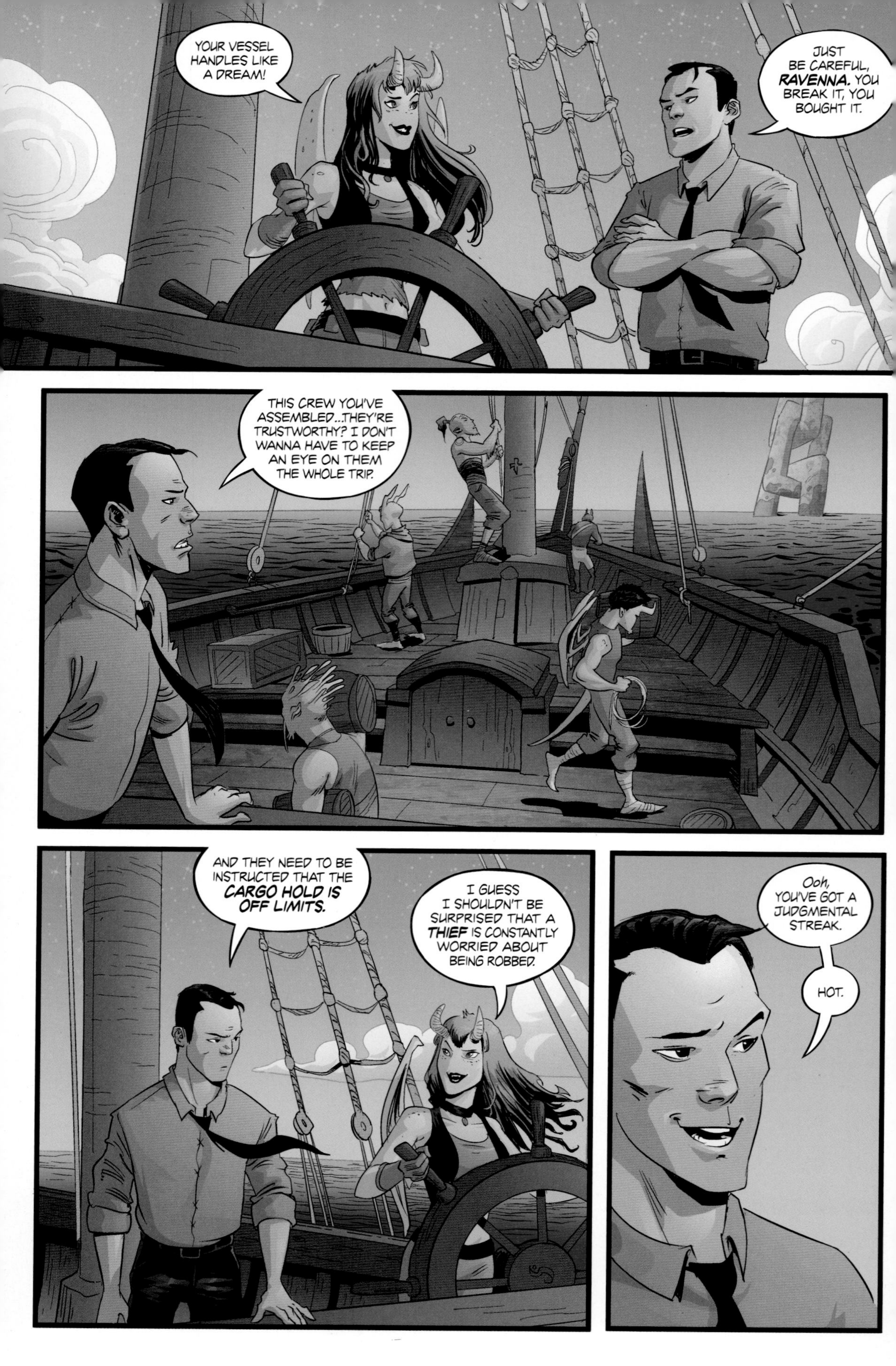
YOUR VESSEL HANDLES LIKE A DREAM!
JUST BE CAREFUL, **RAVENNA.** YOU BREAK IT, YOU BOUGHT IT.
THIS CREW YOU'VE ASSEMBLED...THEY'RE TRUSTWORTHY? I DON'T WANNA HAVE TO KEEP AN EYE ON THEM THE WHOLE TRIP.
AND THEY NEED TO BE INSTRUCTED THAT THE **CARGO HOLD IS OFF LIMITS.**
I GUESS I SHOULDN'T BE SURPRISED THAT A **THIEF** IS CONSTANTLY WORRIED ABOUT BEING ROBBED.
Ooh, YOU'VE GOT A JUDGMENTAL STREAK.
HOT.

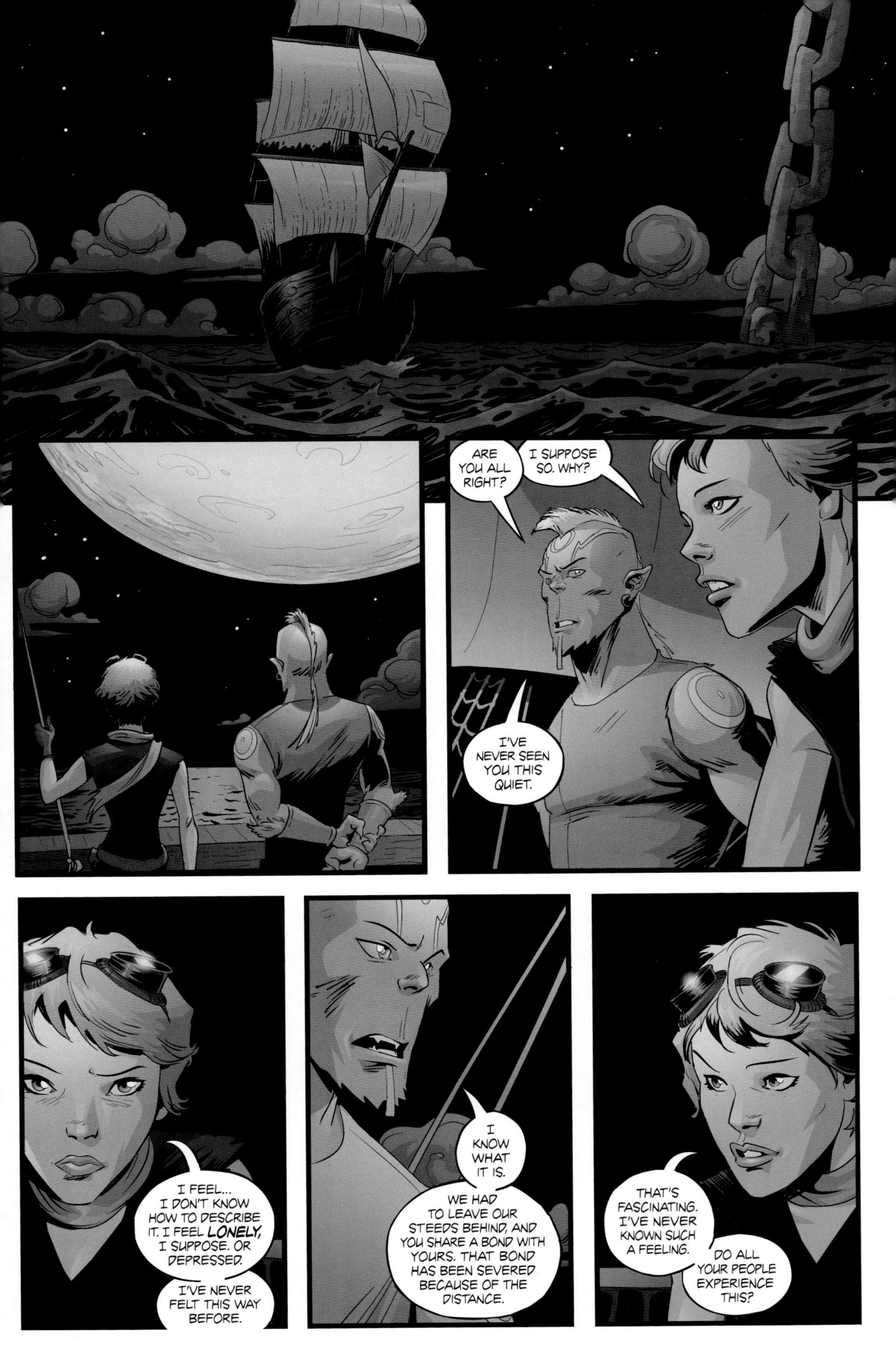
ARE YOU ALL RIGHT?
I SUPPOSE SO. WHY?
I'VE NEVER SEEN YOU THIS QUIET.
I FEEL... I DON'T KNOW HOW TO DESCRIBE IT. I FEEL LONELY, I SUPPOSE. OR DEPRESSED.
I'VE NEVER FELT THIS WAY BEFORE.
I KNOW WHAT IT IS.
WE HAD TO LEAVE OUR STEEDS BEHIND, AND YOU SHARE A BOND WITH YOURS. THAT BOND HAS BEEN SEVERED BECAUSE OF THE DISTANCE.
THAT'S FASCINATING. I'VE NEVER KNOWN SUCH A FEELING.
DO ALL YOUR PEOPLE EXPERIENCE THIS?

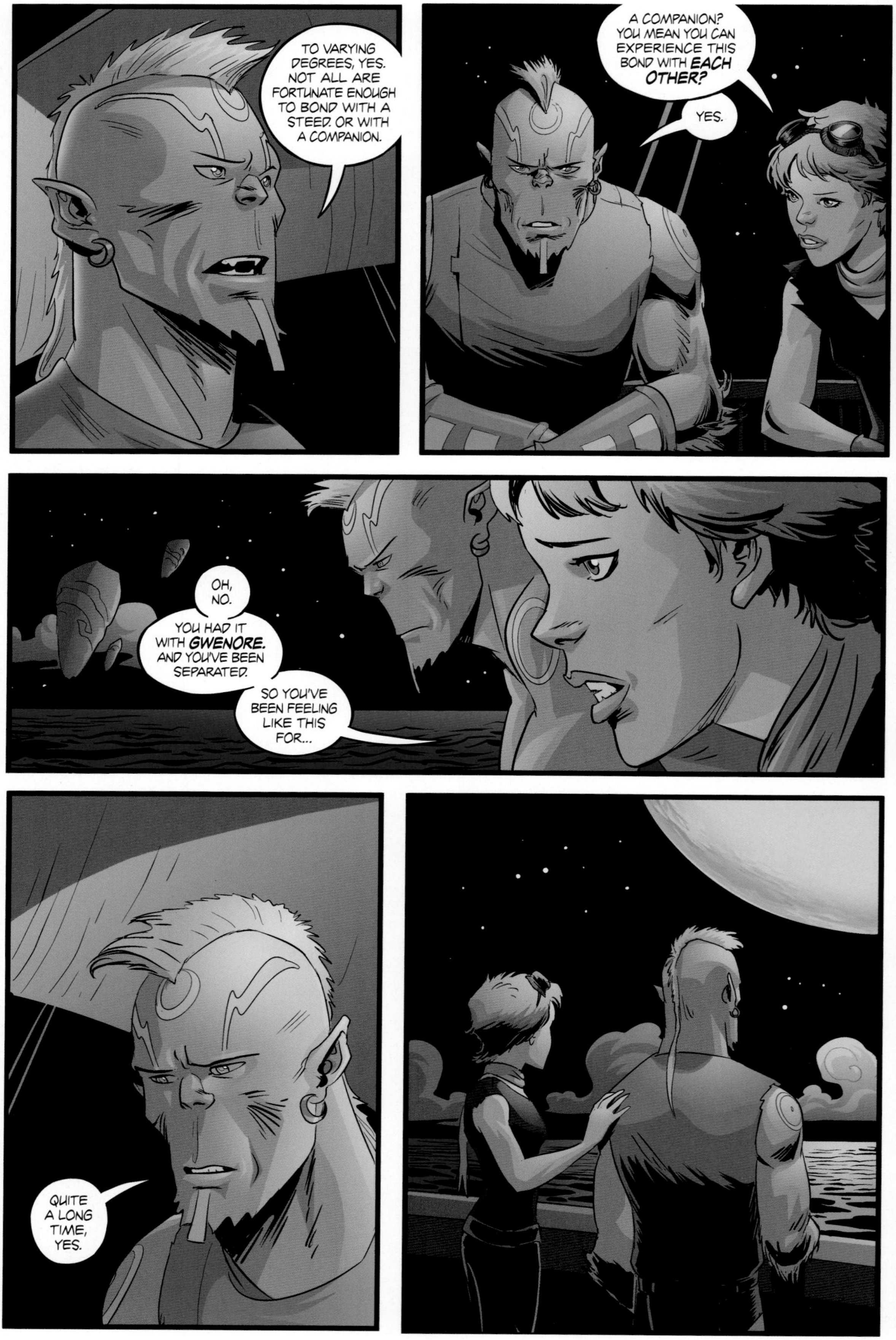
TO VARYING DEGREES, YES. NOT ALL ARE FORTUNATE ENOUGH TO BOND WITH A STEED. OR WITH A COMPANION.
A COMPANION? YOU MEAN YOU CAN EXPERIENCE THIS BOND WITH **EACH OTHER?**
YES.
OH, NO.
YOU HAD IT WITH **GWENORE.** AND YOU'VE BEEN SEPARATED.
SO YOU'VE BEEN FEELING LIKE THIS FOR...
QUITE A LONG TIME, YES.

IT'S THE SAME EVERY TIME.

HANS OF HE HIMHEN KHG HHD HHD DHF OBSHN

KOHHG KHKHH OHOOH DHHK HHHHH

YOU TAKE ME TO THAT OTHER ROOM.

YOU SHOUT AT ME IN A TONGUE I CANNOT UNDERSTAND.

AND YOU GROW FRUSTRATED AND ANGRY WHEN I CANNOT ANSWER.

SO THIS TIME, LET'S TRY SOMETHING DIFFERENT.

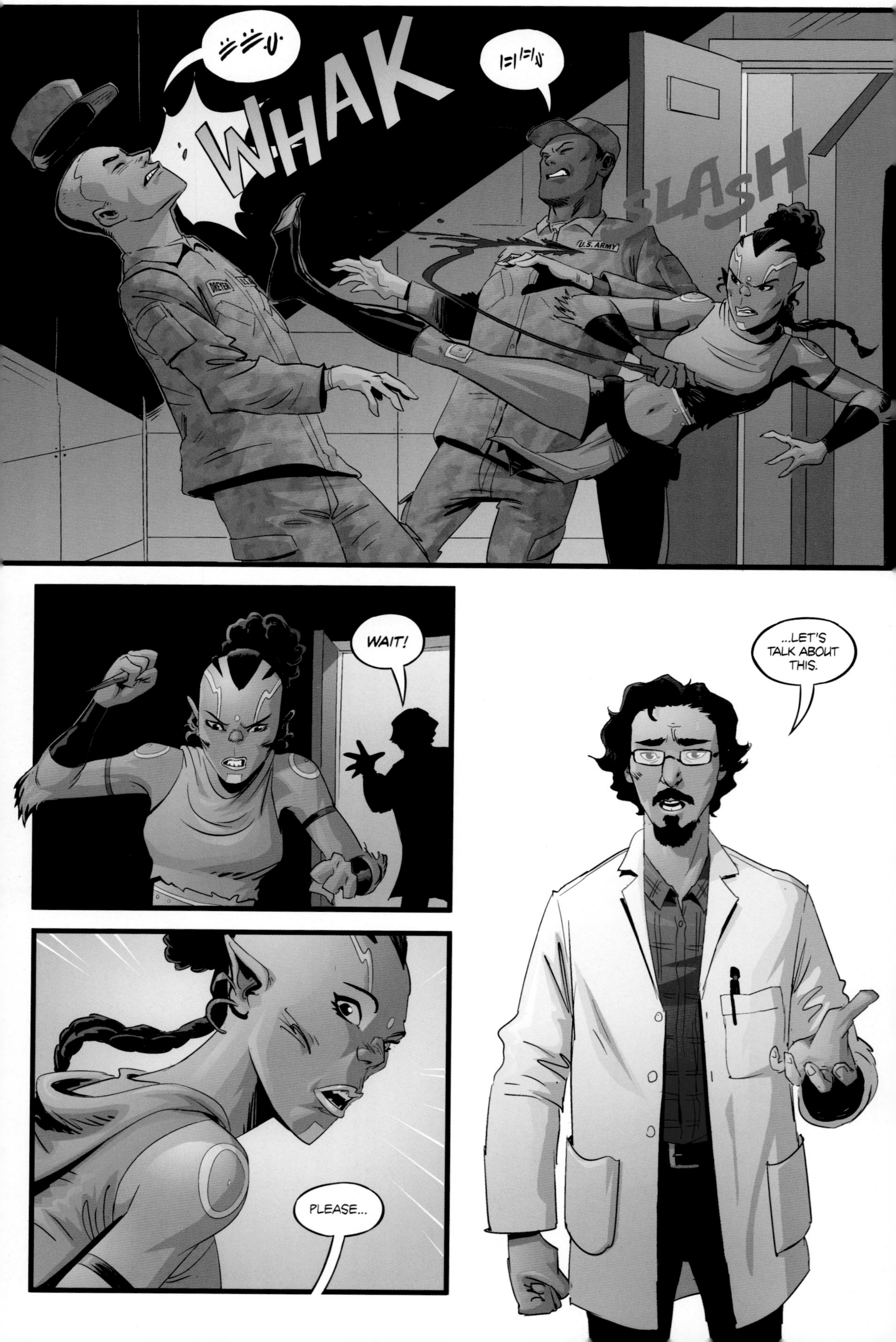
WHAK
SLASH
DREYER
U.S. ARMY
WAIT!
...LET'S TALK ABOUT THIS.
PLEASE...

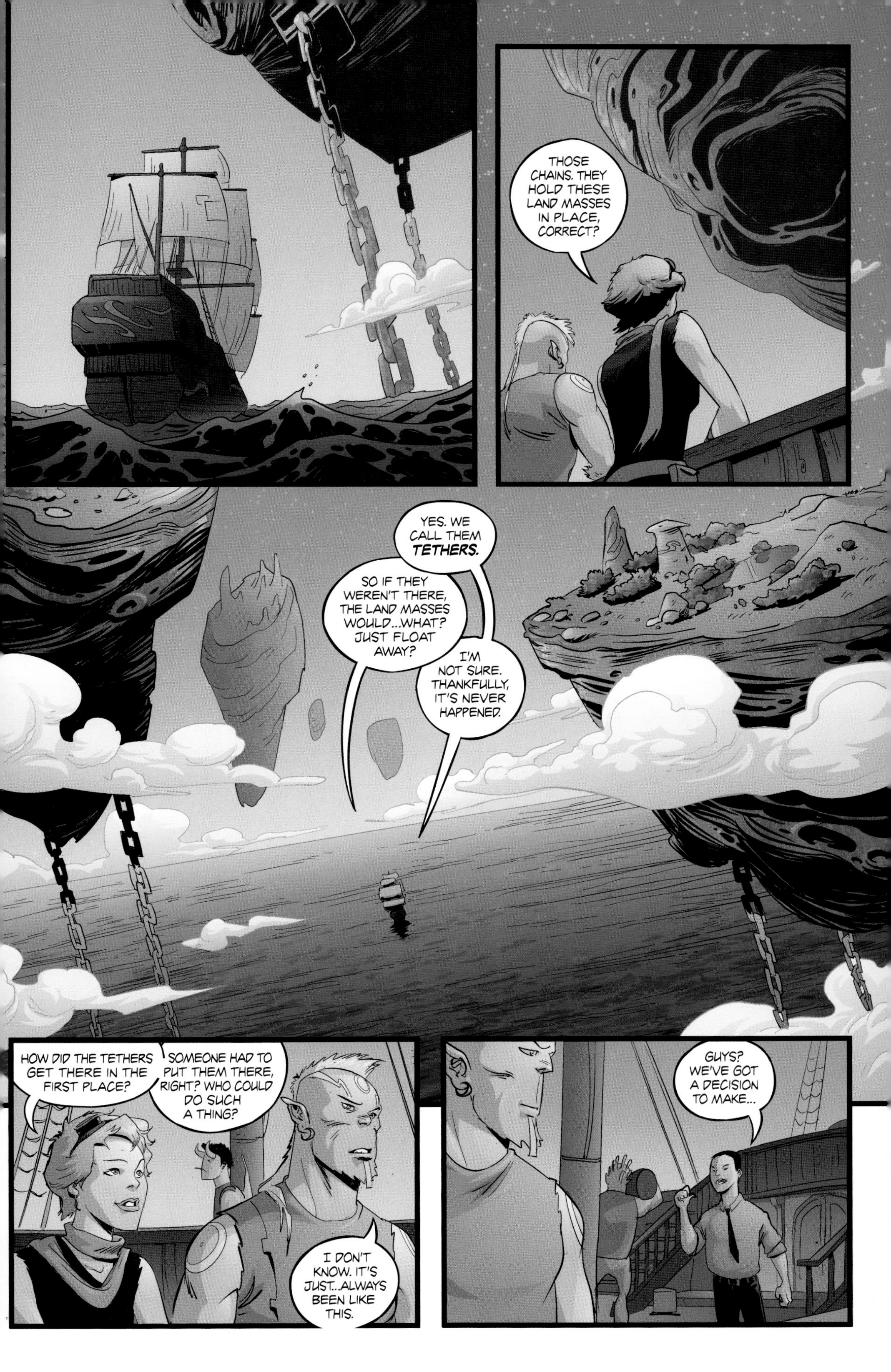
THOSE CHAINS. THEY HOLD THESE LAND MASSES IN PLACE, CORRECT?
YES. WE CALL THEM TETHERS.
SO IF THEY WEREN'T THERE, THE LAND MASSES WOULD...WHAT? JUST FLOAT AWAY?
I'M NOT SURE. THANKFULLY, IT'S NEVER HAPPENED.
HOW DID THE TETHERS GET THERE IN THE FIRST PLACE?
SOMEONE HAD TO PUT THEM THERE, RIGHT? WHO COULD DO SUCH A THING?
I DON'T KNOW. IT'S JUST...ALWAYS BEEN LIKE THIS.
GUYS? WE'VE GOT A DECISION TO MAKE...

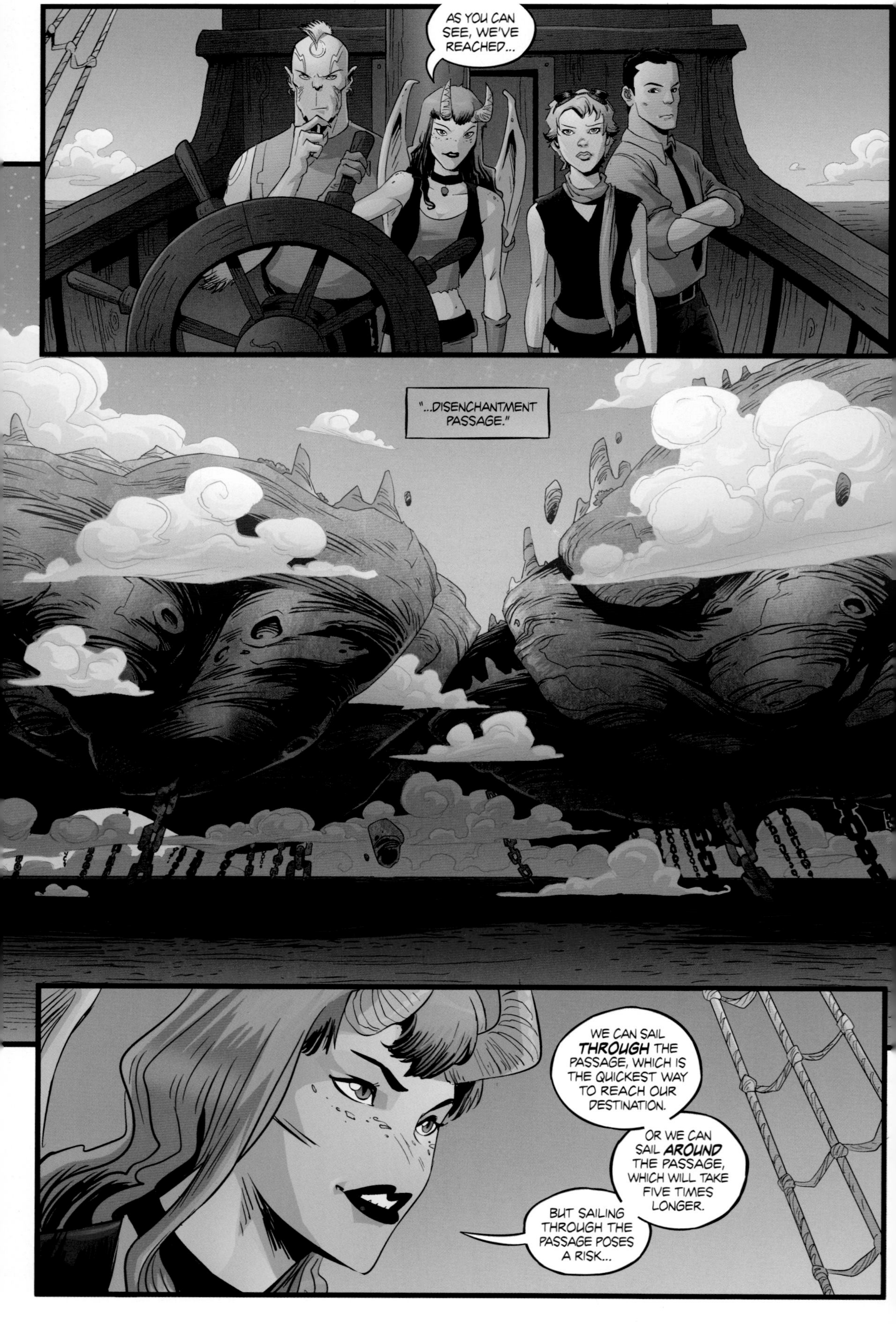

AS YOU CAN SEE, WE'VE REACHED...
"...DISENCHANTMENT PASSAGE."
WE CAN SAIL THROUGH THE PASSAGE, WHICH IS THE QUICKEST WAY TO REACH OUR DESTINATION.
OR WE CAN SAIL AROUND THE PASSAGE, WHICH WILL TAKE FIVE TIMES LONGER.
BUT SAILING THROUGH THE PASSAGE POSES A RISK...

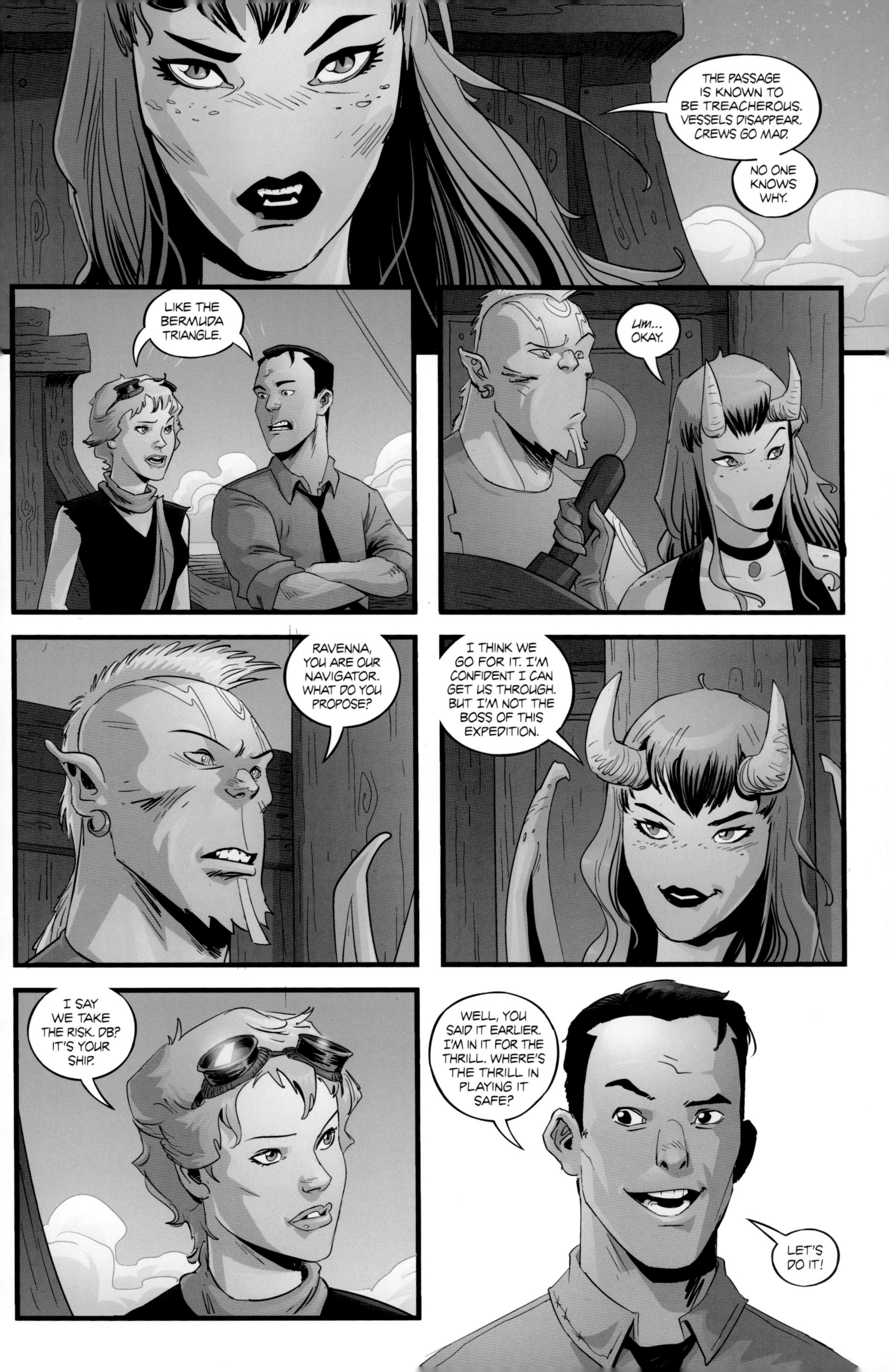
THE PASSAGE IS KNOWN TO BE TREACHEROUS. VESSELS DISAPPEAR. CREWS GO MAD.
NO ONE KNOWS WHY.
LIKE THE BERMUDA TRIANGLE.
UM... OKAY.
RAVENNA, YOU ARE OUR NAVIGATOR. WHAT DO YOU PROPOSE?
I THINK WE GO FOR IT. I'M CONFIDENT I CAN GET US THROUGH. BUT I'M NOT THE BOSS OF THIS EXPEDITION.
I SAY WE TAKE THE RISK. DB? IT'S YOUR SHIP.
WELL, YOU SAID IT EARLIER. I'M IN IT FOR THE THRILL. WHERE'S THE THRILL IN PLAYING IT SAFE?
LET'S DO IT!

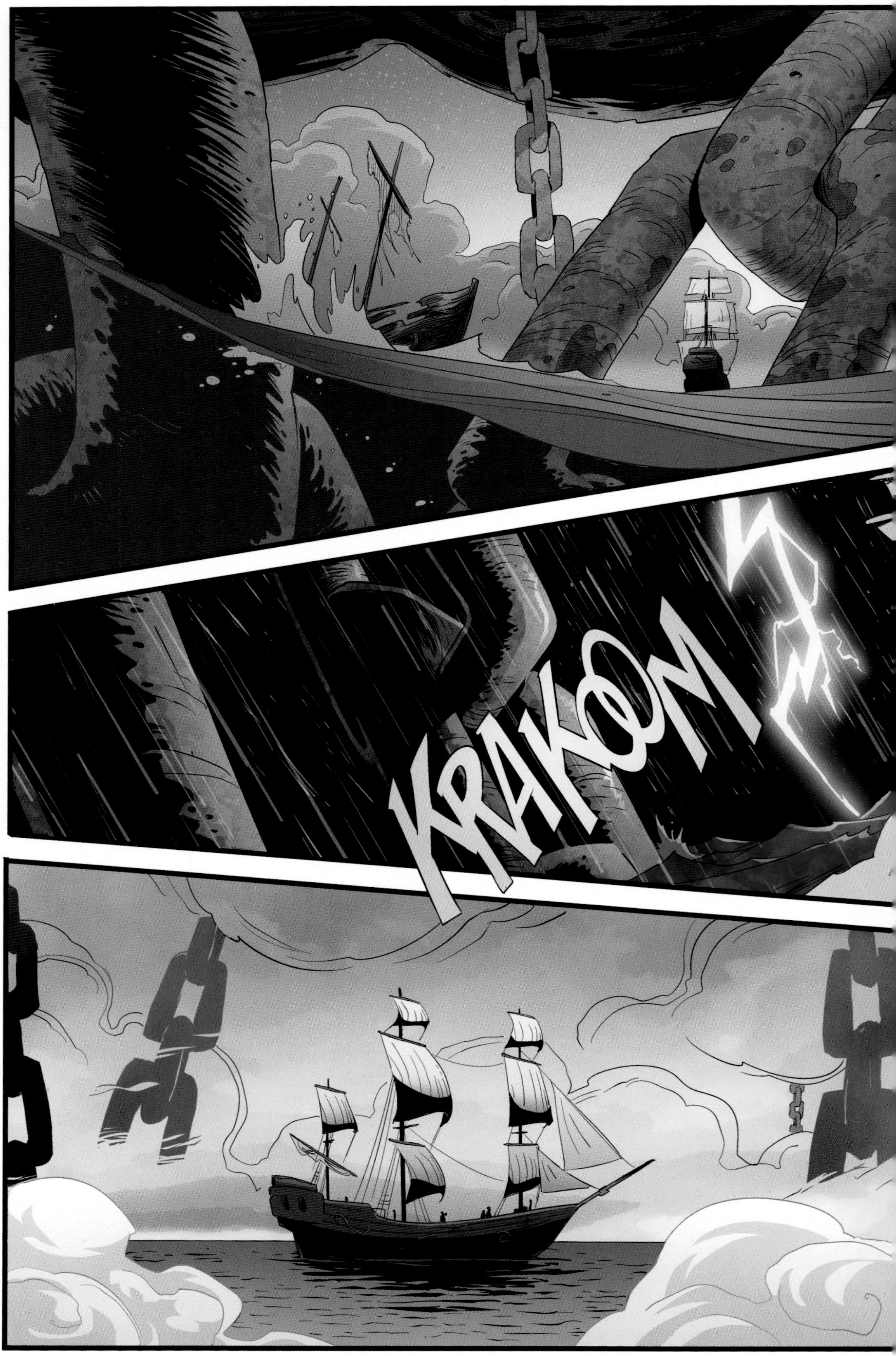
KRAKOOM

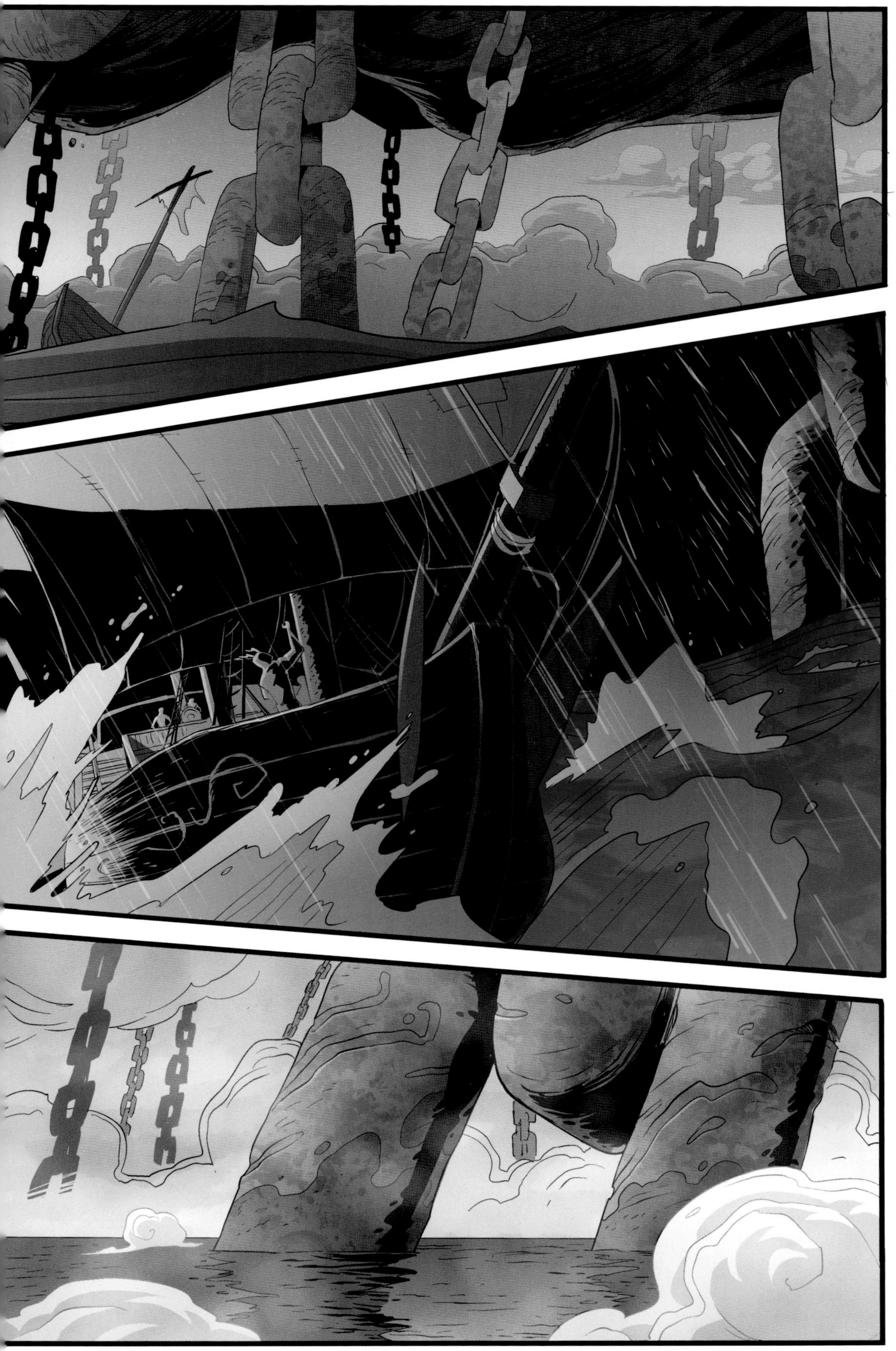

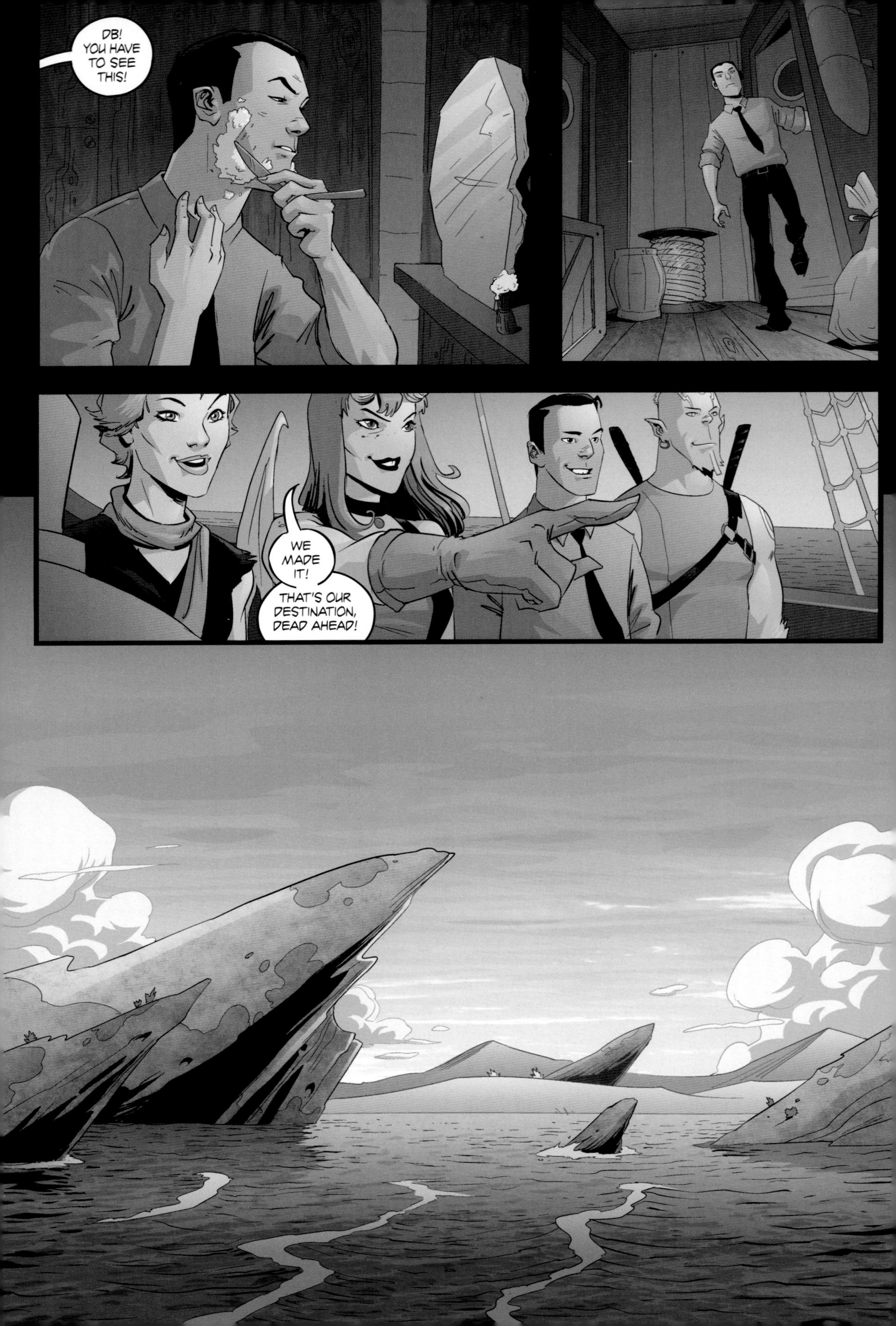
DB! YOU HAVE TO SEE THIS!
WE MADE IT!
THAT'S OUR DESTINATION, DEAD AHEAD!

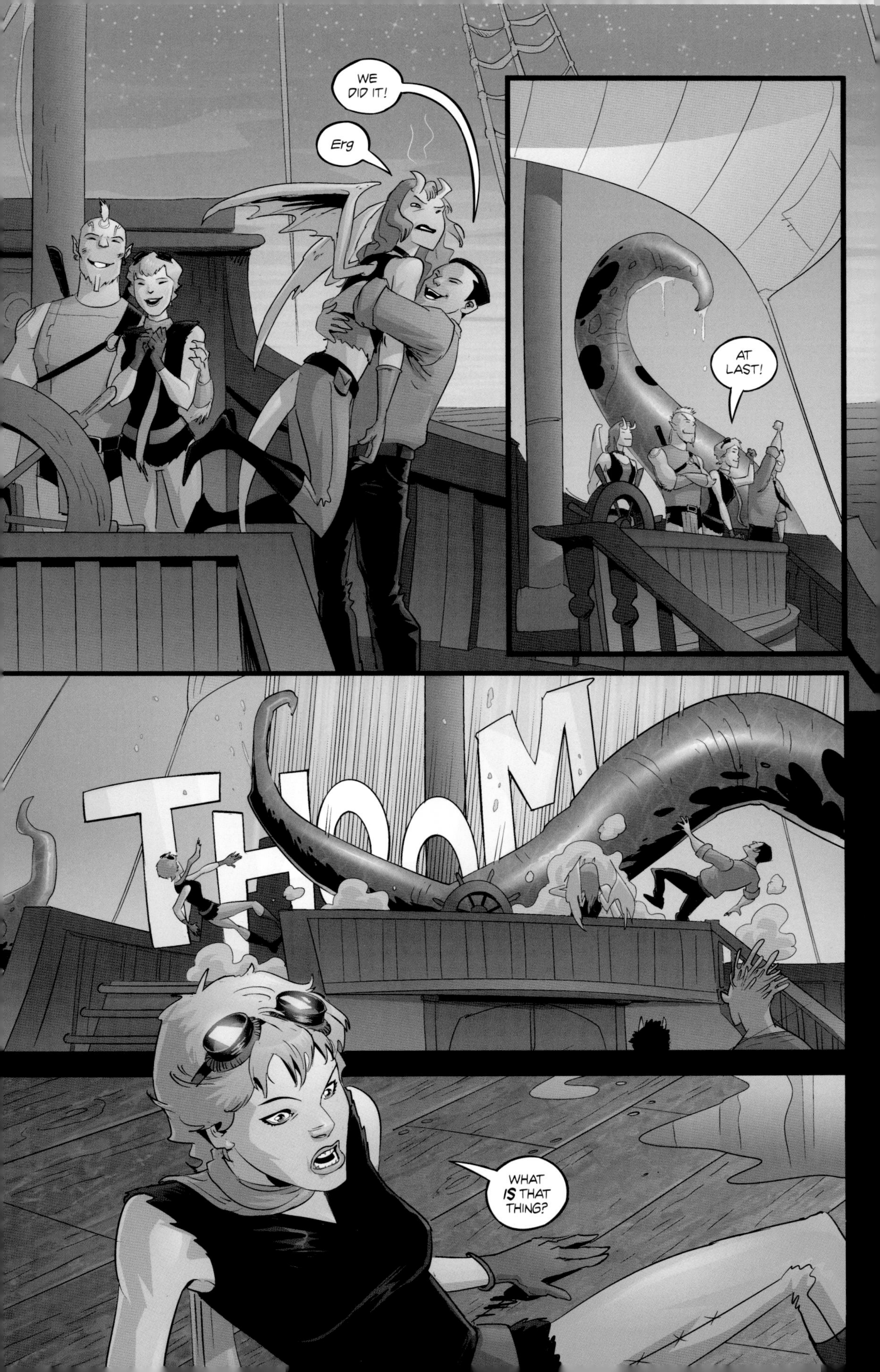
WE DID IT!
Erg
AT LAST!
THOOM
WHAT IS THAT THING?

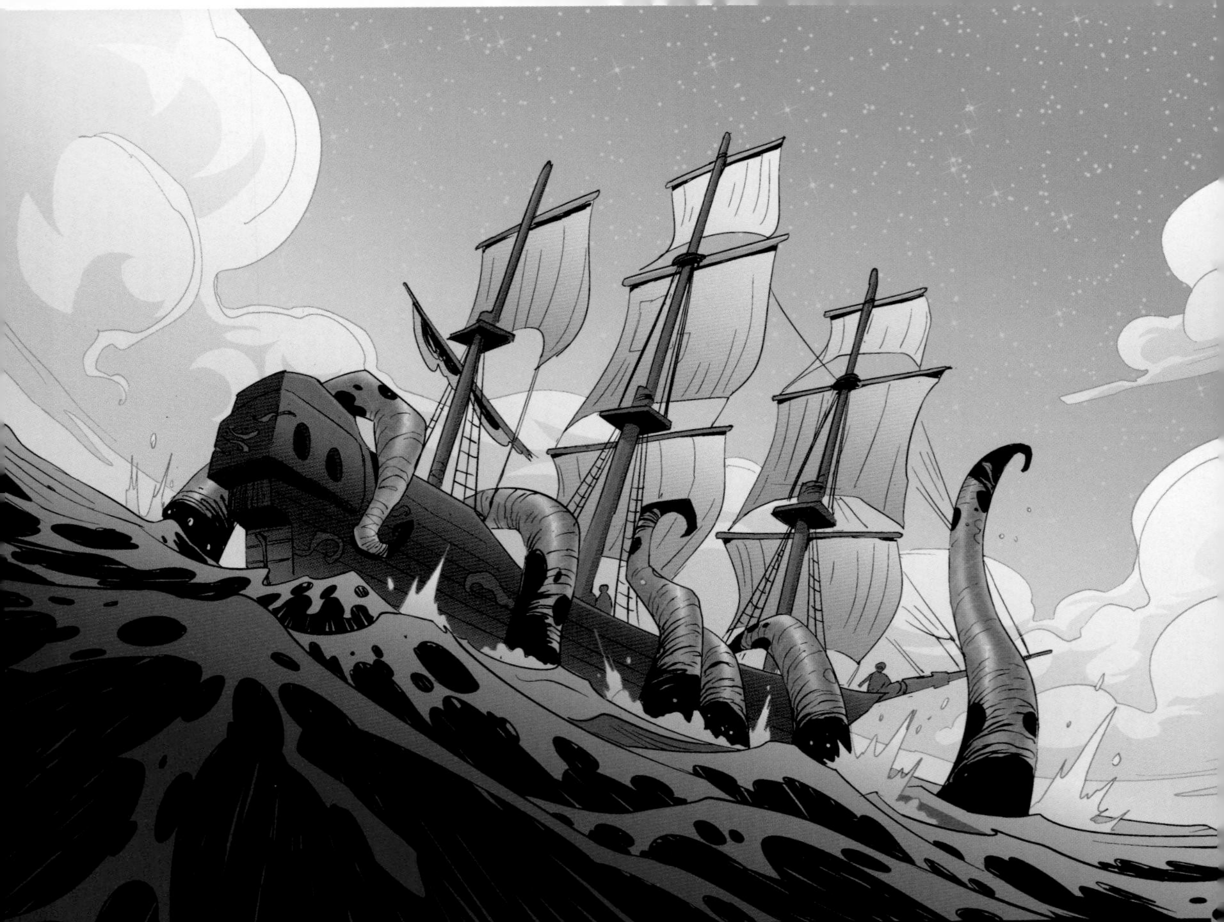

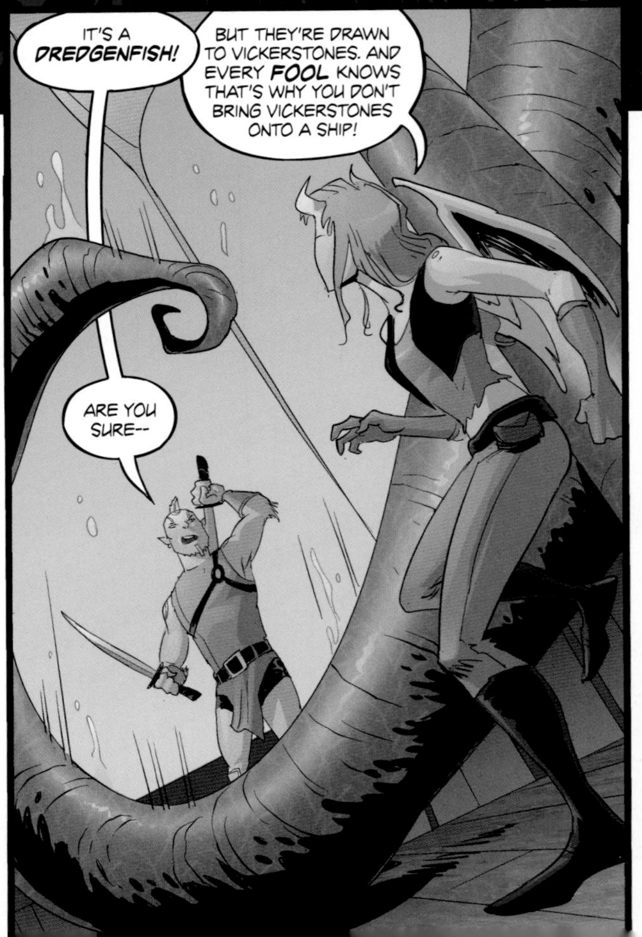
IT'S A DREDGENFISH!
BUT THEY'RE DRAWN TO VICKERSTONES. AND EVERY FOOL KNOWS THAT'S WHY YOU DON'T BRING VICKERSTONES ONTO A SHIP!
ARE YOU SURE--

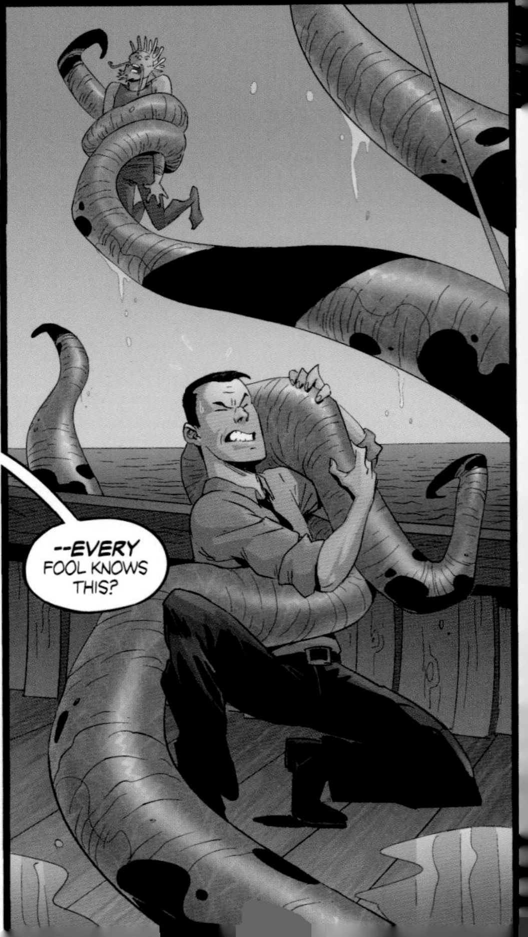
--EVERY FOOL KNOWS THIS?

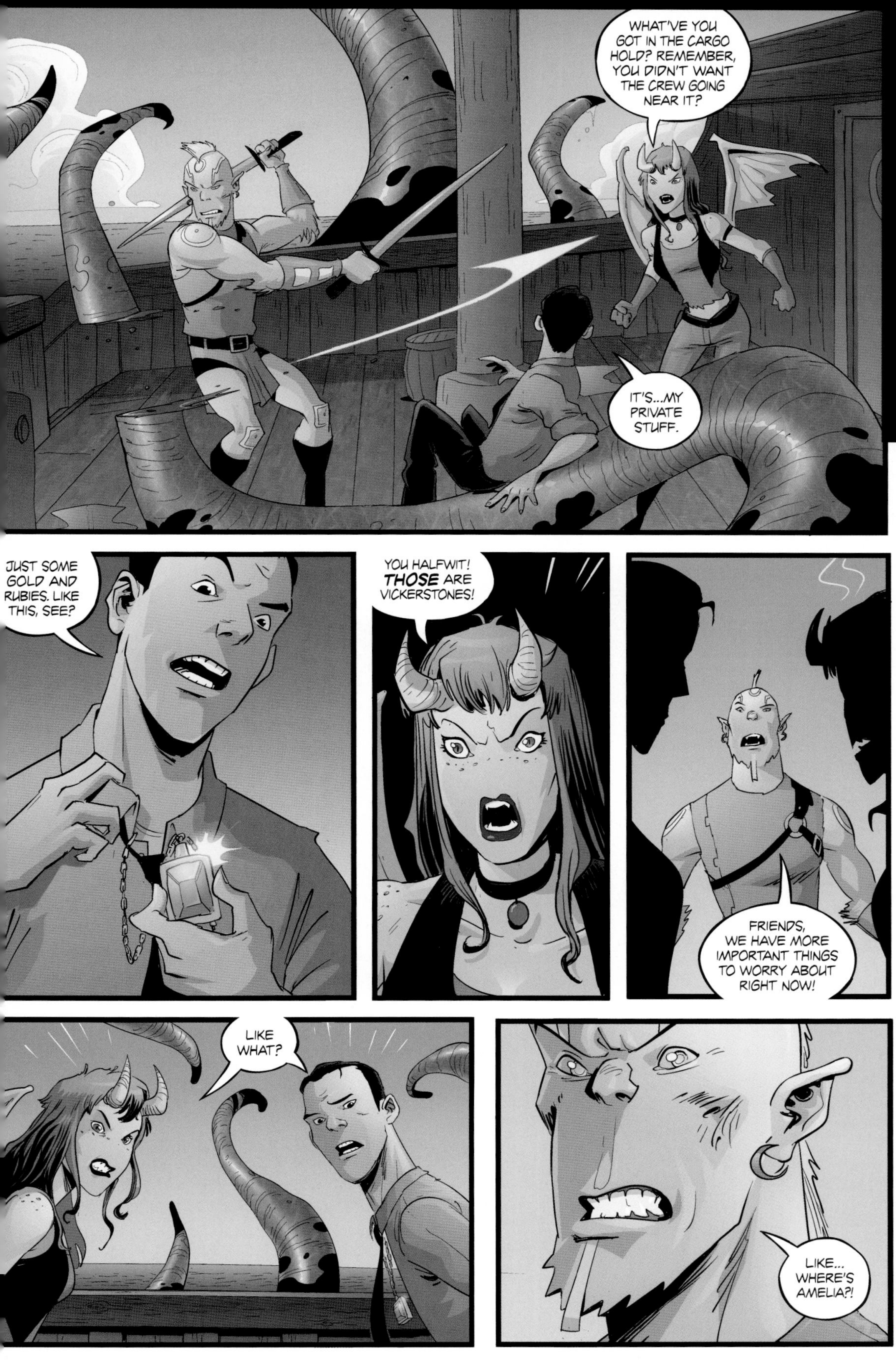
WHAT'VE YOU GOT IN THE CARGO HOLD? REMEMBER, YOU DIDN'T WANT THE CREW GOING NEAR IT?
IT'S...MY PRIVATE STUFF.
JUST SOME GOLD AND RUBIES. LIKE THIS, SEE?
YOU HALFWIT! THOSE ARE VICKERSTONES!
FRIENDS, WE HAVE MORE IMPORTANT THINGS TO WORRY ABOUT RIGHT NOW!
LIKE WHAT?
LIKE... WHERE'S AMELIA?!

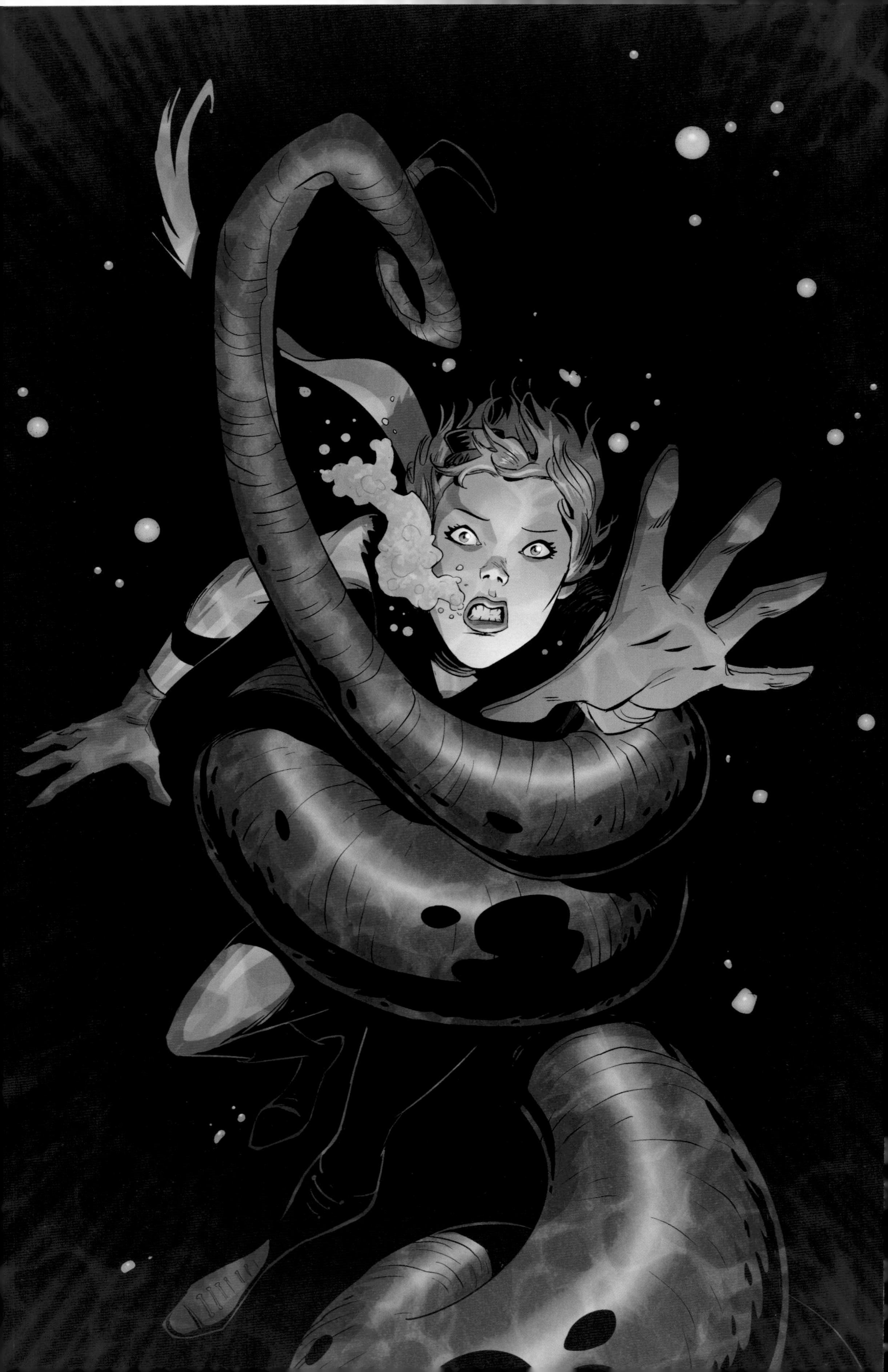

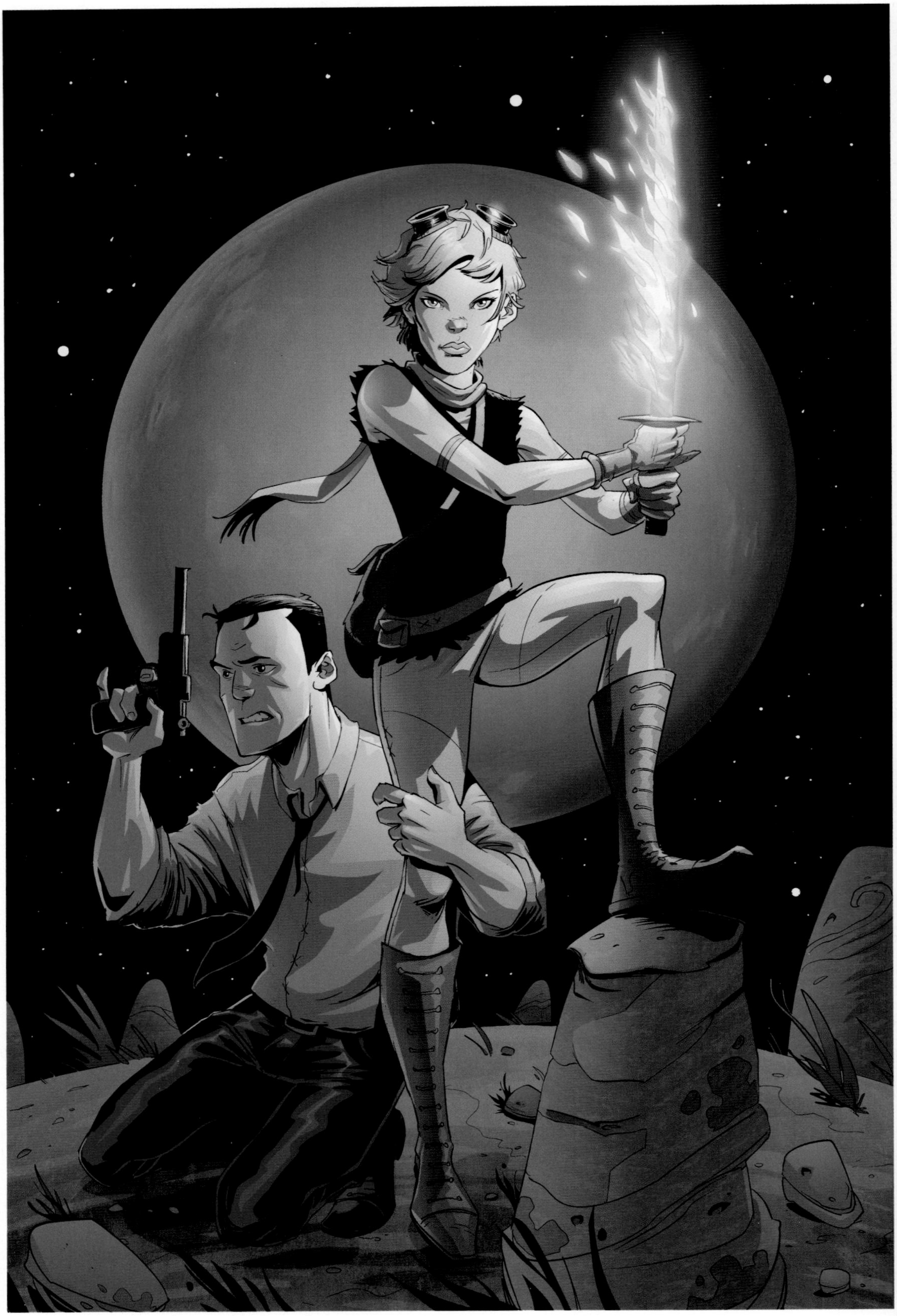

CHAPTER 3

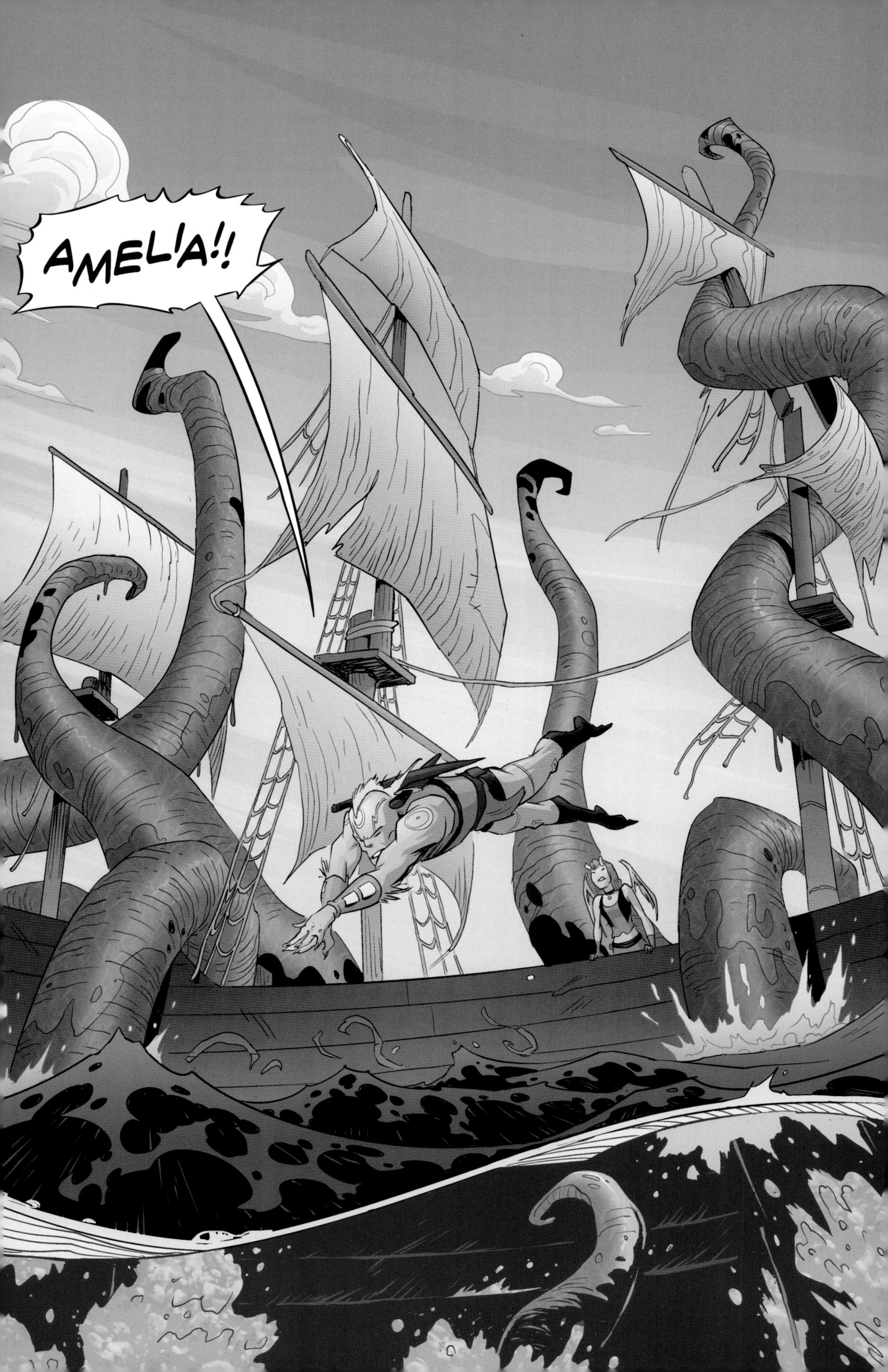
AMELIA!!

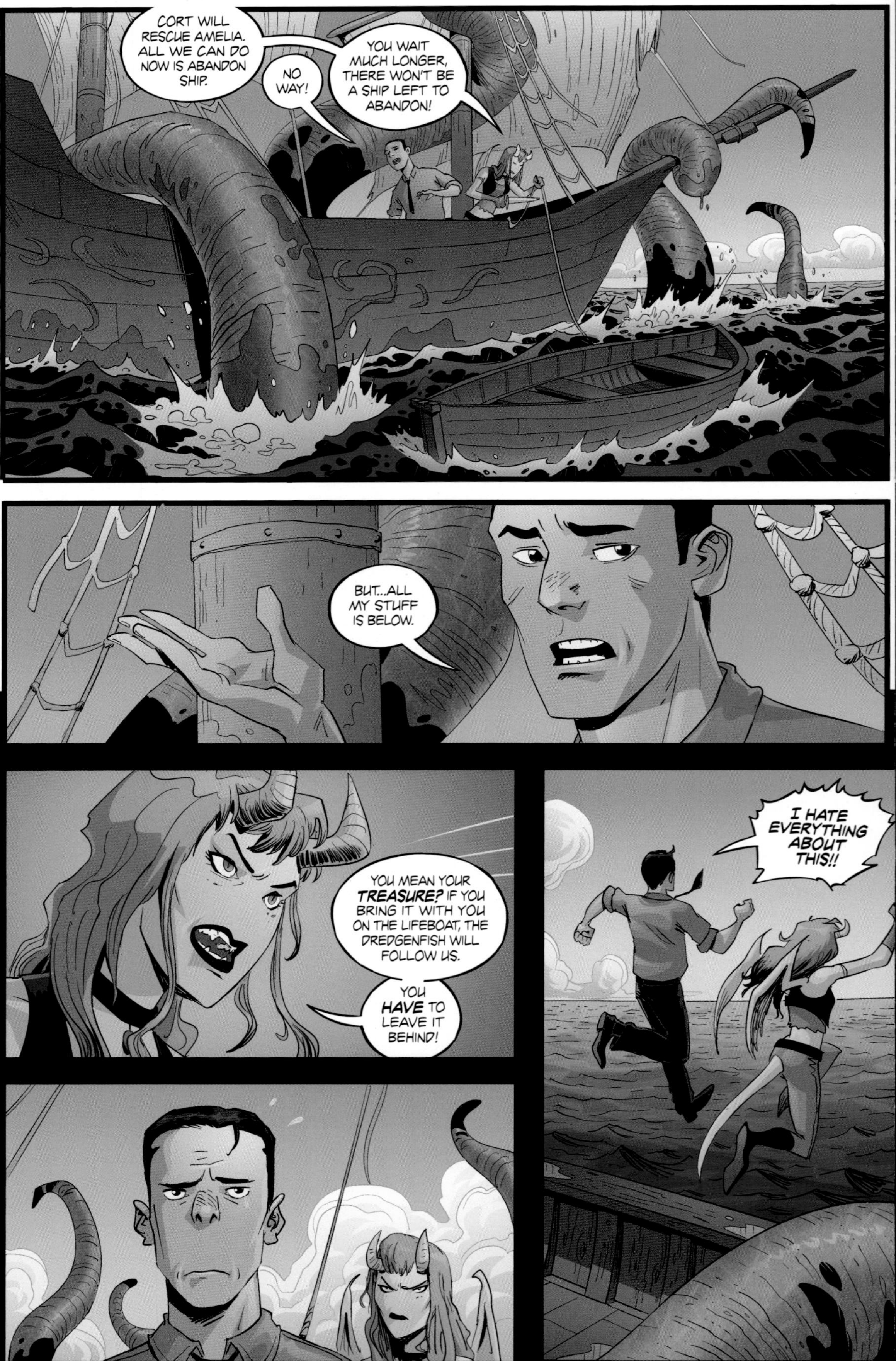
CORT WILL RESCUE AMELIA. ALL WE CAN DO NOW IS ABANDON SHIP.
NO WAY!
YOU WAIT MUCH LONGER, THERE WON'T BE A SHIP LEFT TO ABANDON!
BUT...ALL MY STUFF IS BELOW.
YOU MEAN YOUR TREASURE? IF YOU BRING IT WITH YOU ON THE LIFEBOAT, THE DREDGENFISH WILL FOLLOW US.
YOU HAVE TO LEAVE IT BEHIND!
I HATE EVERYTHING ABOUT THIS!!

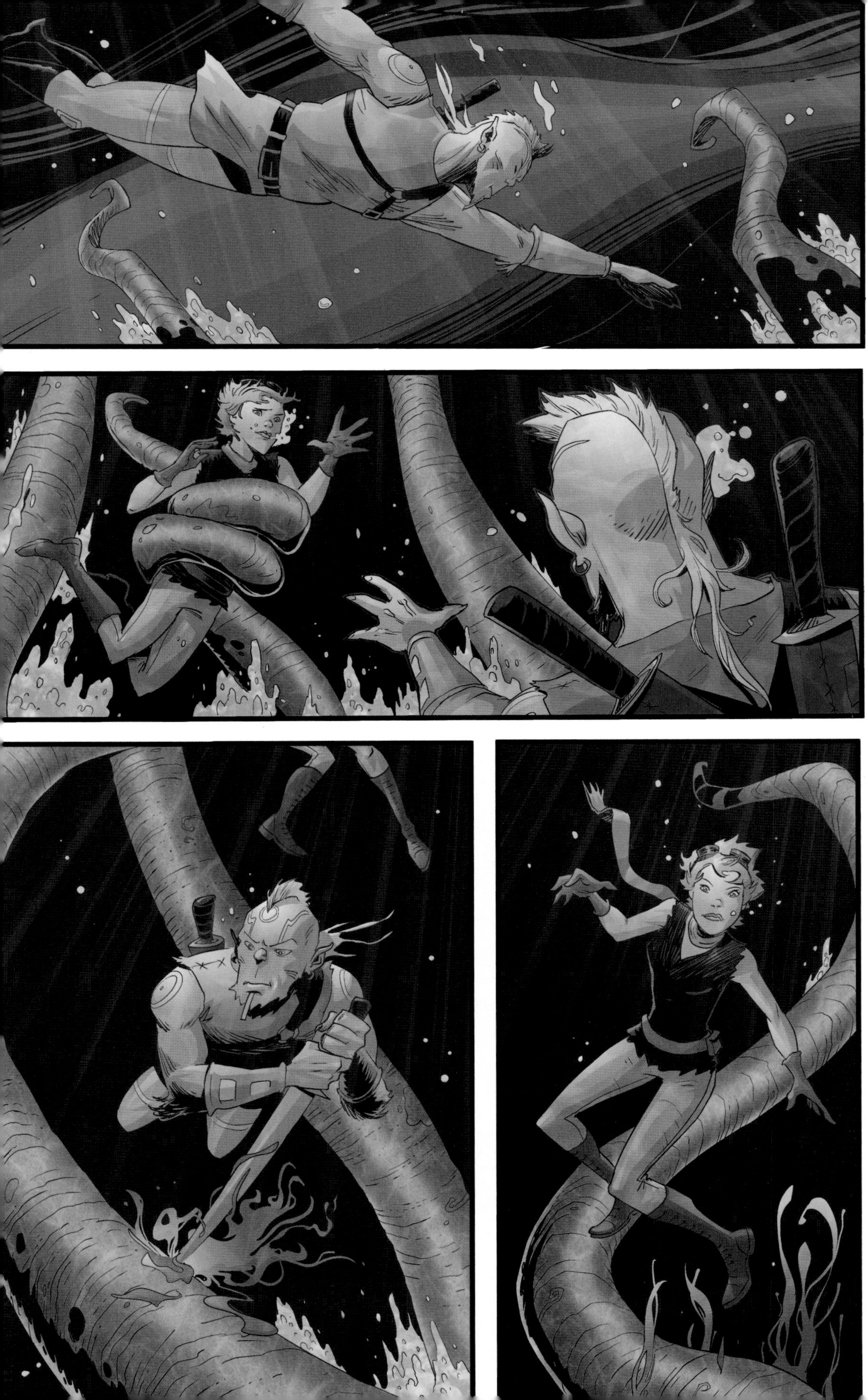

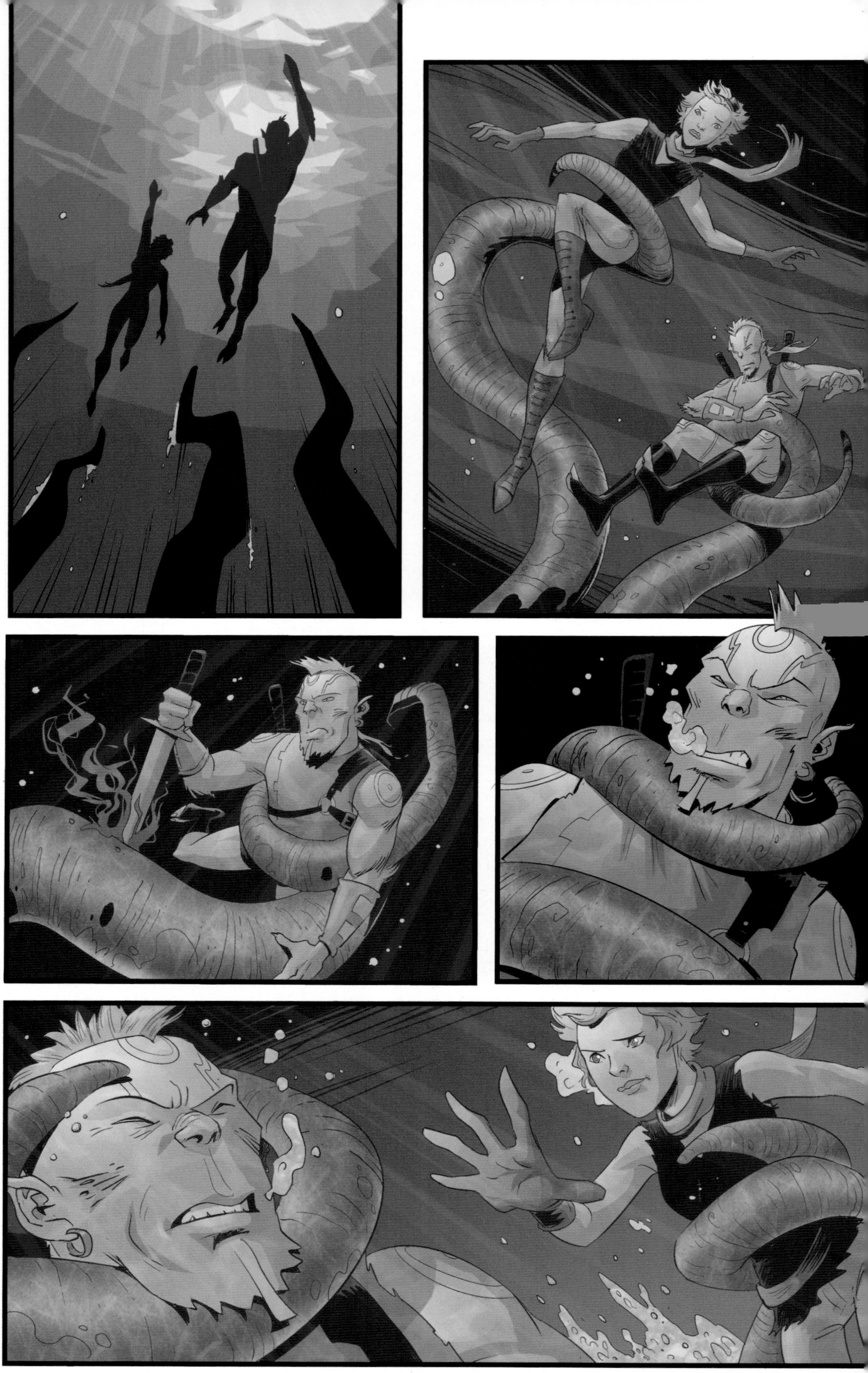

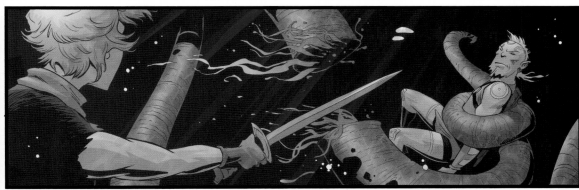

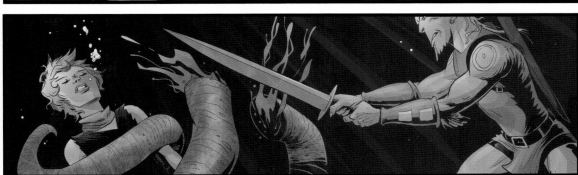

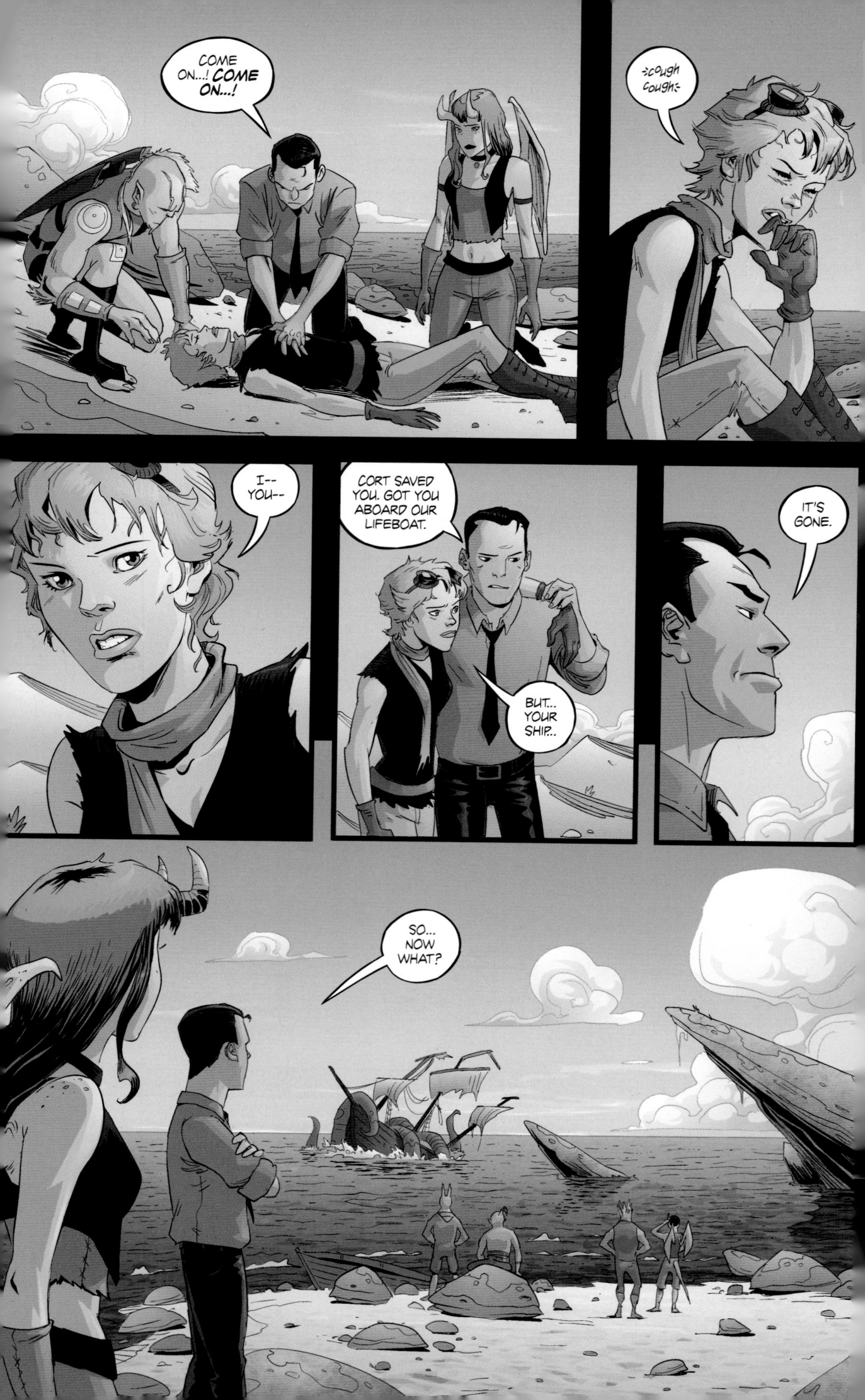
COME ON...! COME ON...!
cough cough
I-- YOU--
CORT SAVED YOU. GOT YOU ABOARD OUR LIFEBOAT.
BUT... YOUR SHIP...
IT'S GONE.
SO... NOW WHAT?

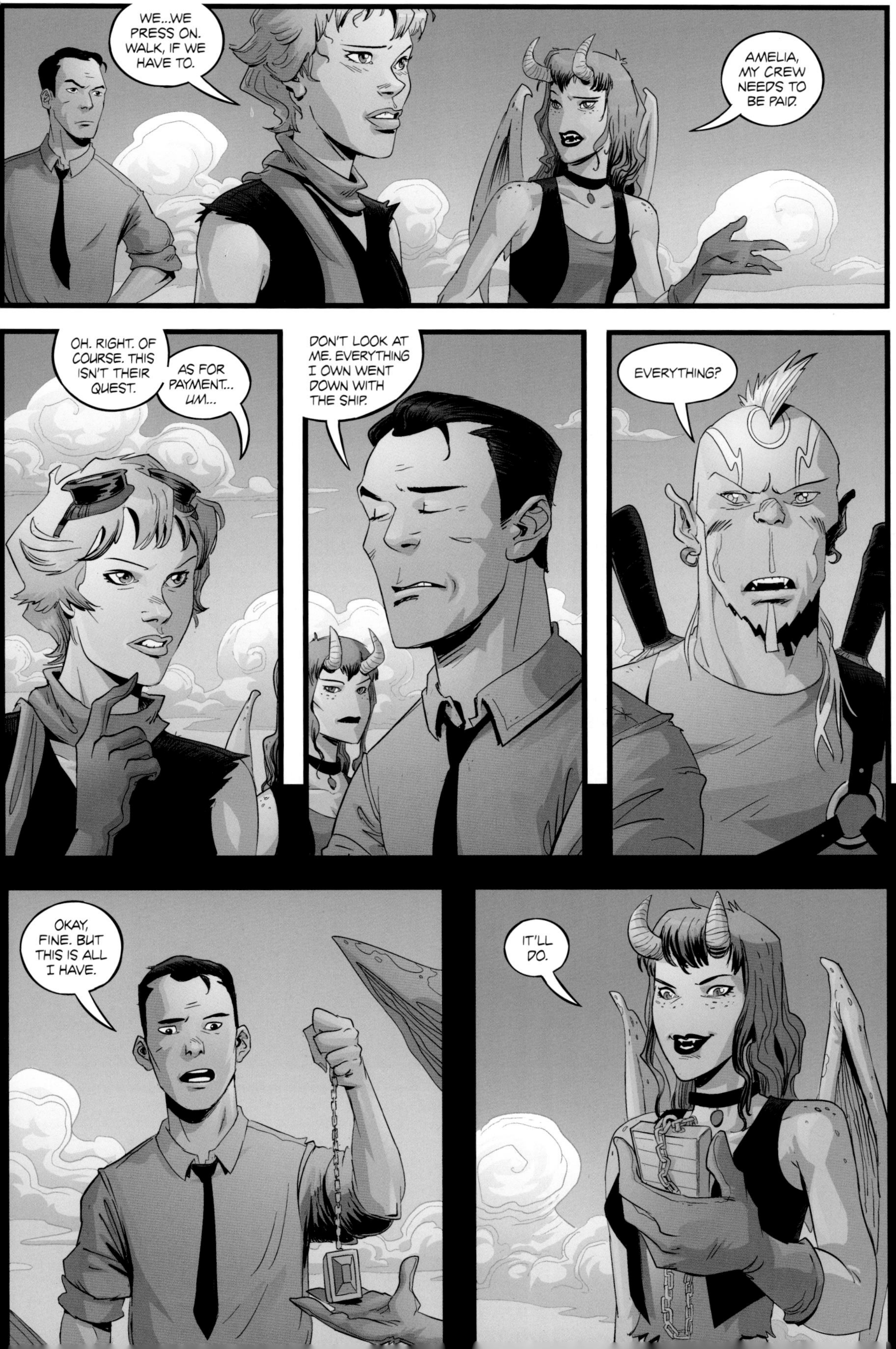
WE...WE PRESS ON. WALK, IF WE HAVE TO.
AMELIA, MY CREW NEEDS TO BE PAID.
OH. RIGHT. OF COURSE. THIS ISN'T THEIR QUEST.
AS FOR PAYMENT... UM...
DON'T LOOK AT ME. EVERYTHING I OWN WENT DOWN WITH THE SHIP.
EVERYTHING?
OKAY, FINE. BUT THIS IS ALL I HAVE.
IT'LL DO.

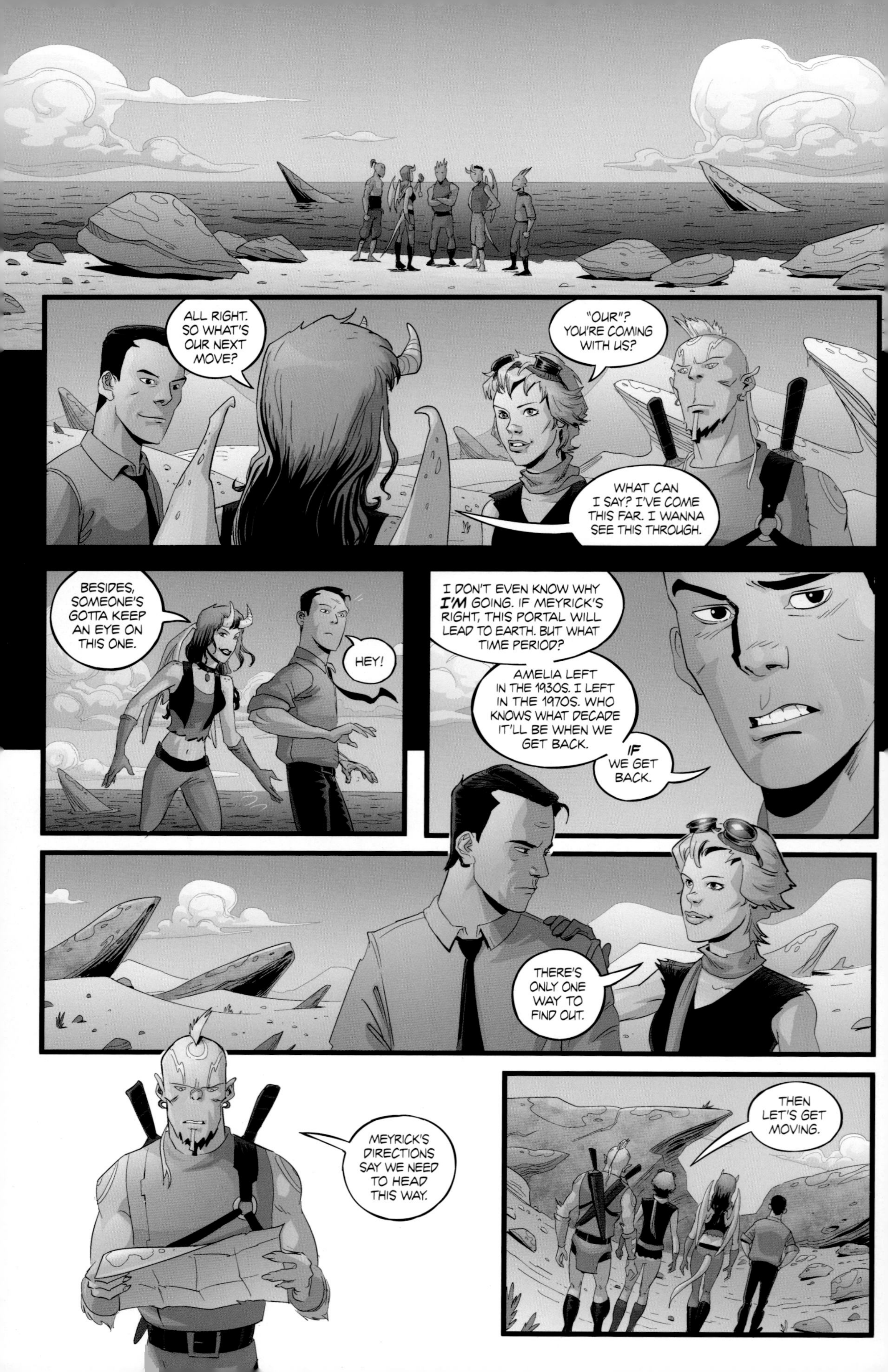
ALL RIGHT. SO WHAT'S OUR NEXT MOVE?
"OUR"? YOU'RE COMING WITH US?
WHAT CAN I SAY? I'VE COME THIS FAR. I WANNA SEE THIS THROUGH.
BESIDES, SOMEONE'S GOTTA KEEP AN EYE ON THIS ONE.
HEY!
I DON'T EVEN KNOW WHY ***I'M*** GOING. IF MEYRICK'S RIGHT, THIS PORTAL WILL LEAD TO EARTH. BUT WHAT TIME PERIOD?
AMELIA LEFT IN THE 1930S. I LEFT IN THE 1970S. WHO KNOWS WHAT DECADE IT'LL BE WHEN WE GET BACK.
IF WE GET BACK.
THERE'S ONLY ONE WAY TO FIND OUT.
MEYRICK'S DIRECTIONS SAY WE NEED TO HEAD THIS WAY.
THEN LET'S GET MOVING.

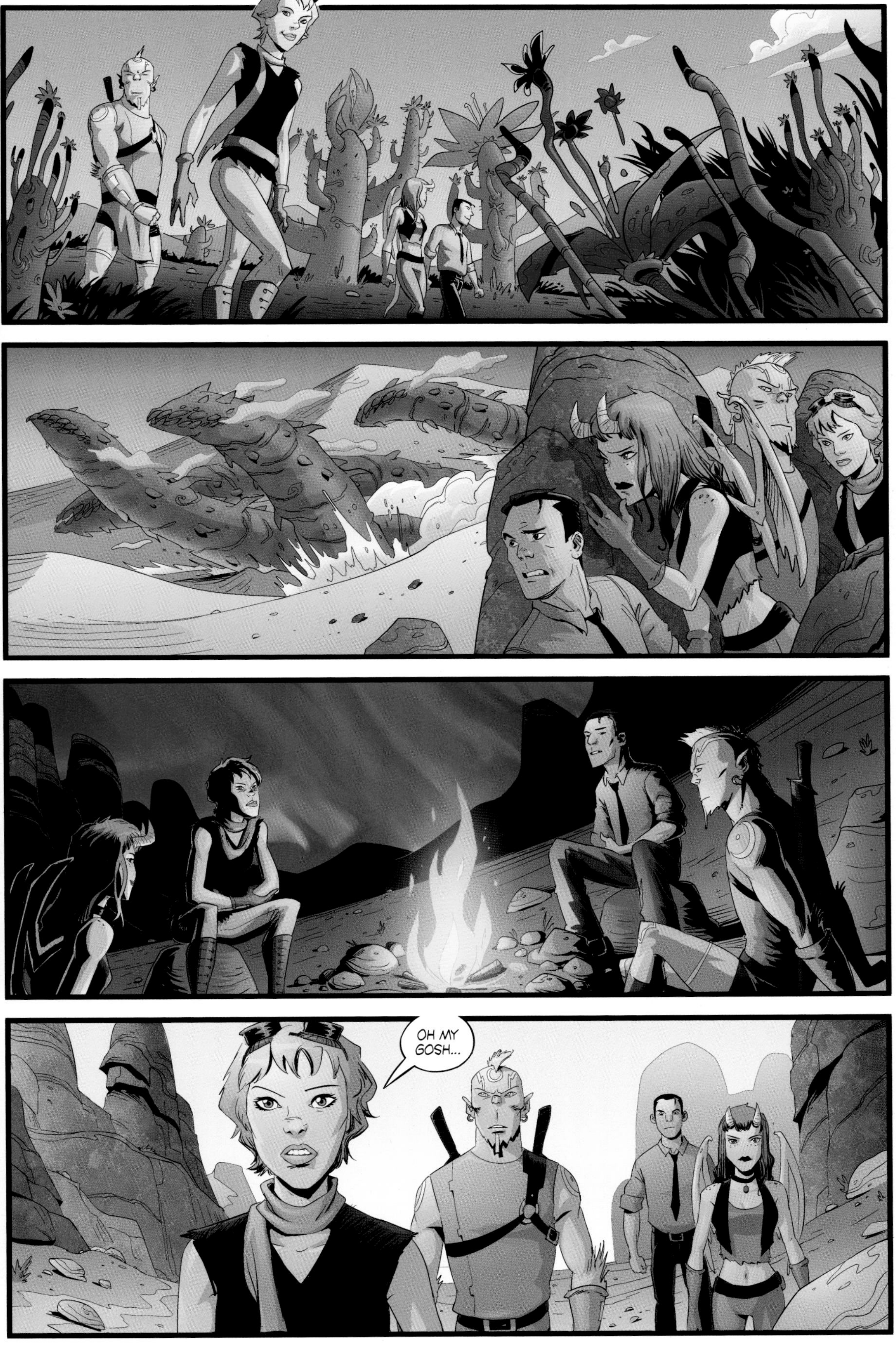
OH MY GOSH...

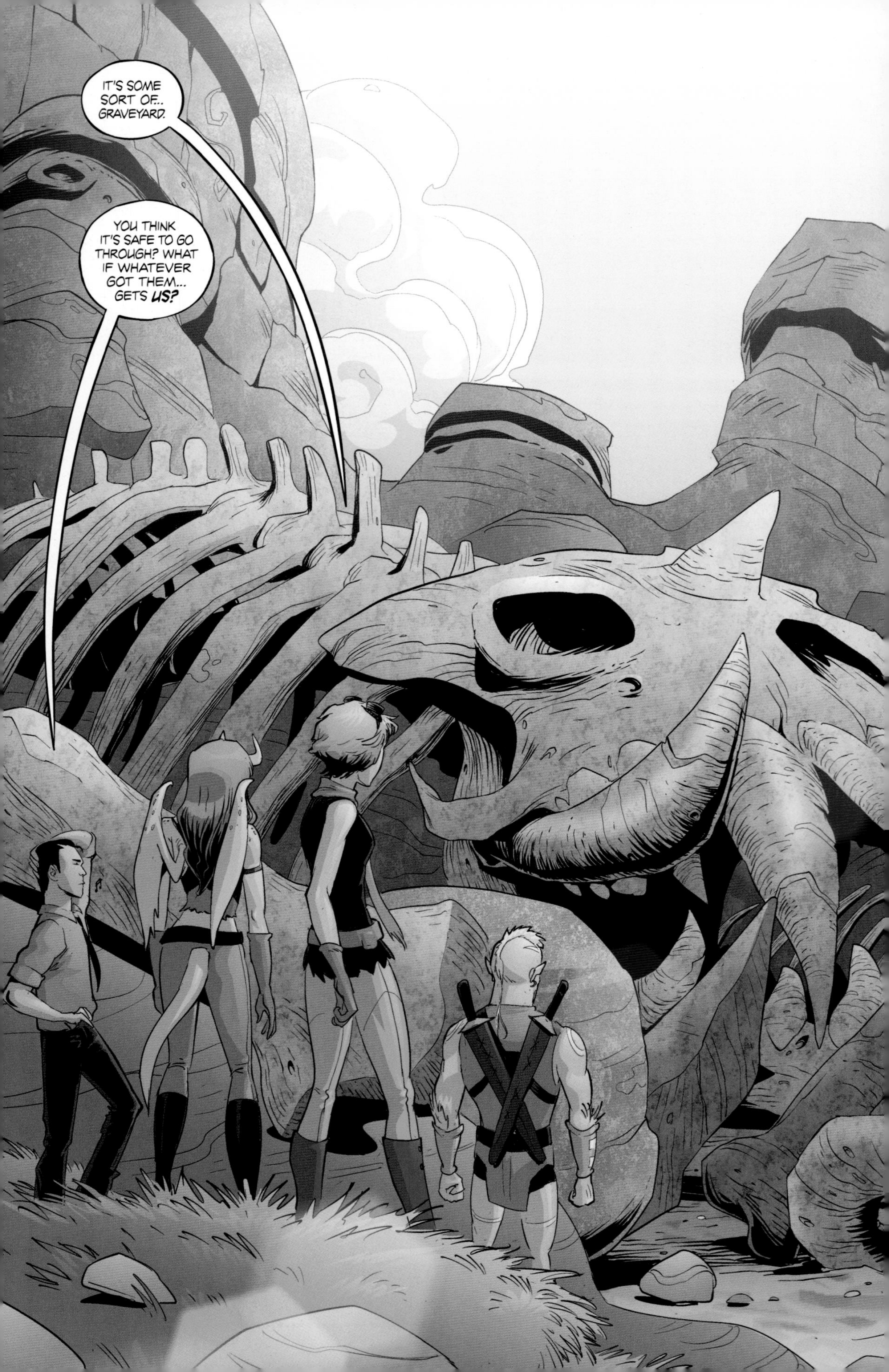
IT'S SOME SORT OF.. GRAVEYARD.
YOU THINK IT'S SAFE TO GO THROUGH? WHAT IF WHATEVER GOT THEM... GETS **US?**

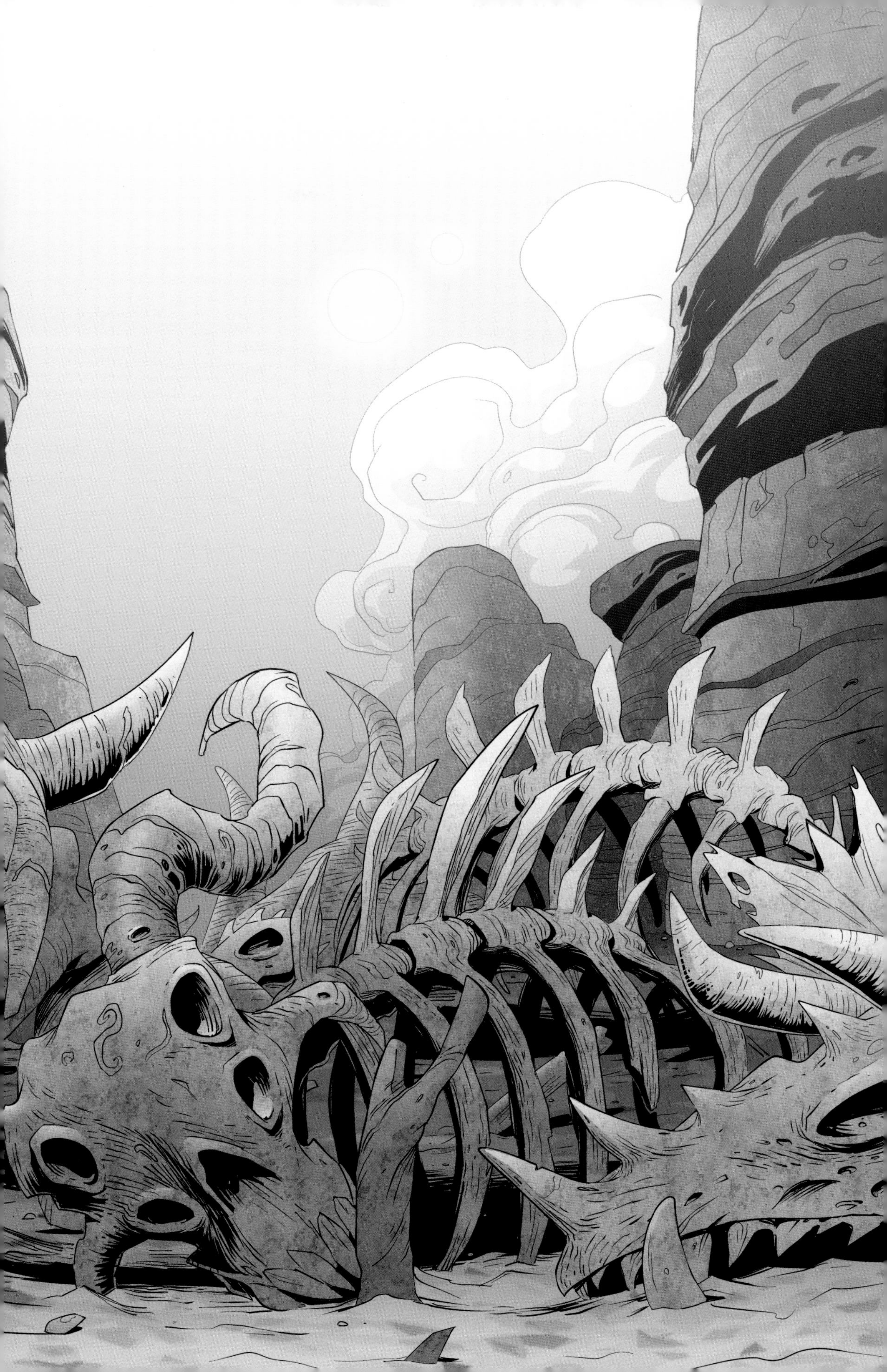

I DON'T THINK WE HAVE A CHOICE. THE **PORTAL** SHOULD BE JUST THROUGH THIS VALLEY.

BUT LOOK AT THOSE MOUNTAINS. IT WOULD TAKE **DAYS** TO FIND ANOTHER WAY AROUND.

THAT SETTLES IT. WE GO THROUGH.

COME ON. I'LL PROTECT YOU.

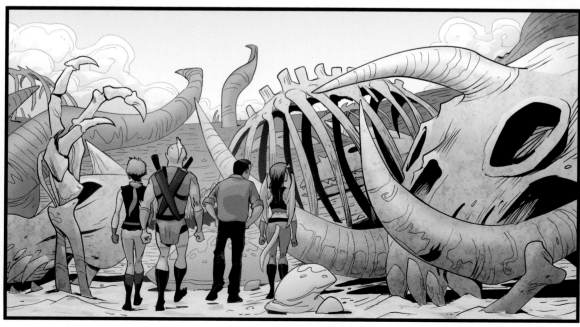

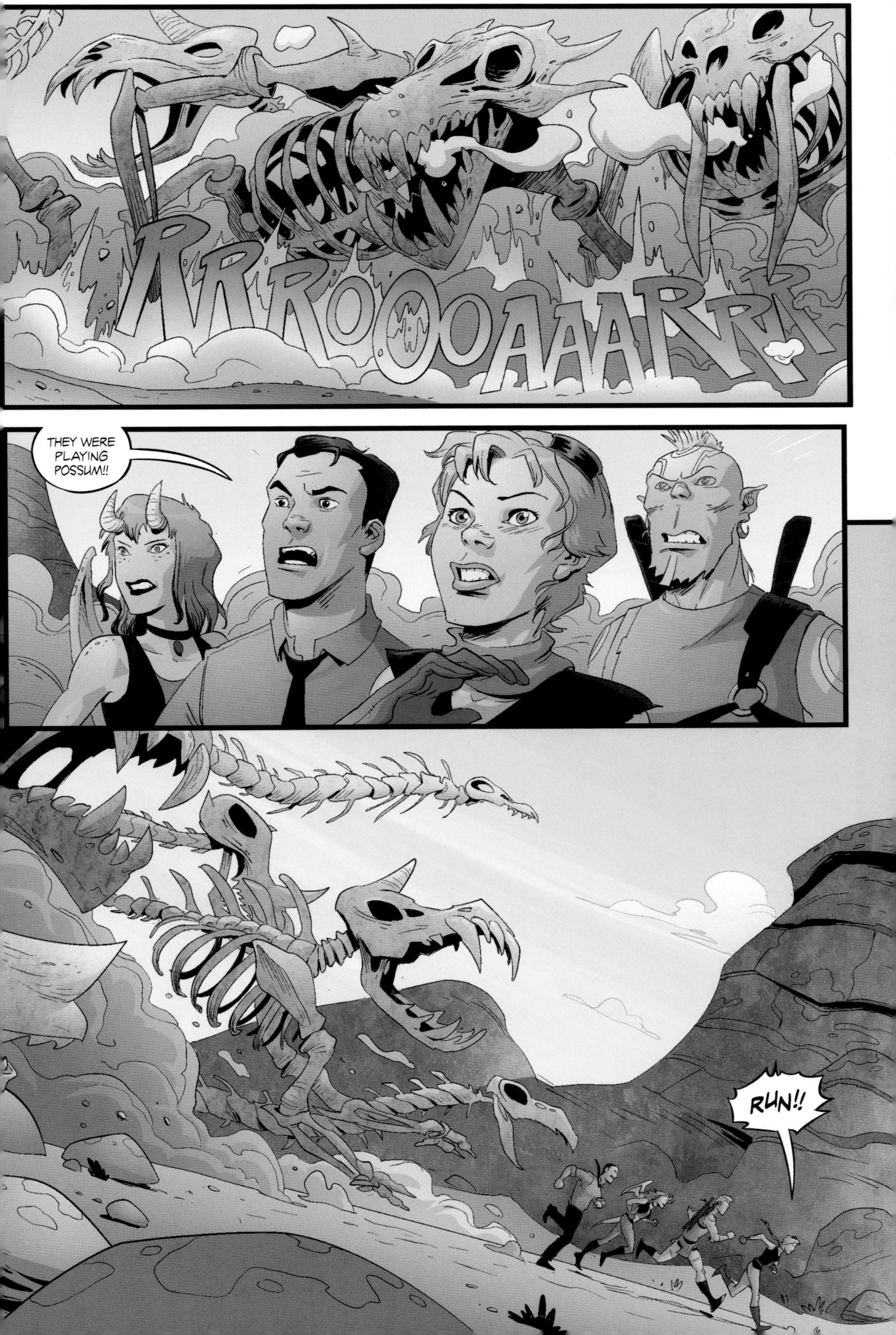
RRROOOAAARRR
THEY WERE PLAYING POSSUM!!
RUN!!

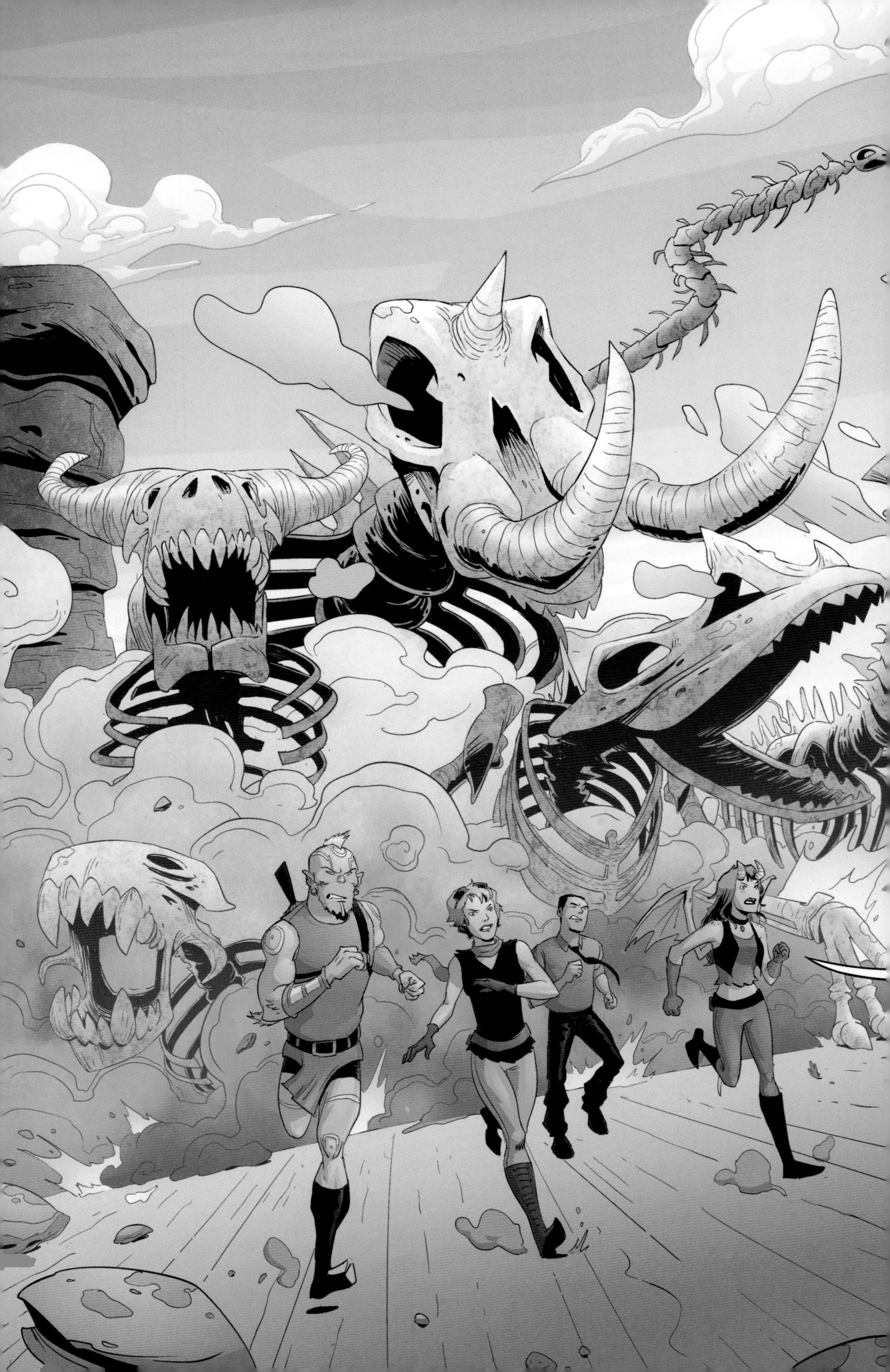

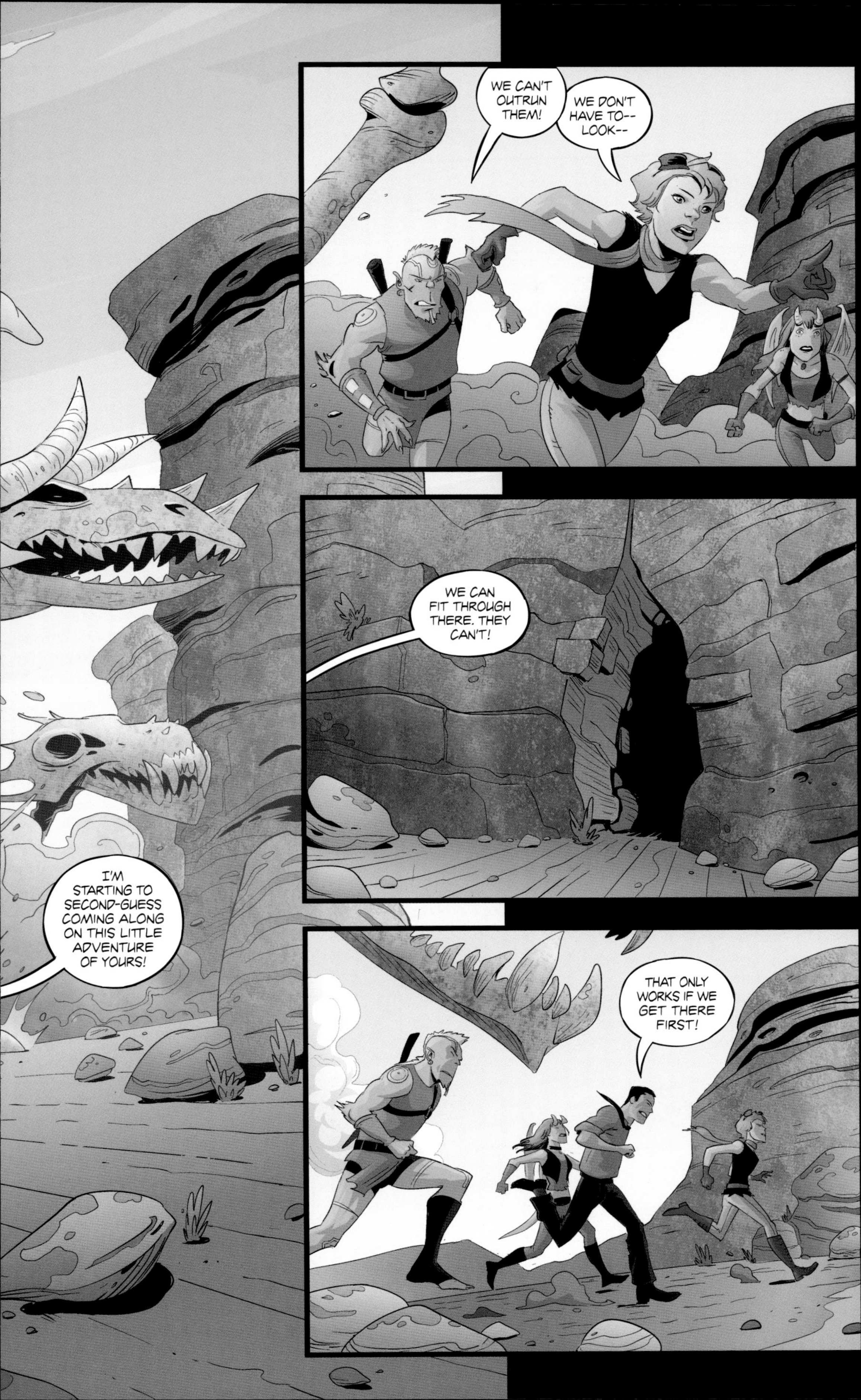

WE CAN'T OUTRUN THEM!
WE DON'T HAVE TO-- LOOK--
WE CAN FIT THROUGH THERE. THEY CAN'T!
I'M STARTING TO SECOND-GUESS COMING ALONG ON THIS LITTLE ADVENTURE OF YOURS!
THAT ONLY WORKS IF WE GET THERE FIRST!

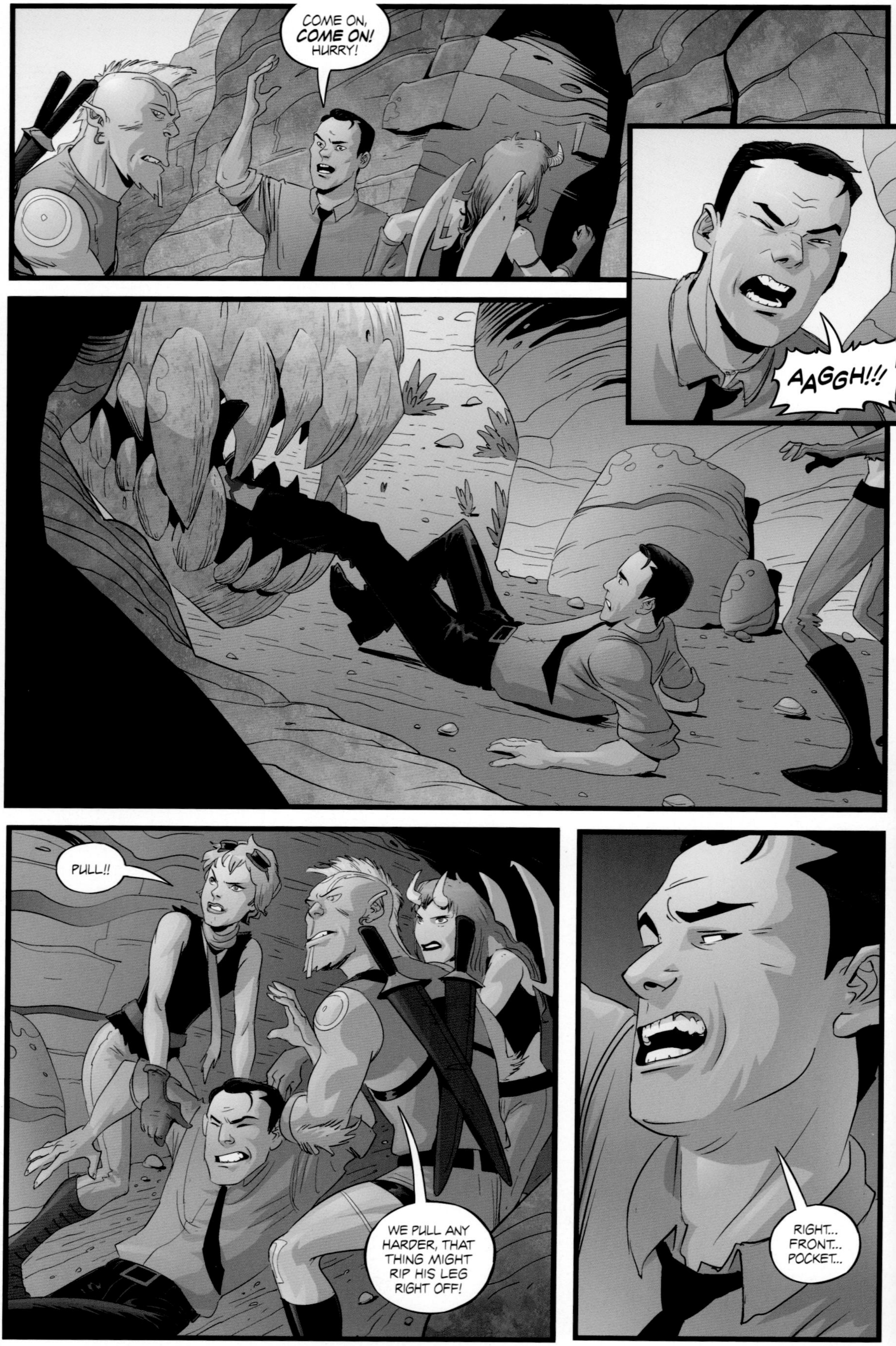
COME ON, COME ON! HURRY!
AAGGH!!!
PULL!!
WE PULL ANY HARDER, THAT THING MIGHT RIP HIS LEG RIGHT OFF!
RIGHT... FRONT... POCKET...

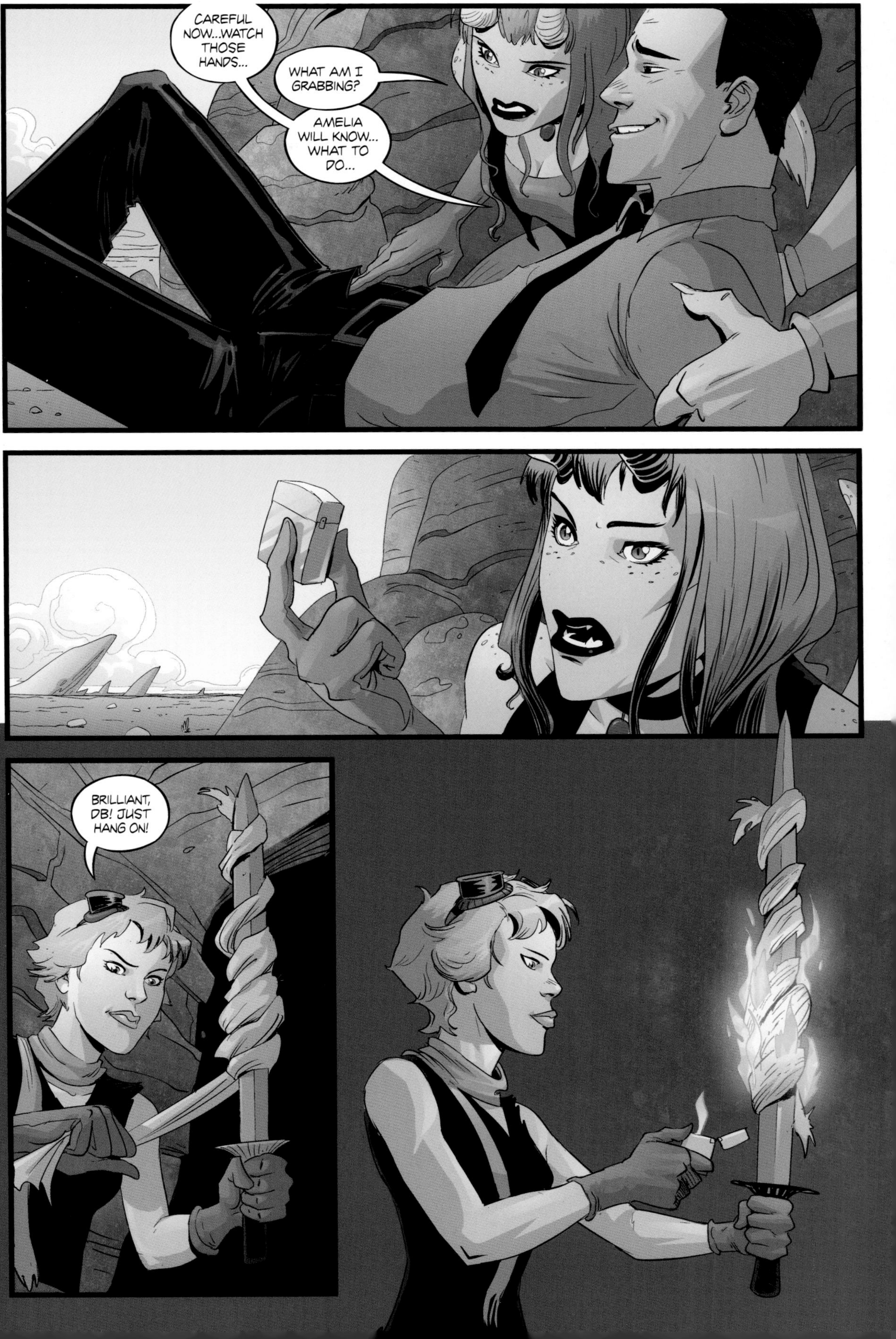
CAREFUL NOW...WATCH THOSE HANDS...
WHAT AM I GRABBING?
AMELIA WILL KNOW... WHAT TO DO...
BRILLIANT, DB! JUST HANG ON!

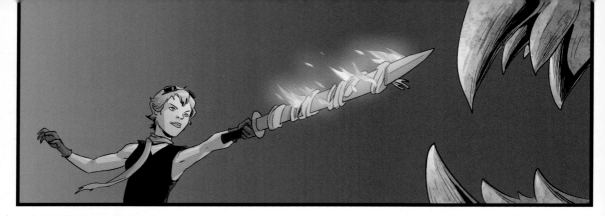

AAARRROOOO

TH-THANKS, GUYS.

DON'T READ TOO MUCH INTO IT. I JUST WANT TO MAKE SURE YOU GET THROUGH THAT PORTAL AND FAR AWAY FROM MY PEOPLE.

I LOVE YOU TOO, MAN.

EVERYONE... LOOK...

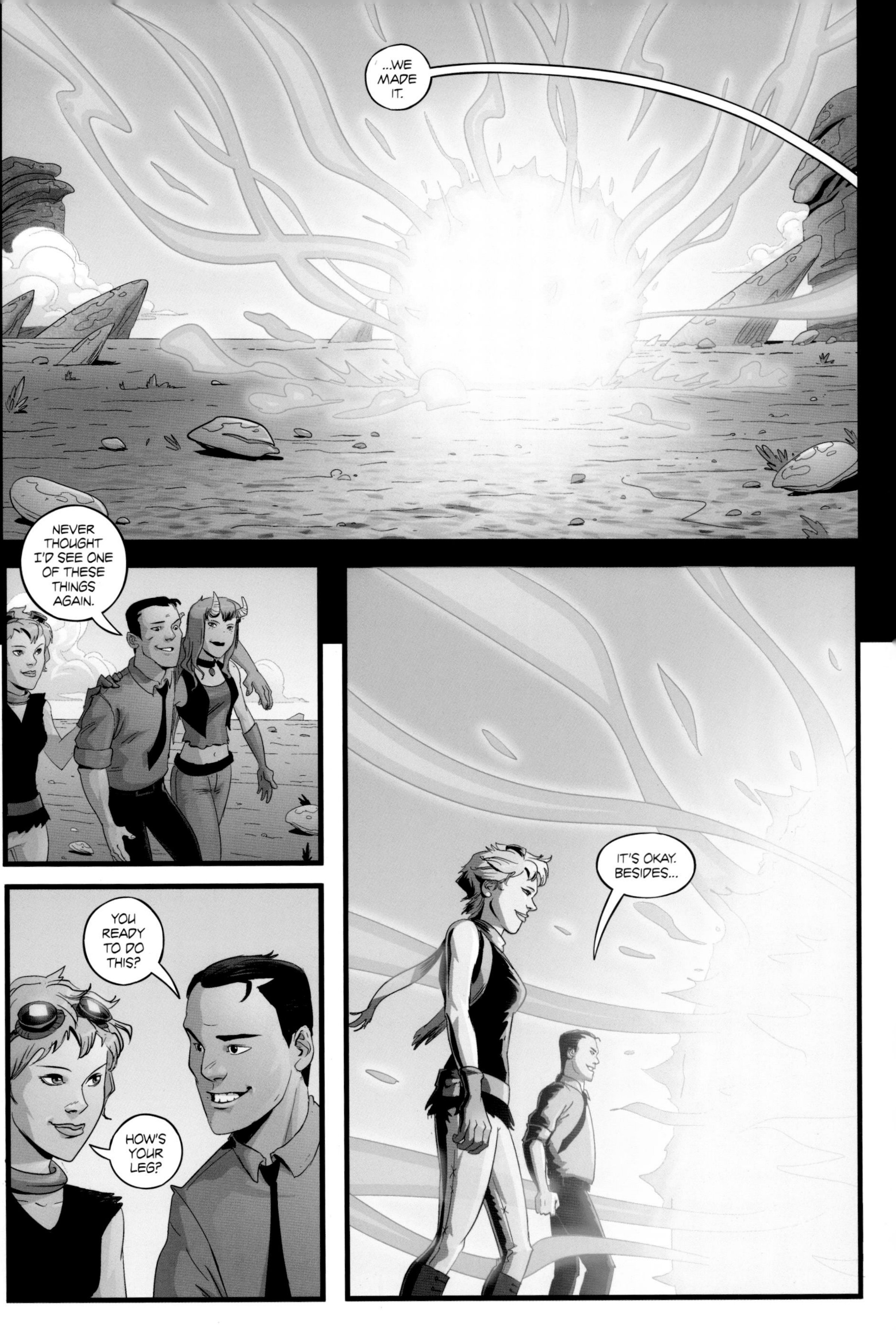
...WE MADE IT.
NEVER THOUGHT I'D SEE ONE OF THESE THINGS AGAIN.
YOU READY TO DO THIS?
HOW'S YOUR LEG?
IT'S OKAY. BESIDES...

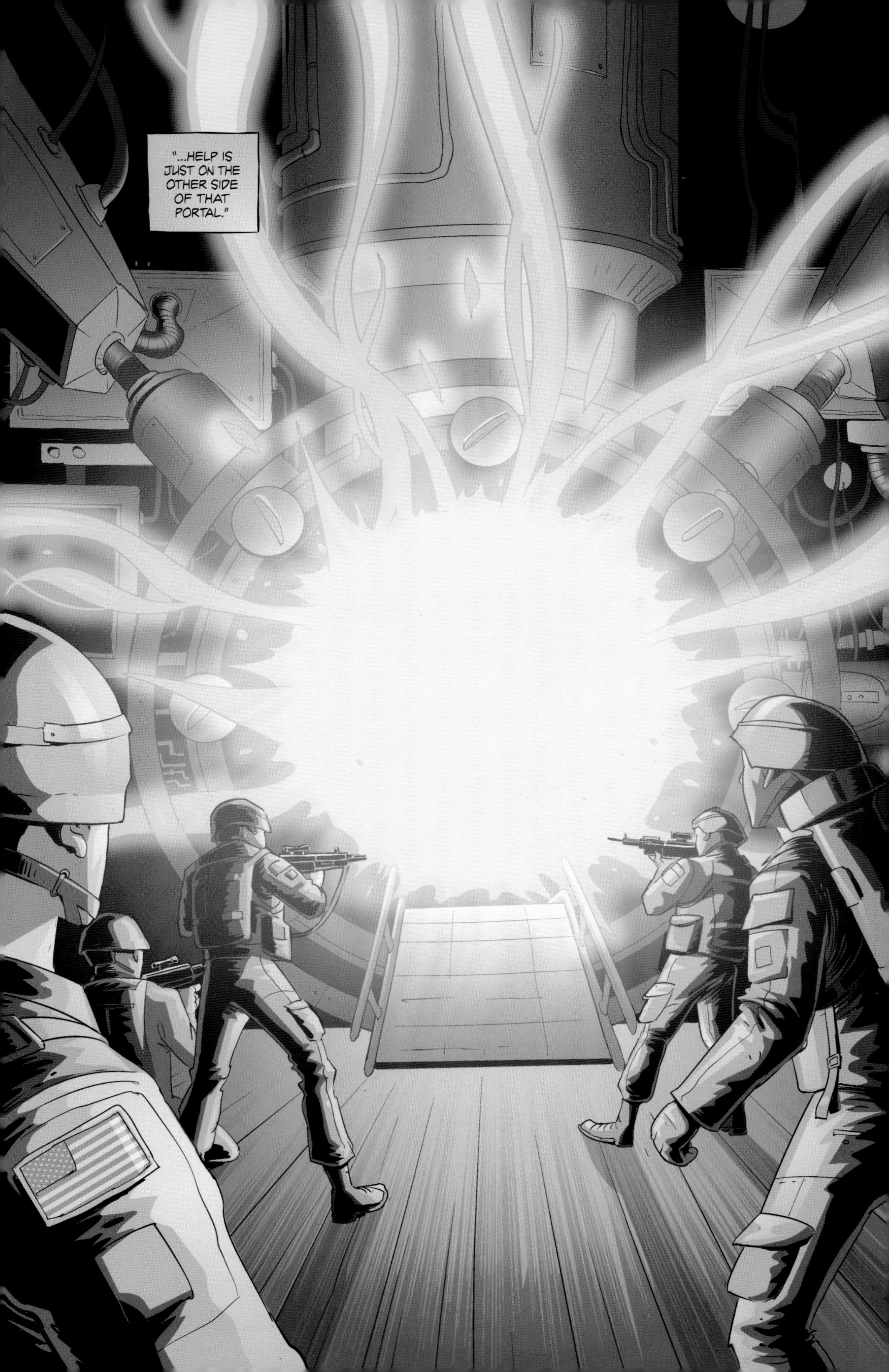
"...HELP IS JUST ON THE OTHER SIDE OF THAT PORTAL."

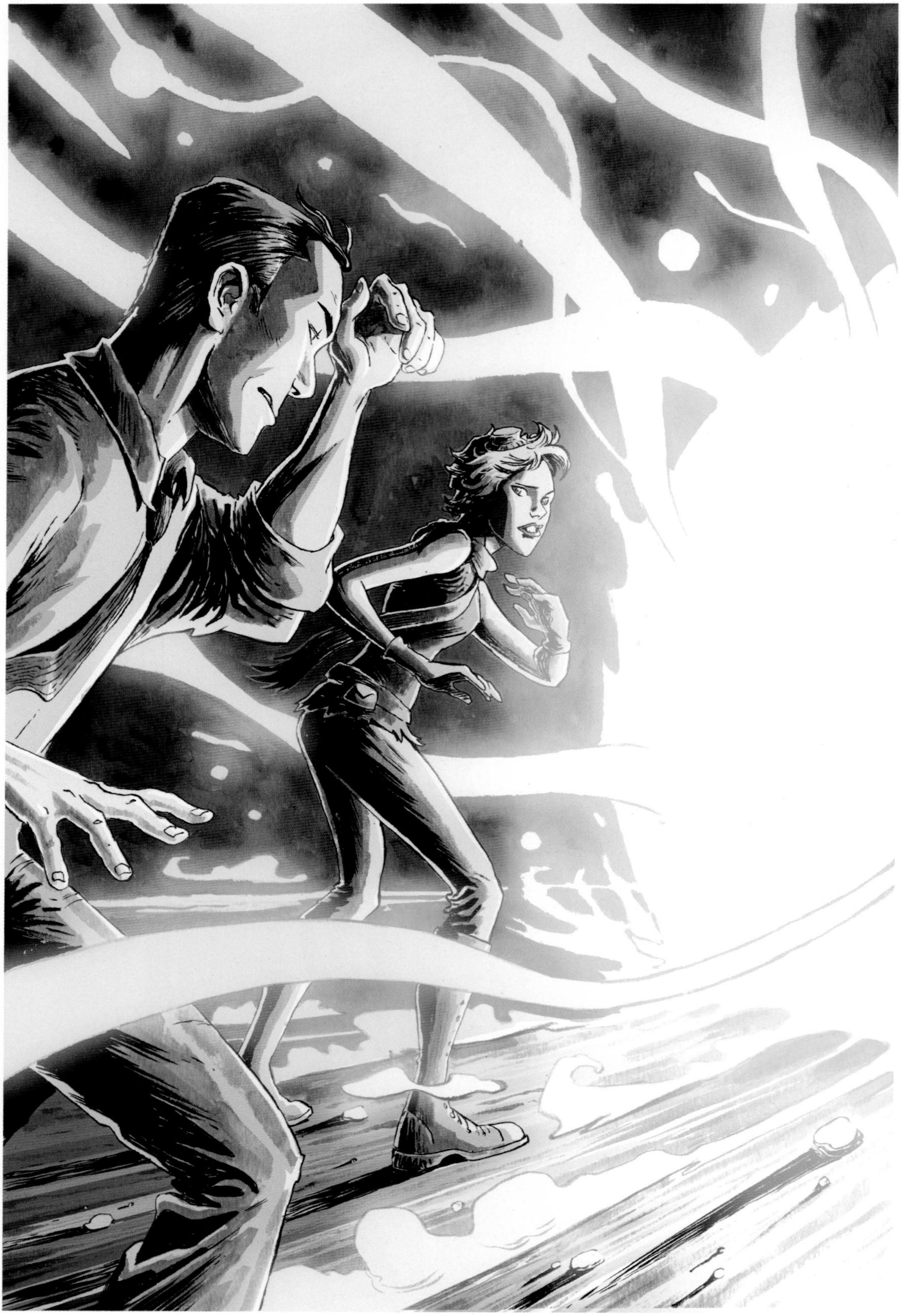

CHAPTER 4

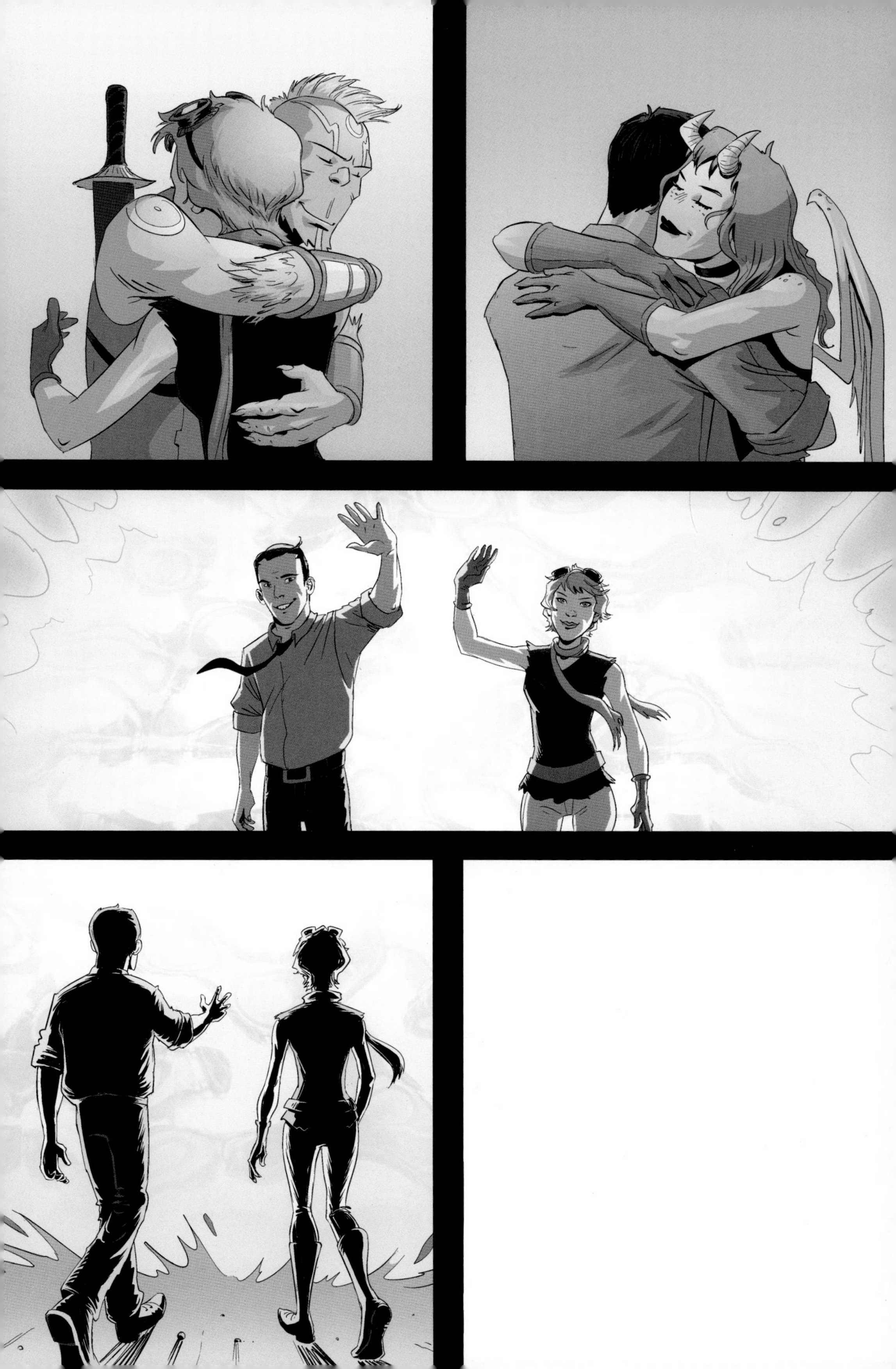

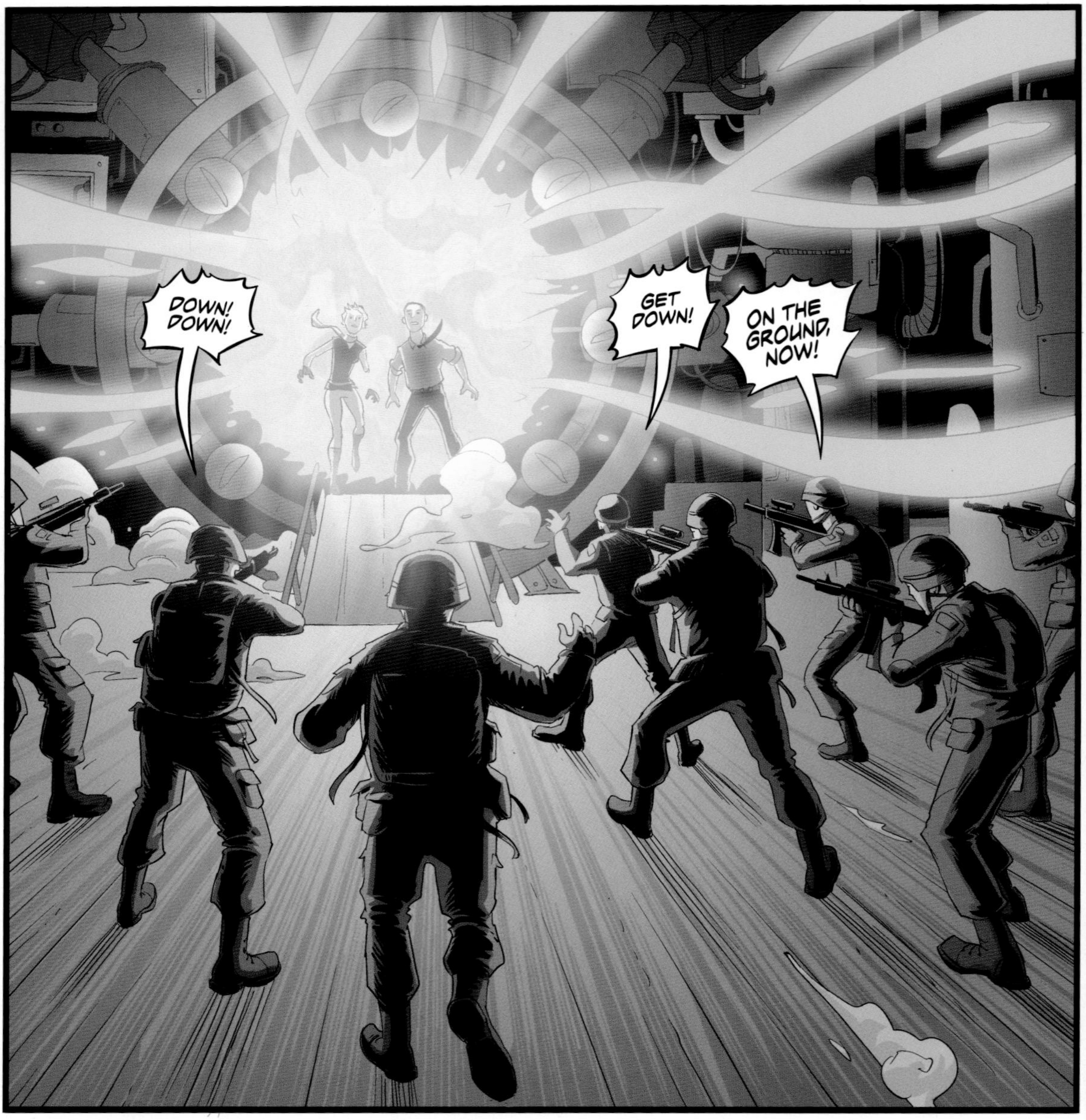
DOWN! DOWN!
GET DOWN!
ON THE GROUND, NOW!

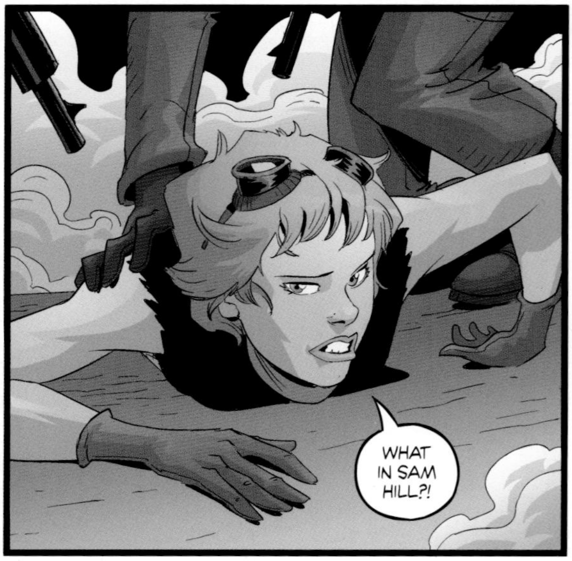
WHAT IN SAM HILL?!

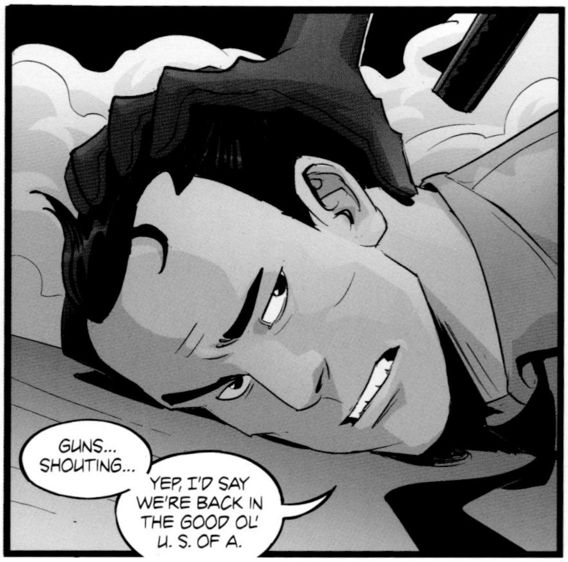
GUNS... SHOUTING...
YEP, I'D SAY WE'RE BACK IN THE GOOD OL' U. S. OF A.

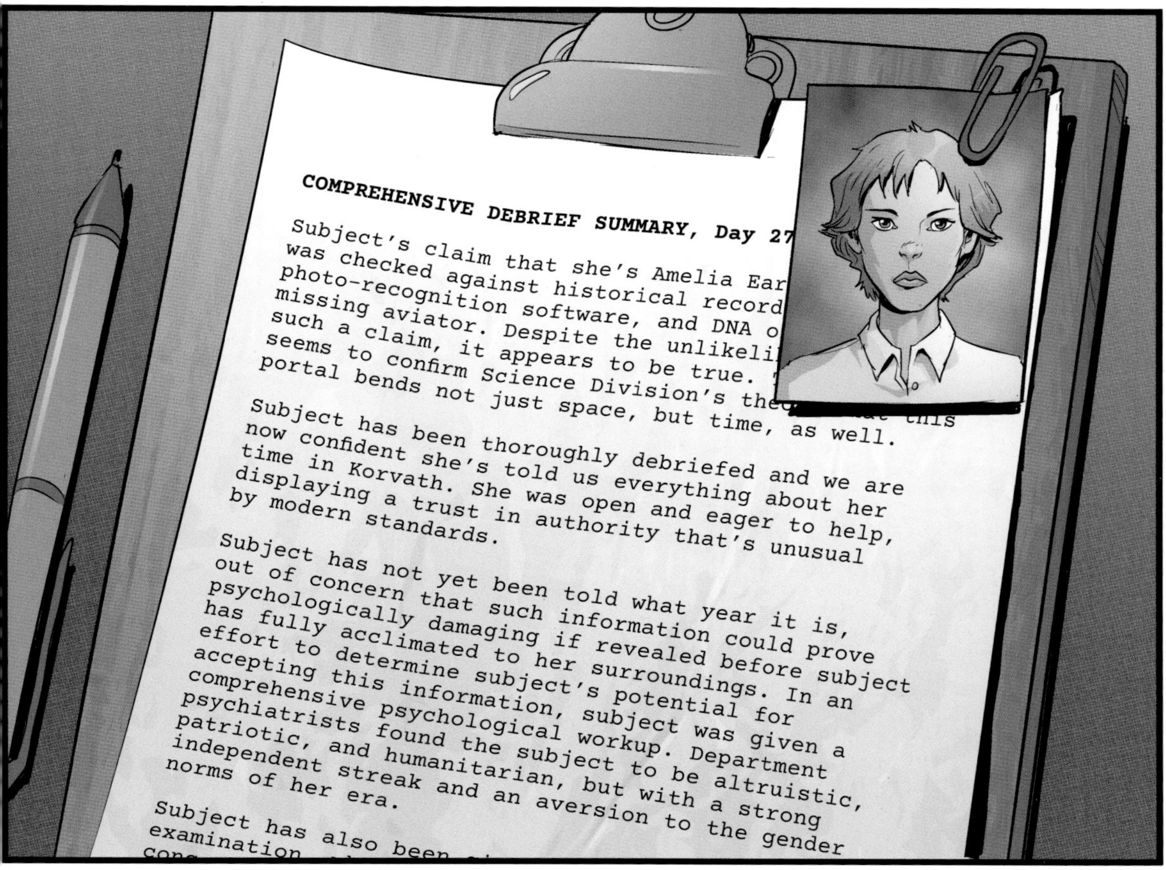
COMPREHENSIVE DEBRIEF SUMMARY, Day 27
Subject's claim that she's Amelia Ear
was checked against historical record
photo-recognition software, and DNA o
missing aviator. Despite the unlikeli
such a claim, it appears to be true.
seems to confirm Science Division's the
portal bends not just space, but time, as well.
Subject has been thoroughly debriefed and we are now confident she's told us everything about her time in Korvath. She was open and eager to help, displaying a trust in authority that's unusual by modern standards.
Subject has not yet been told what year it is, out of concern that such information could prove psychologically damaging if revealed before subject has fully acclimated to her surroundings. In an effort to determine subject's potential for accepting this information, subject was given a comprehensive psychological workup. Department psychiatrists found the subject to be altruistic, patriotic, and humanitarian, but with a strong independent streak and an aversion to the gender norms of her era.
Subject has also been
examination

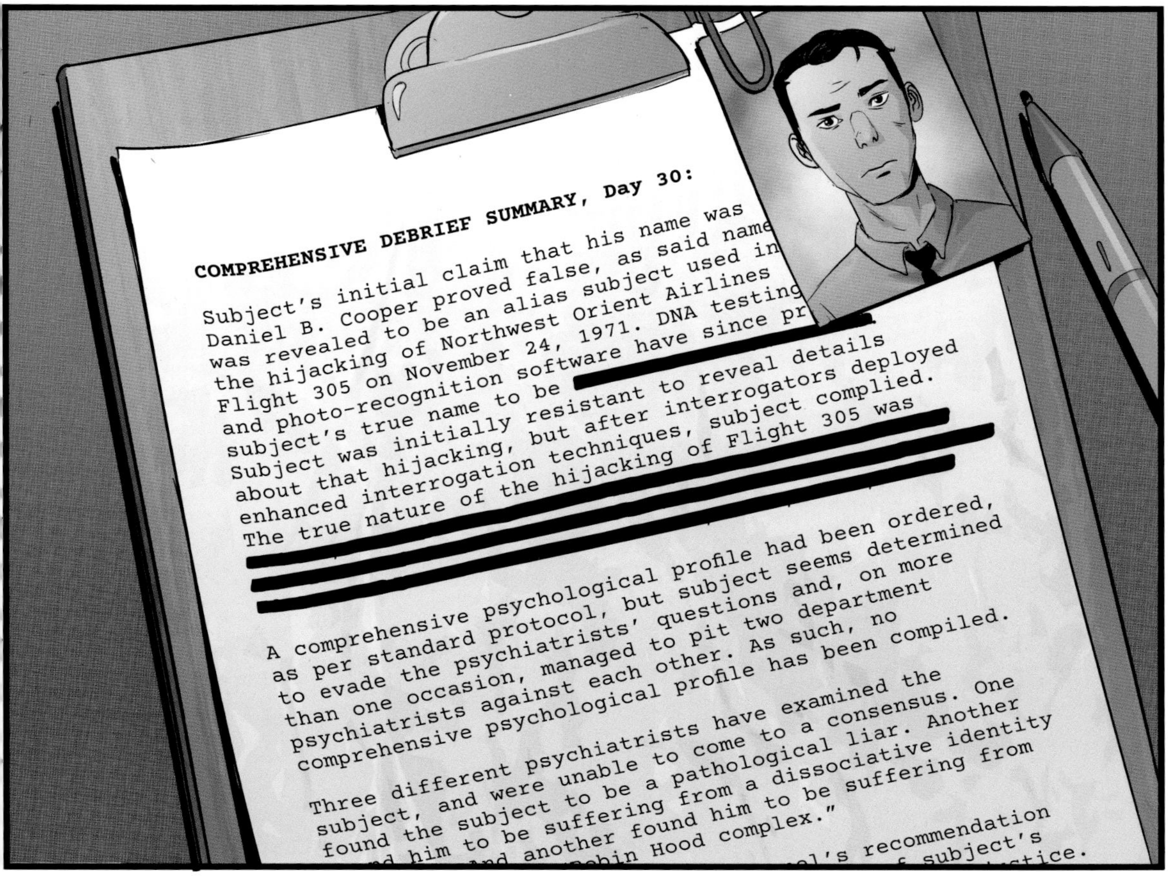
COMPREHENSIVE DEBRIEF SUMMARY, Day 30:
Subject's initial claim that his name was
Daniel B. Cooper proved false, as said name
was revealed to be an alias subject used in
the hijacking of Northwest Orient Airlines
Flight 305 on November 24, 1971. DNA testing
and photo-recognition software have since pr
subject's true name to be [redacted]
Subject was initially resistant to reveal details
about that hijacking, but after interrogators deployed
enhanced interrogation techniques, subject complied.
The true nature of the hijacking of Flight 305 was [redacted]
A comprehensive psychological profile had been ordered, as per standard protocol, but subject seems determined to evade the psychiatrists' questions and, on more than one occasion, managed to pit two department psychiatrists against each other. As such, no comprehensive psychological profile has been compiled.
Three different psychiatrists have examined the subject, and were unable to come to a consensus. One found the subject to be a pathological liar. Another found him to be suffering from a dissociative identity
and another found him to be suffering from
Robin Hood complex."
recommendation
subject's

KNOCK KNOCK

COME IN.

MISS EARHART. HOW'RE YOU DOING TODAY?

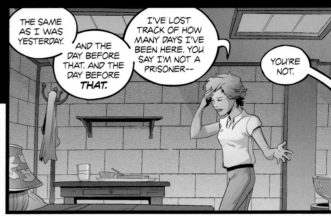

THE SAME AS I WAS YESTERDAY. AND THE DAY BEFORE THAT. AND THE DAY BEFORE *THAT.*

I'VE LOST TRACK OF HOW MANY DAYS I'VE BEEN HERE. YOU SAY I'M NOT A PRISONER--

YOU'RE NOT.

THEN WHY CAN'T I LEAVE?

WE WANT TO MAKE SURE YOU'RE PROPERLY...PREPARED BEFORE YOU LEAVE THIS FACILITY.

PREPARED FOR WHAT?

YOU MIGHT WANT TO SIT DOWN FOR THIS.

WHATEVER YOU HAVE TO SAY, I CAN TAKE IT STANDING UP.

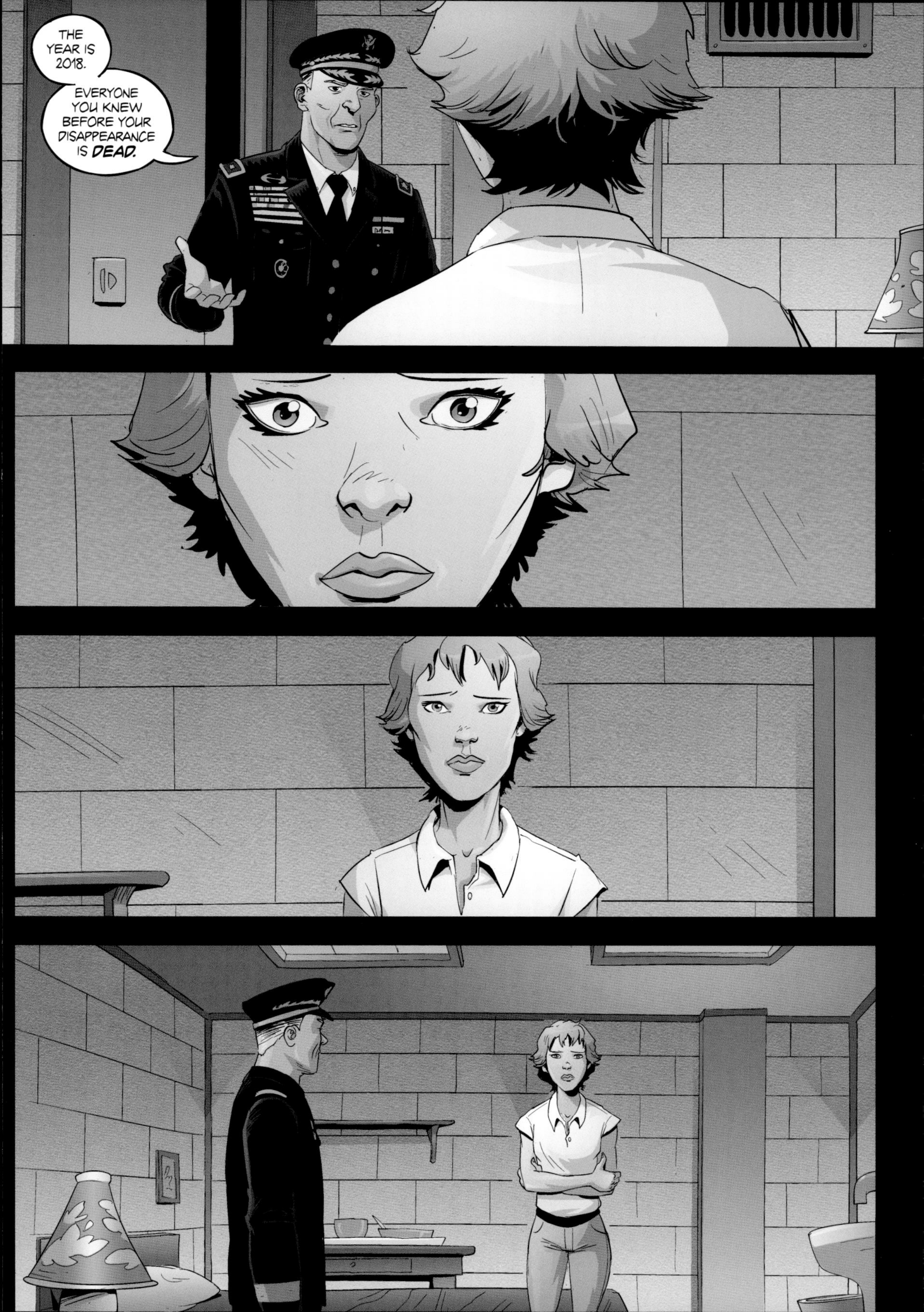
THE YEAR IS 2018.
EVERYONE YOU KNEW BEFORE YOUR DISAPPEARANCE IS **DEAD.**

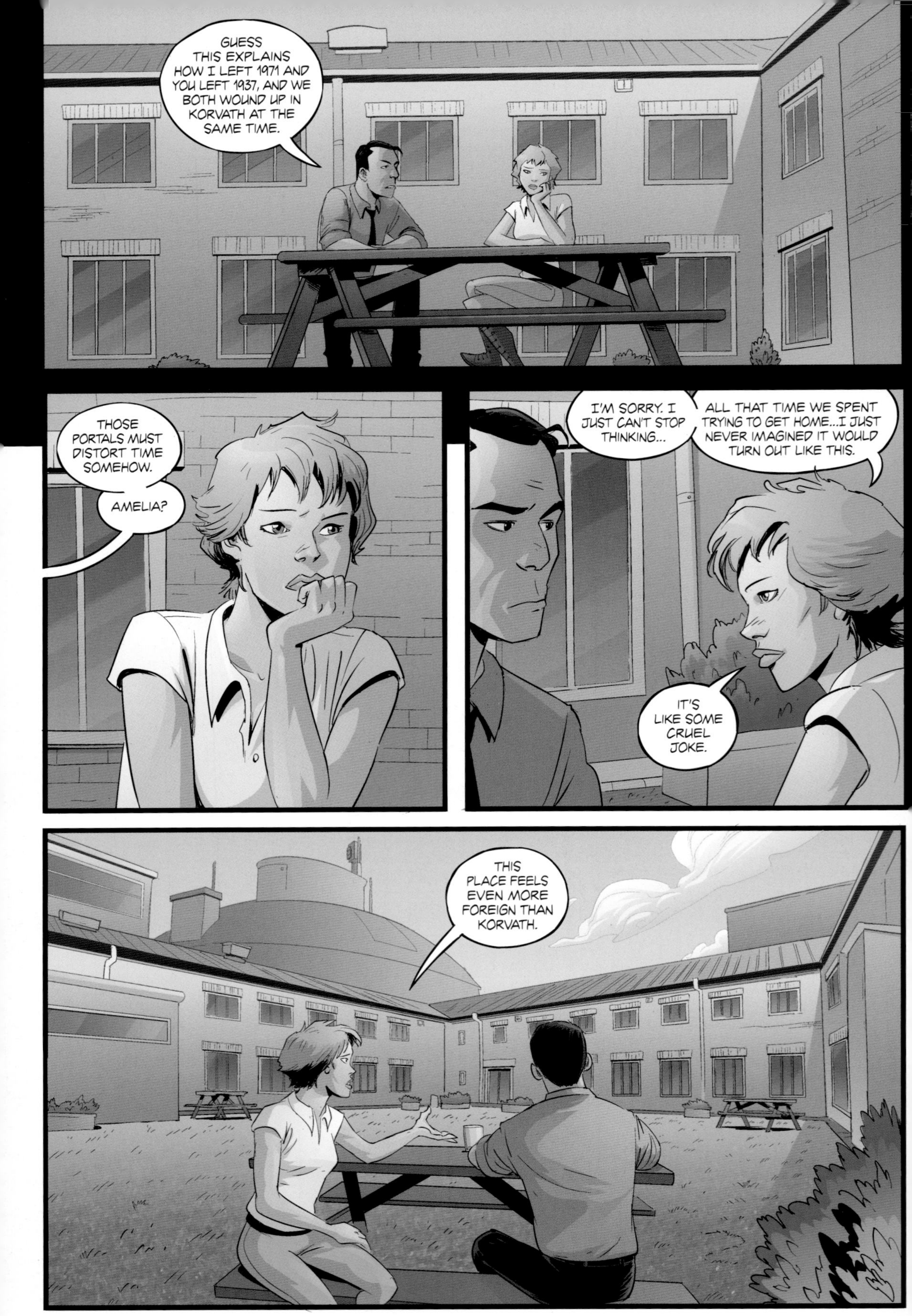
GUESS THIS EXPLAINS HOW I LEFT 1971 AND YOU LEFT 1937, AND WE BOTH WOUND UP IN KORVATH AT THE SAME TIME.
THOSE PORTALS MUST DISTORT TIME SOMEHOW.
AMELIA?
I'M SORRY. I JUST CAN'T STOP THINKING...
ALL THAT TIME WE SPENT TRYING TO GET HOME...I JUST NEVER IMAGINED IT WOULD TURN OUT LIKE THIS.
IT'S LIKE SOME CRUEL JOKE.
THIS PLACE FEELS EVEN MORE FOREIGN THAN KORVATH.

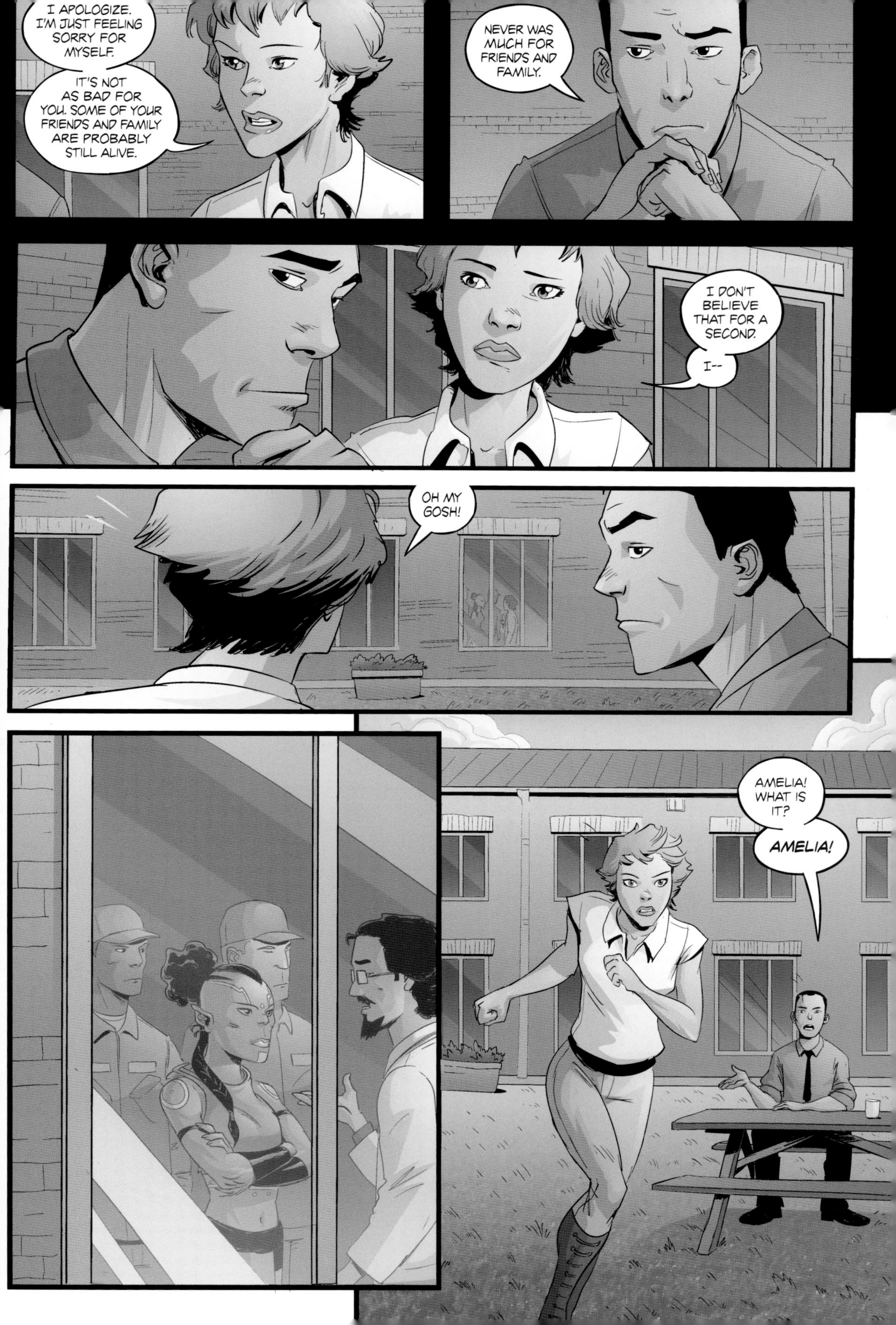
I APOLOGIZE. I'M JUST FEELING SORRY FOR MYSELF.
IT'S NOT AS BAD FOR YOU. SOME OF YOUR FRIENDS AND FAMILY ARE PROBABLY STILL ALIVE.
NEVER WAS MUCH FOR FRIENDS AND FAMILY.
I DON'T BELIEVE THAT FOR A SECOND.
I--
OH MY GOSH!
AMELIA! WHAT IS IT?
AMELIA!

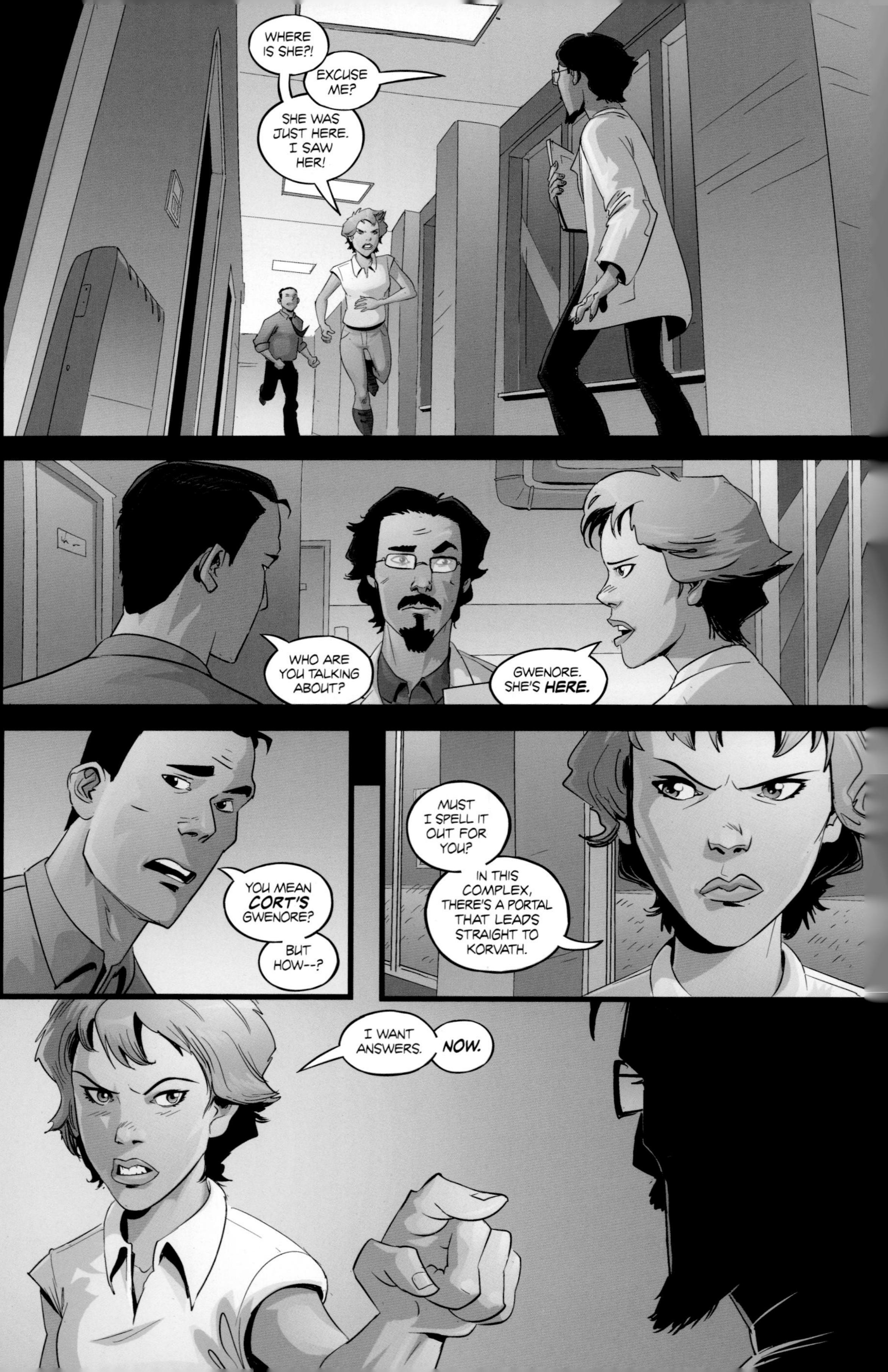
WHERE IS SHE?!
EXCUSE ME?
SHE WAS JUST HERE. I SAW HER!
WHO ARE YOU TALKING ABOUT?
GWENORE. SHE'S **HERE.**
YOU MEAN ***CORT'S*** GWENORE?
BUT HOW--?
MUST I SPELL IT OUT FOR YOU?
IN THIS COMPLEX, THERE'S A PORTAL THAT LEADS STRAIGHT TO KORVATH.
I WANT ANSWERS.
NOW.

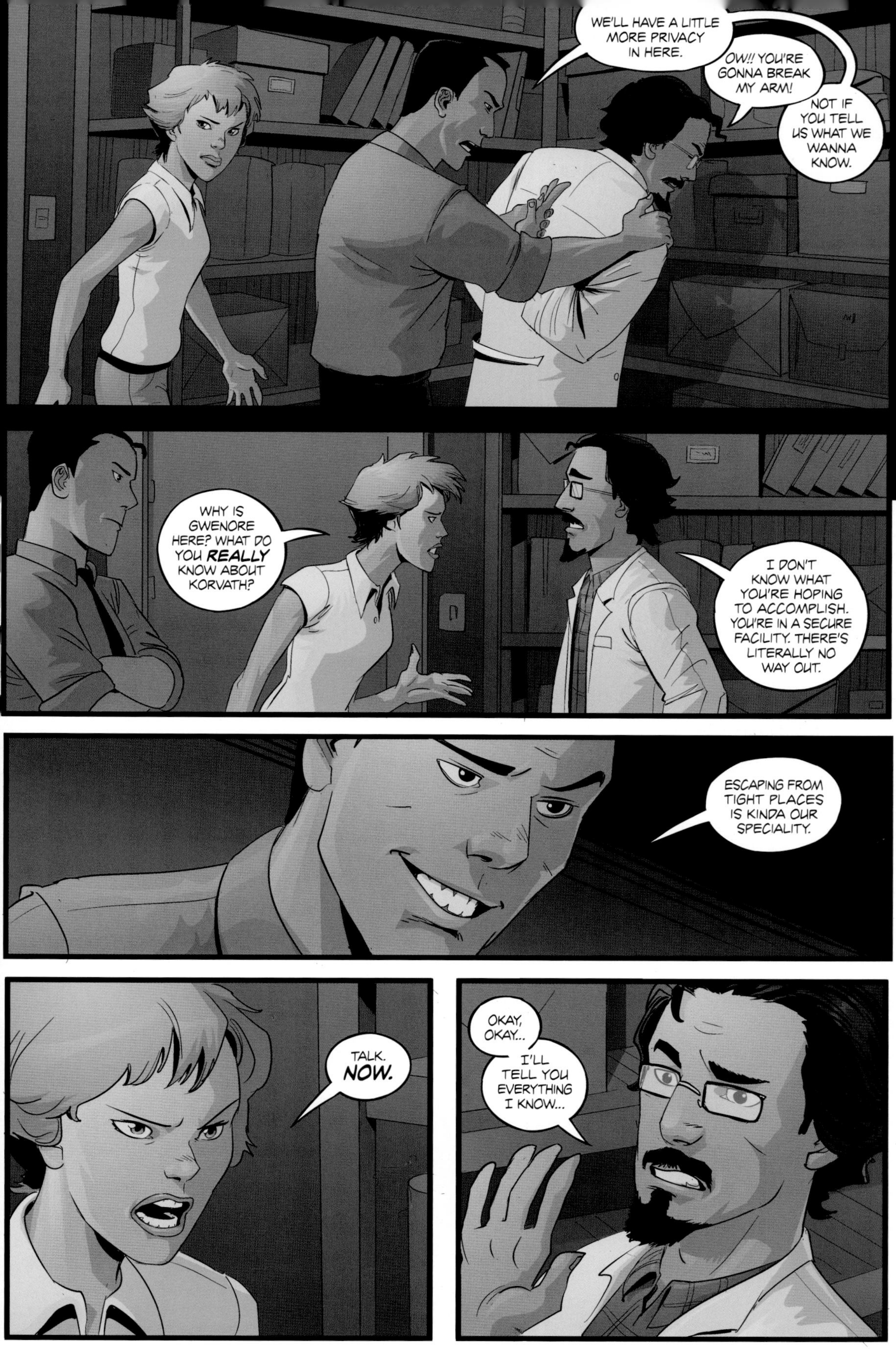
WE'LL HAVE A LITTLE MORE PRIVACY IN HERE.
OW!! YOU'RE GONNA BREAK MY ARM!
NOT IF YOU TELL US WHAT WE WANNA KNOW.
WHY IS GWENORE HERE? WHAT DO YOU REALLY KNOW ABOUT KORVATH?
I DON'T KNOW WHAT YOU'RE HOPING TO ACCOMPLISH. YOU'RE IN A SECURE FACILITY. THERE'S LITERALLY NO WAY OUT.
ESCAPING FROM TIGHT PLACES IS KINDA OUR SPECIALITY.
TALK. NOW.
OKAY, OKAY...
I'LL TELL YOU EVERYTHING I KNOW...

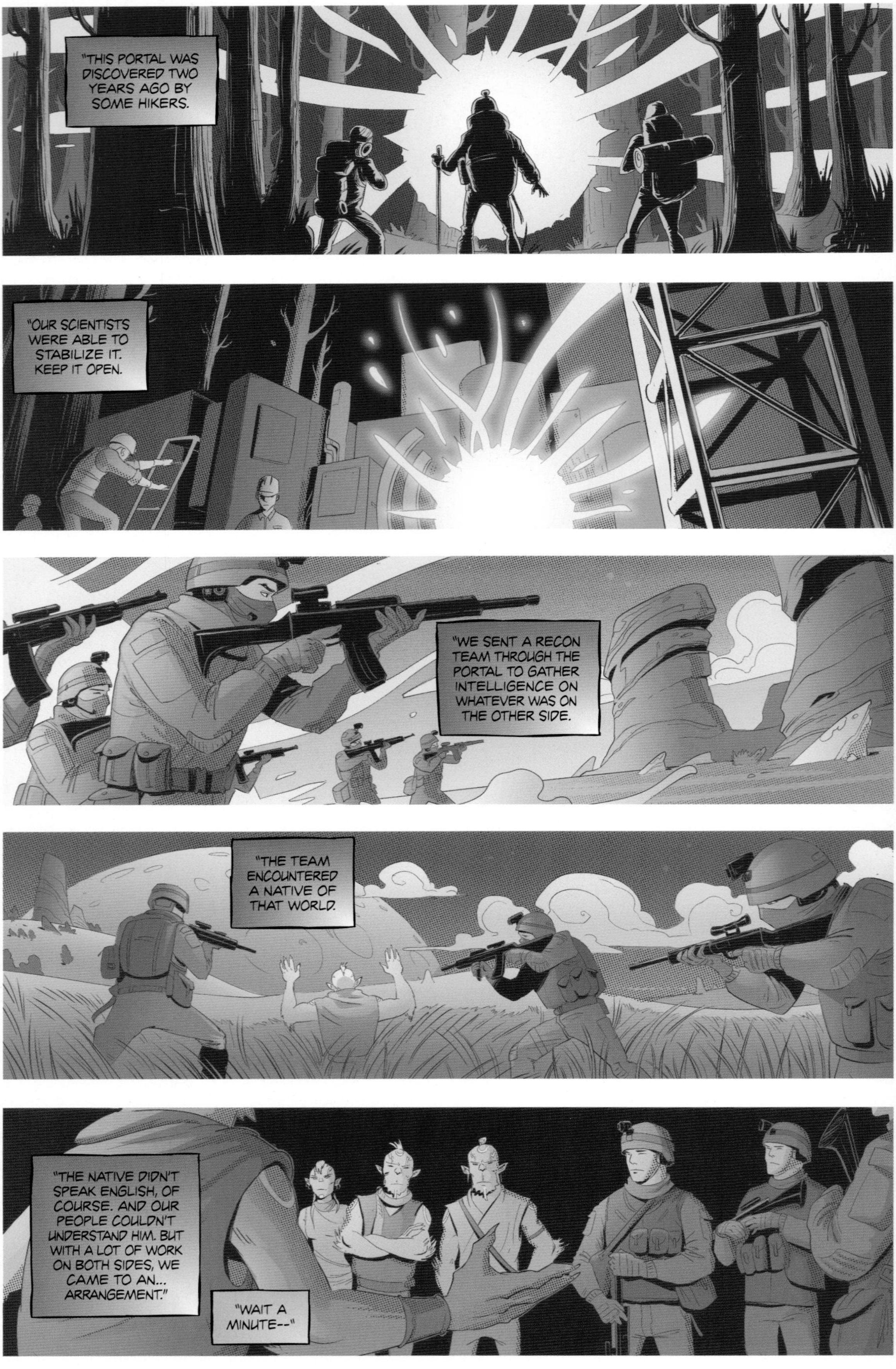
"THIS PORTAL WAS DISCOVERED TWO YEARS AGO BY SOME HIKERS.
"OUR SCIENTISTS WERE ABLE TO STABILIZE IT. KEEP IT OPEN.
"WE SENT A RECON TEAM THROUGH THE PORTAL TO GATHER INTELLIGENCE ON WHATEVER WAS ON THE OTHER SIDE.
"THE TEAM ENCOUNTERED A NATIVE OF THAT WORLD.
"THE NATIVE DIDN'T SPEAK ENGLISH, OF COURSE. AND OUR PEOPLE COULDN'T UNDERSTAND HIM. BUT WITH A LOT OF WORK ON BOTH SIDES, WE CAME TO AN... ARRANGEMENT."
"WAIT A MINUTE--"

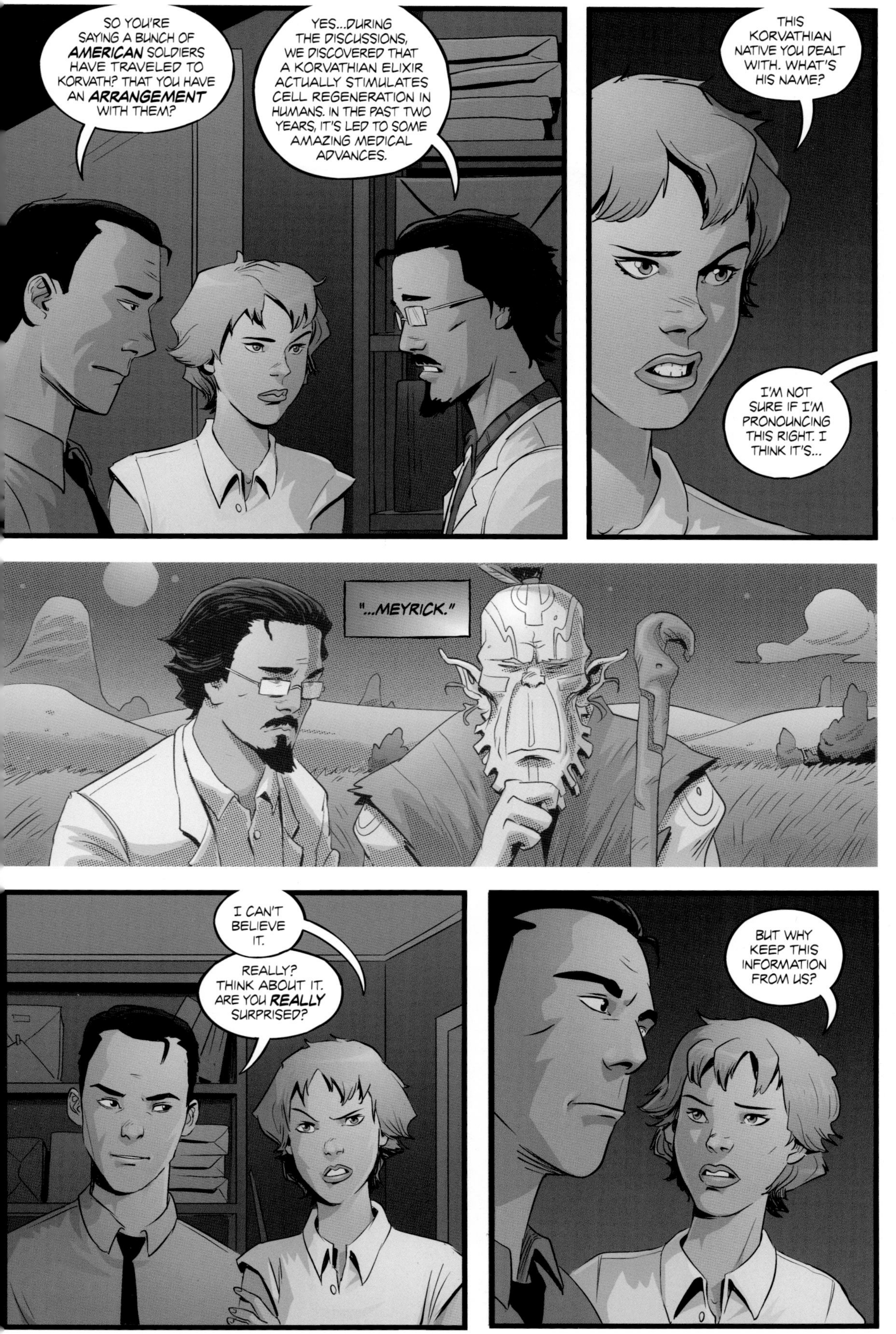
SO YOU'RE SAYING A BUNCH OF **AMERICAN** SOLDIERS HAVE TRAVELED TO KORVATH? THAT YOU HAVE AN **ARRANGEMENT** WITH THEM?
YES...DURING THE DISCUSSIONS, WE DISCOVERED THAT A KORVATHIAN ELIXIR ACTUALLY STIMULATES CELL REGENERATION IN HUMANS. IN THE PAST TWO YEARS, IT'S LED TO SOME AMAZING MEDICAL ADVANCES.
THIS KORVATHIAN NATIVE YOU DEALT WITH. WHAT'S HIS NAME?
I'M NOT SURE IF I'M PRONOUNCING THIS RIGHT. I THINK IT'S...
"...MEYRICK."
I CAN'T BELIEVE IT.
REALLY? THINK ABOUT IT. ARE YOU **REALLY** SURPRISED?
BUT WHY KEEP THIS INFORMATION FROM US?

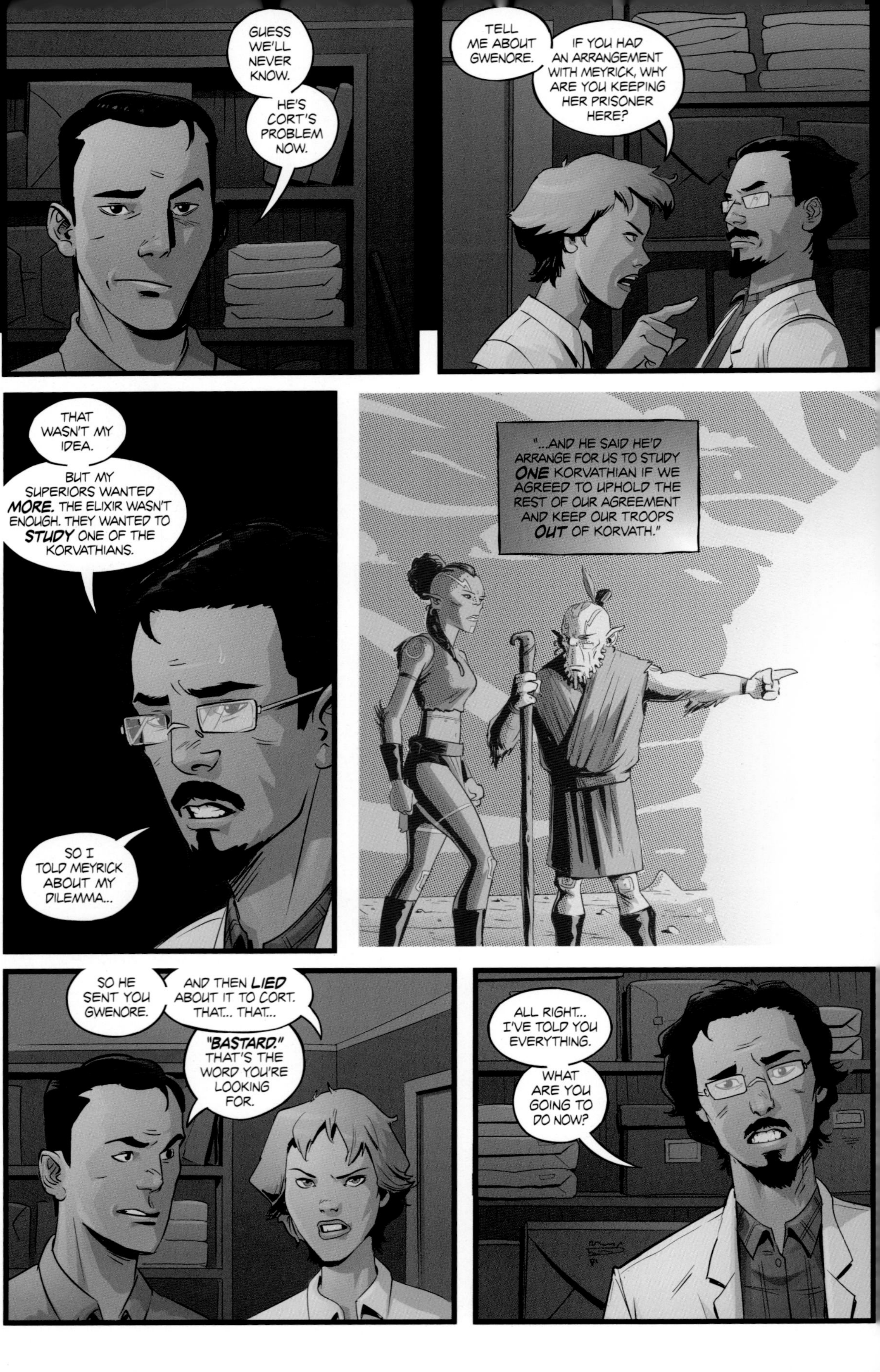
GUESS WE'LL NEVER KNOW.
HE'S CORT'S PROBLEM NOW.
TELL ME ABOUT GWENORE.
IF YOU HAD AN ARRANGEMENT WITH MEYRICK, WHY ARE YOU KEEPING HER PRISONER HERE?
THAT WASN'T MY IDEA.
BUT MY SUPERIORS WANTED MORE. THE ELIXIR WASN'T ENOUGH. THEY WANTED TO STUDY ONE OF THE KORVATHIANS.
SO I TOLD MEYRICK ABOUT MY DILEMMA...
"...AND HE SAID HE'D ARRANGE FOR US TO STUDY ONE KORVATHIAN IF WE AGREED TO UPHOLD THE REST OF OUR AGREEMENT AND KEEP OUR TROOPS OUT OF KORVATH."
SO HE SENT YOU GWENORE.
AND THEN LIED ABOUT IT TO CORT. THAT... THAT...
"BASTARD." THAT'S THE WORD YOU'RE LOOKING FOR.
ALL RIGHT... I'VE TOLD YOU EVERYTHING.
WHAT ARE YOU GOING TO DO NOW?

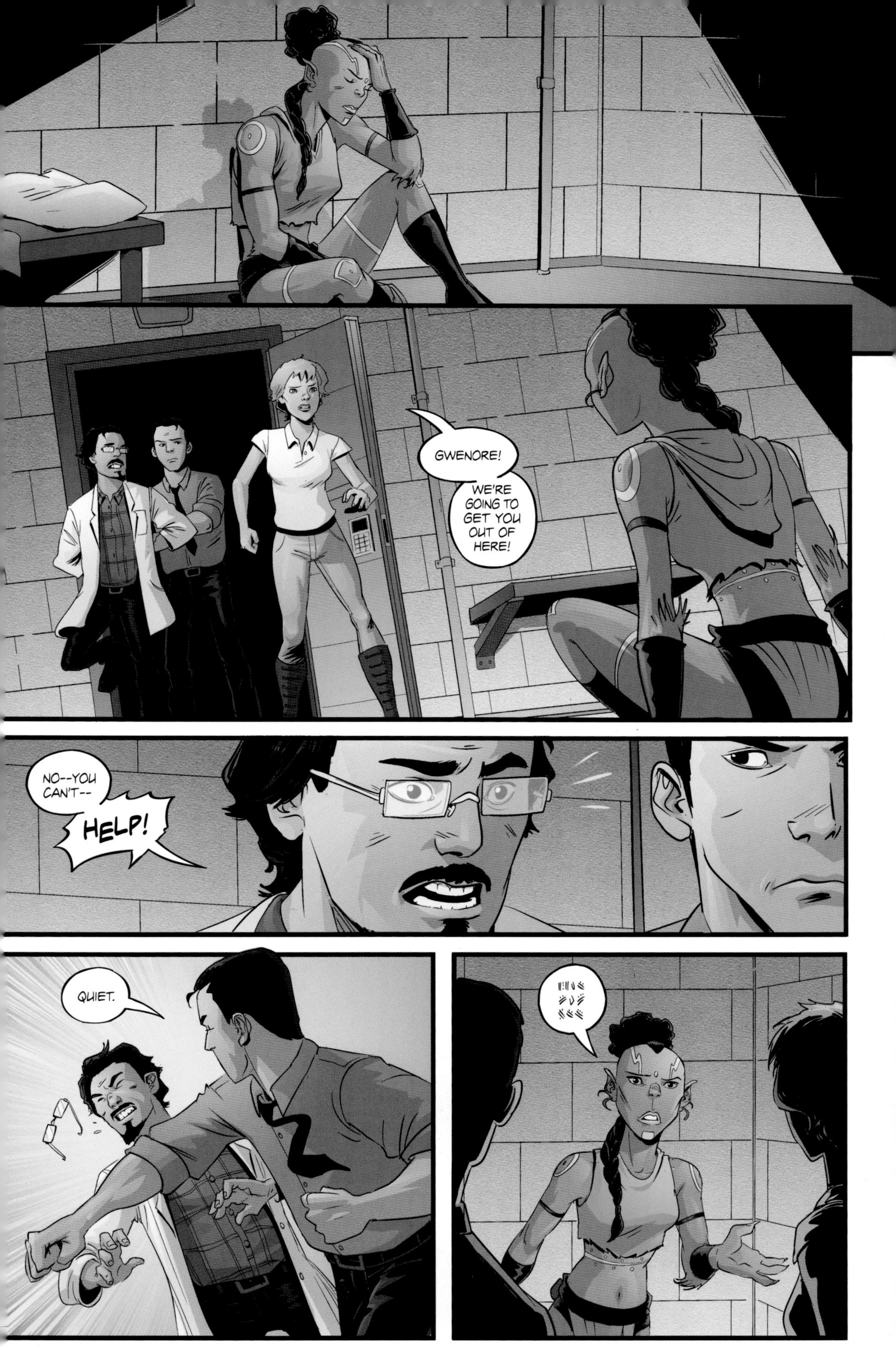
GWENORE!
WE'RE GOING TO GET YOU OUT OF HERE!
NO--YOU CAN'T--
HELP!
QUIET.

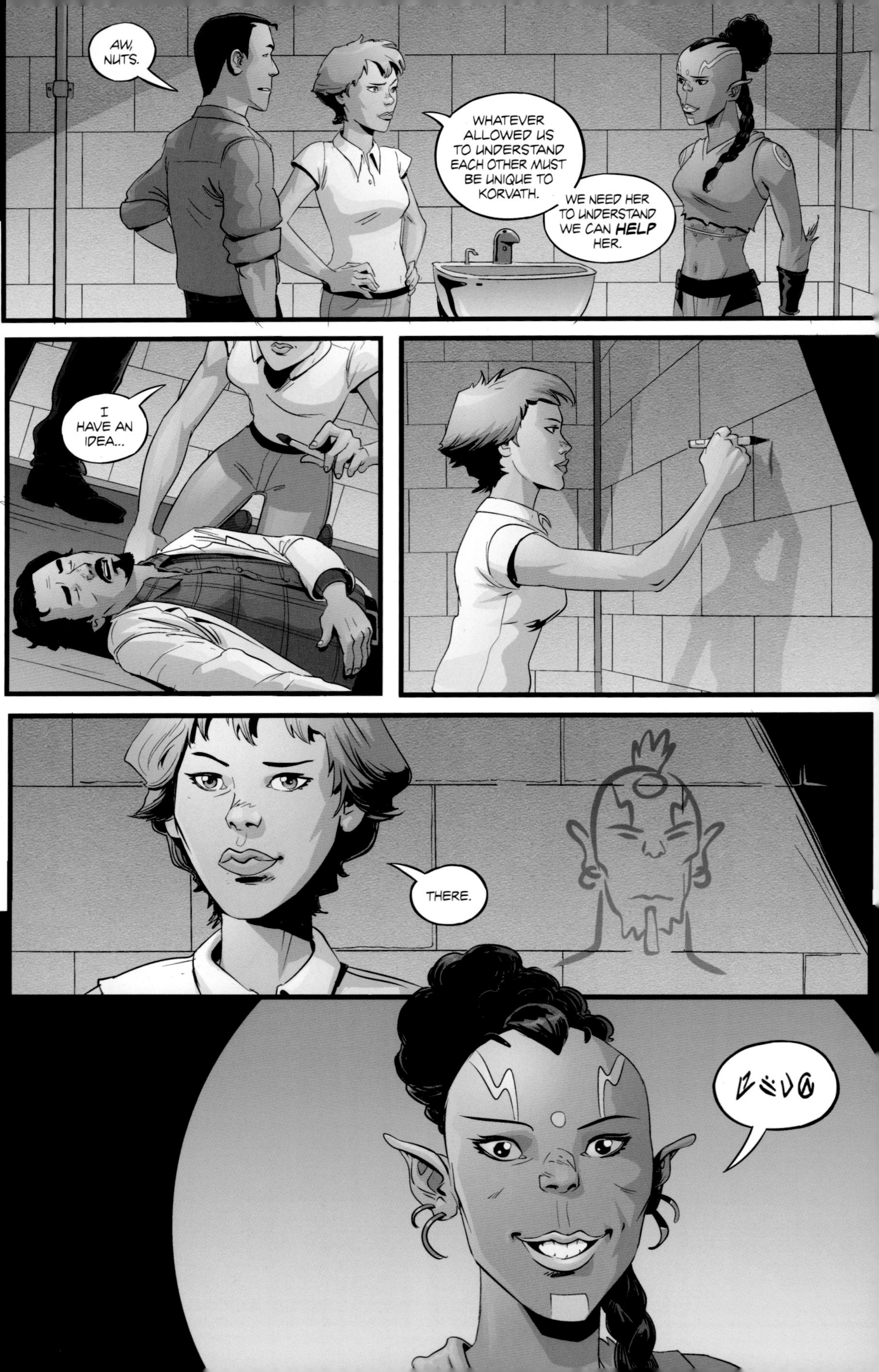
AW, NUTS.
WHATEVER ALLOWED US TO UNDERSTAND EACH OTHER MUST BE UNIQUE TO KORVATH.
WE NEED HER TO UNDERSTAND WE CAN **HELP** HER.
I HAVE AN IDEA...
THERE.

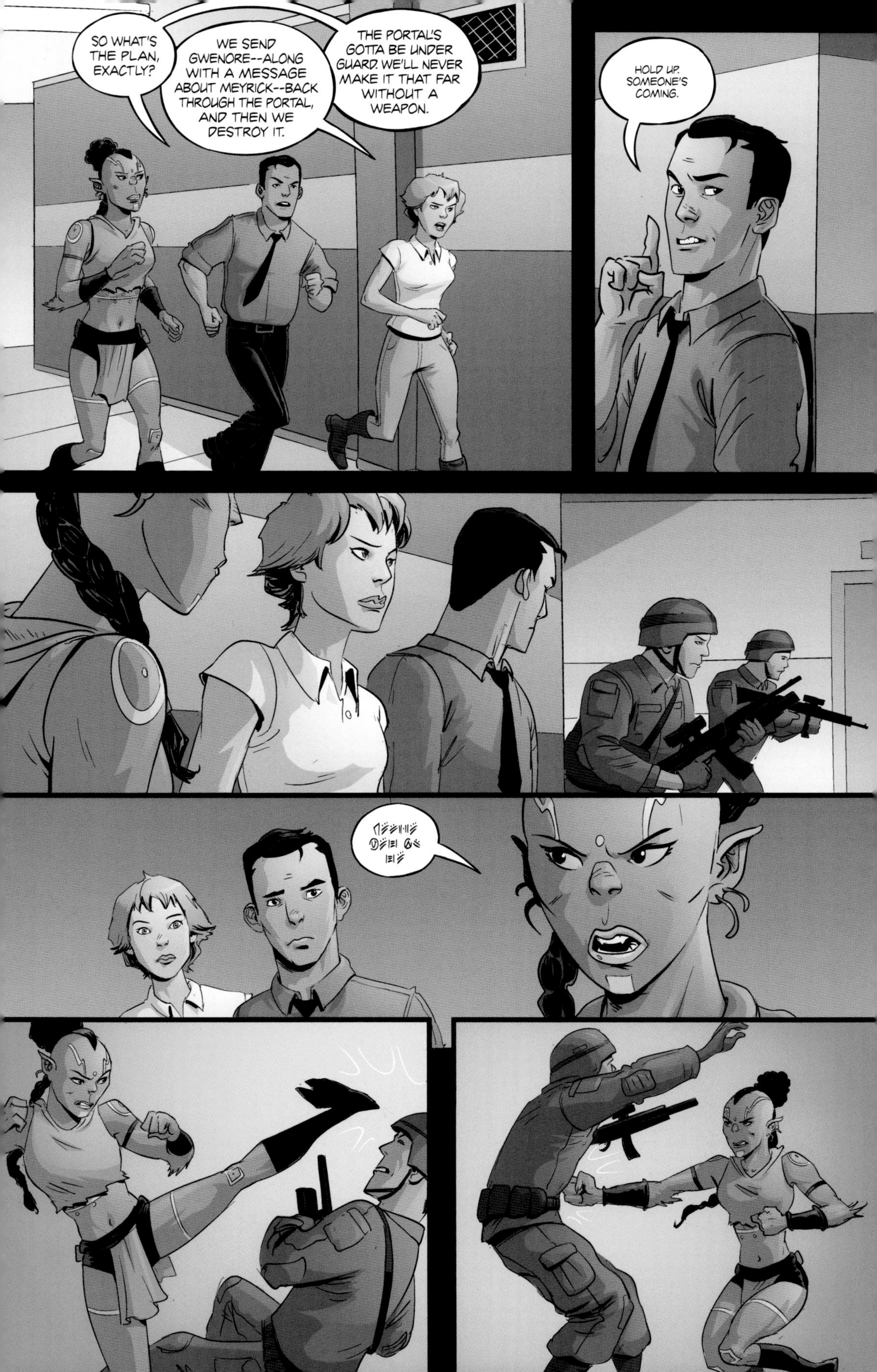
SO WHAT'S THE PLAN, EXACTLY?
WE SEND GWENORE--ALONG WITH A MESSAGE ABOUT MEYRICK--BACK THROUGH THE PORTAL, AND THEN WE DESTROY IT.
THE PORTAL'S GOTTA BE UNDER GUARD. WE'LL NEVER MAKE IT THAT FAR WITHOUT A WEAPON.
HOLD UP. SOMEONE'S COMING.

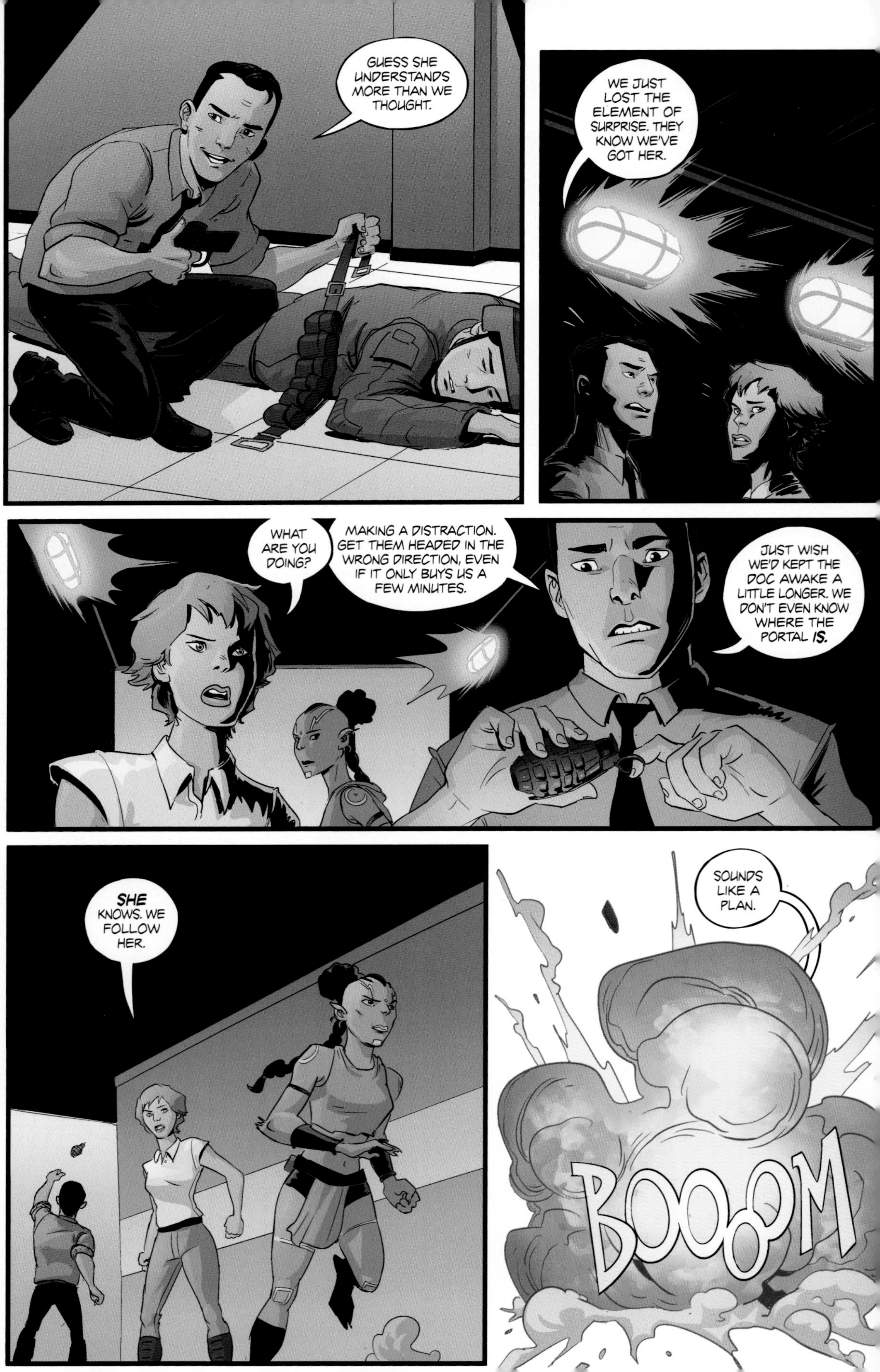
GUESS SHE UNDERSTANDS MORE THAN WE THOUGHT.
WE JUST LOST THE ELEMENT OF SURPRISE. THEY KNOW WE'VE GOT HER.
WHAT ARE YOU DOING?
MAKING A DISTRACTION. GET THEM HEADED IN THE WRONG DIRECTION, EVEN IF IT ONLY BUYS US A FEW MINUTES.
JUST WISH WE'D KEPT THE DOC AWAKE A LITTLE LONGER. WE DON'T EVEN KNOW WHERE THE PORTAL *IS.*
SHE KNOWS. WE FOLLOW HER.
SOUNDS LIKE A PLAN.
BOOOOM

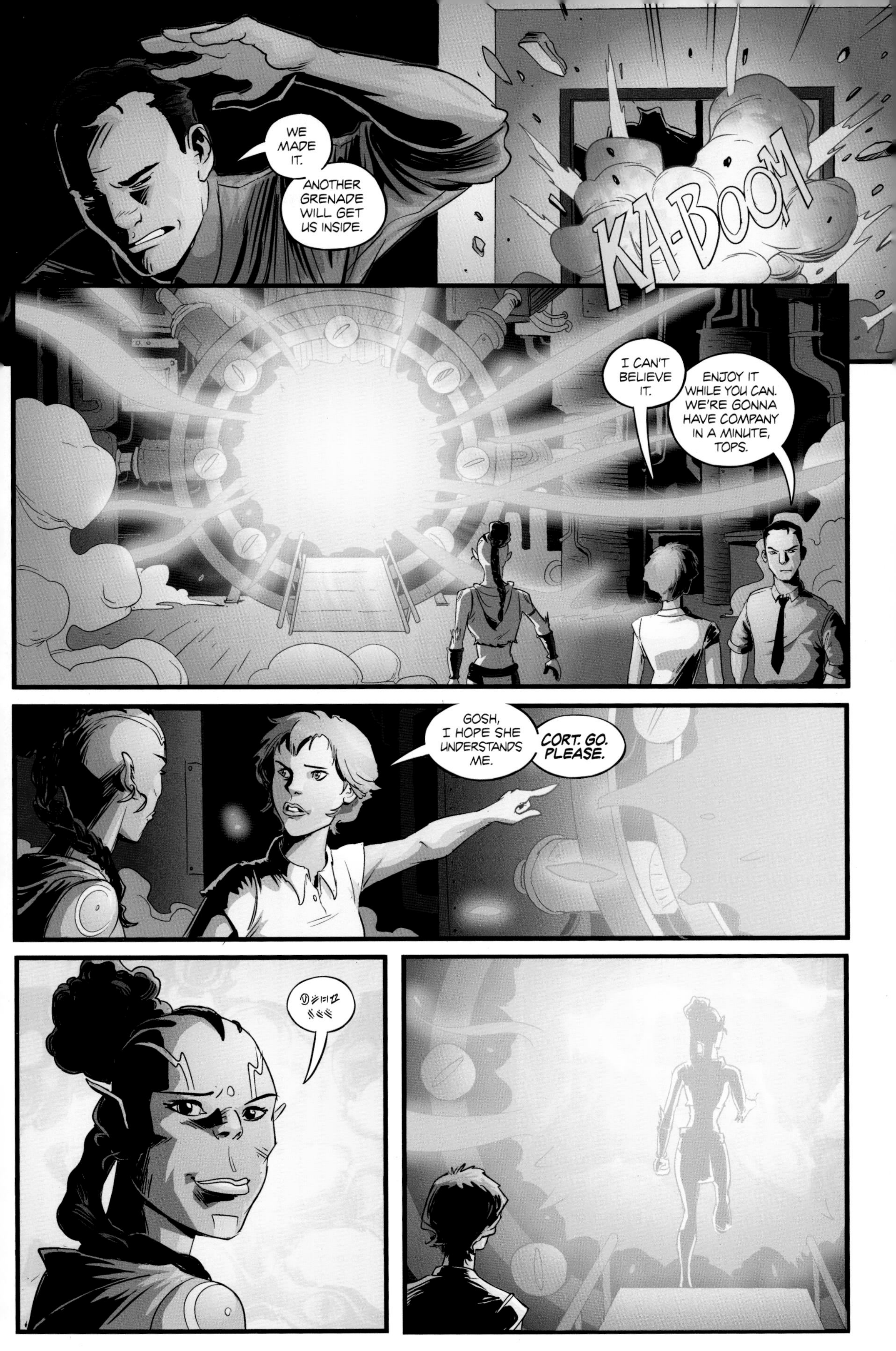
WE MADE IT.
ANOTHER GRENADE WILL GET US INSIDE.
KA-BOOM
I CAN'T BELIEVE IT.
ENJOY IT WHILE YOU CAN. WE'RE GONNA HAVE COMPANY IN A MINUTE, TOPS.
GOSH, I HOPE SHE UNDERSTANDS ME.
CORT. GO. PLEASE.

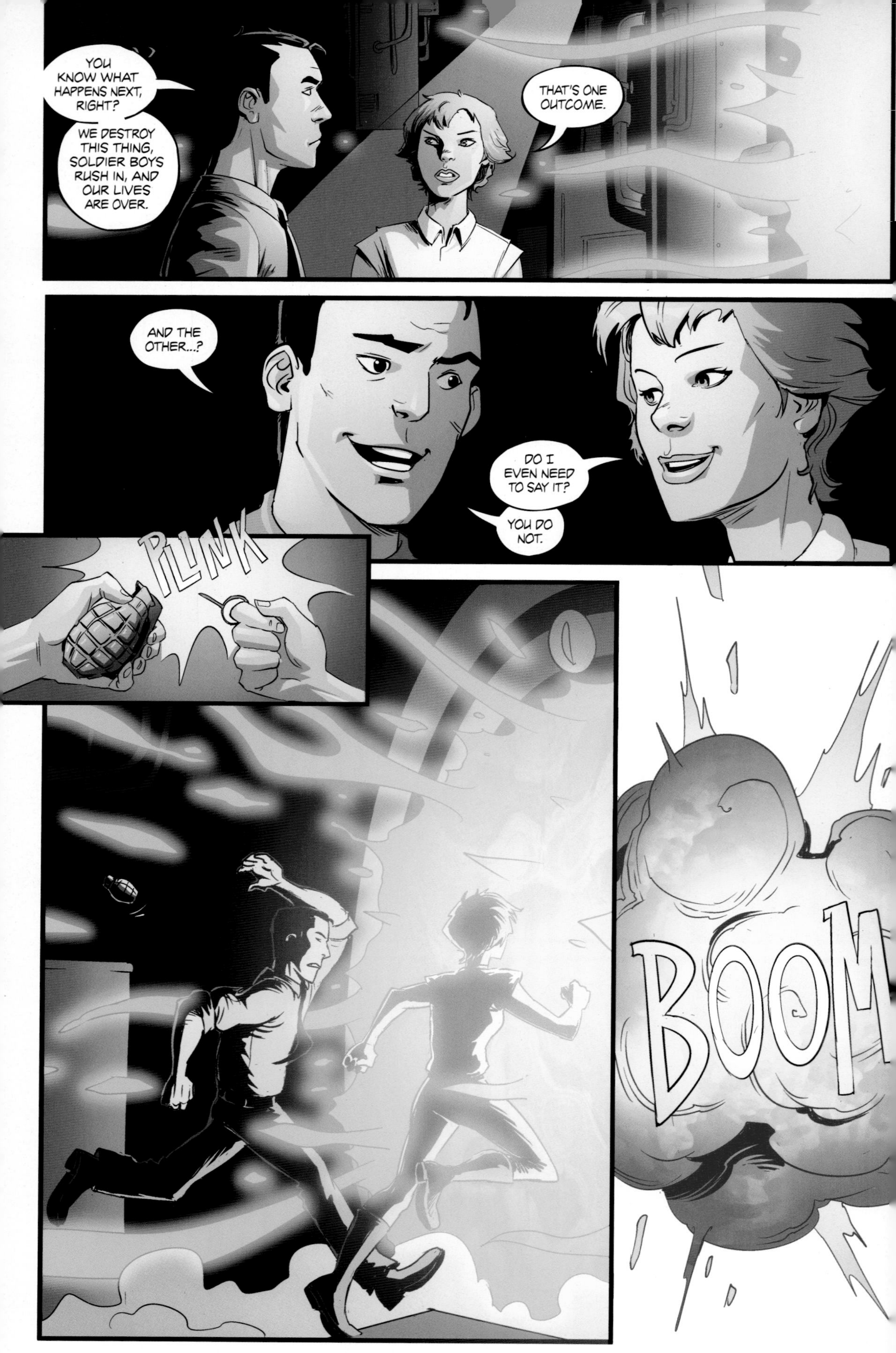
YOU KNOW WHAT HAPPENS NEXT, RIGHT?
WE DESTROY THIS THING, SOLDIER BOYS RUSH IN, AND OUR LIVES ARE OVER.
THAT'S ONE OUTCOME.
AND THE OTHER...?
DO I EVEN NEED TO SAY IT?
YOU DO NOT.
PLINK
BOOM

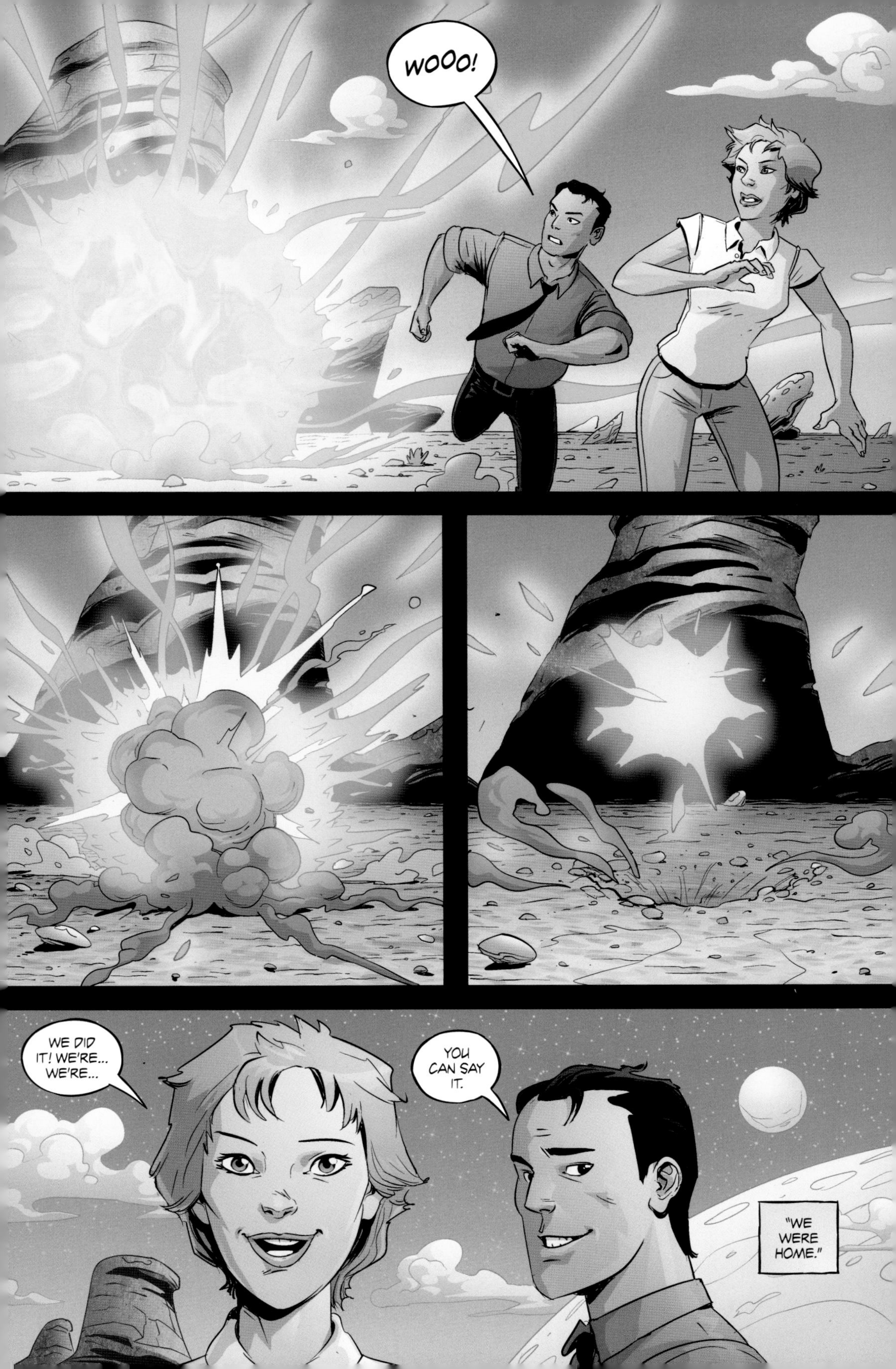
WOOO!
WE DID IT! WE'RE... WE'RE...
YOU CAN SAY IT.
"WE WERE HOME."

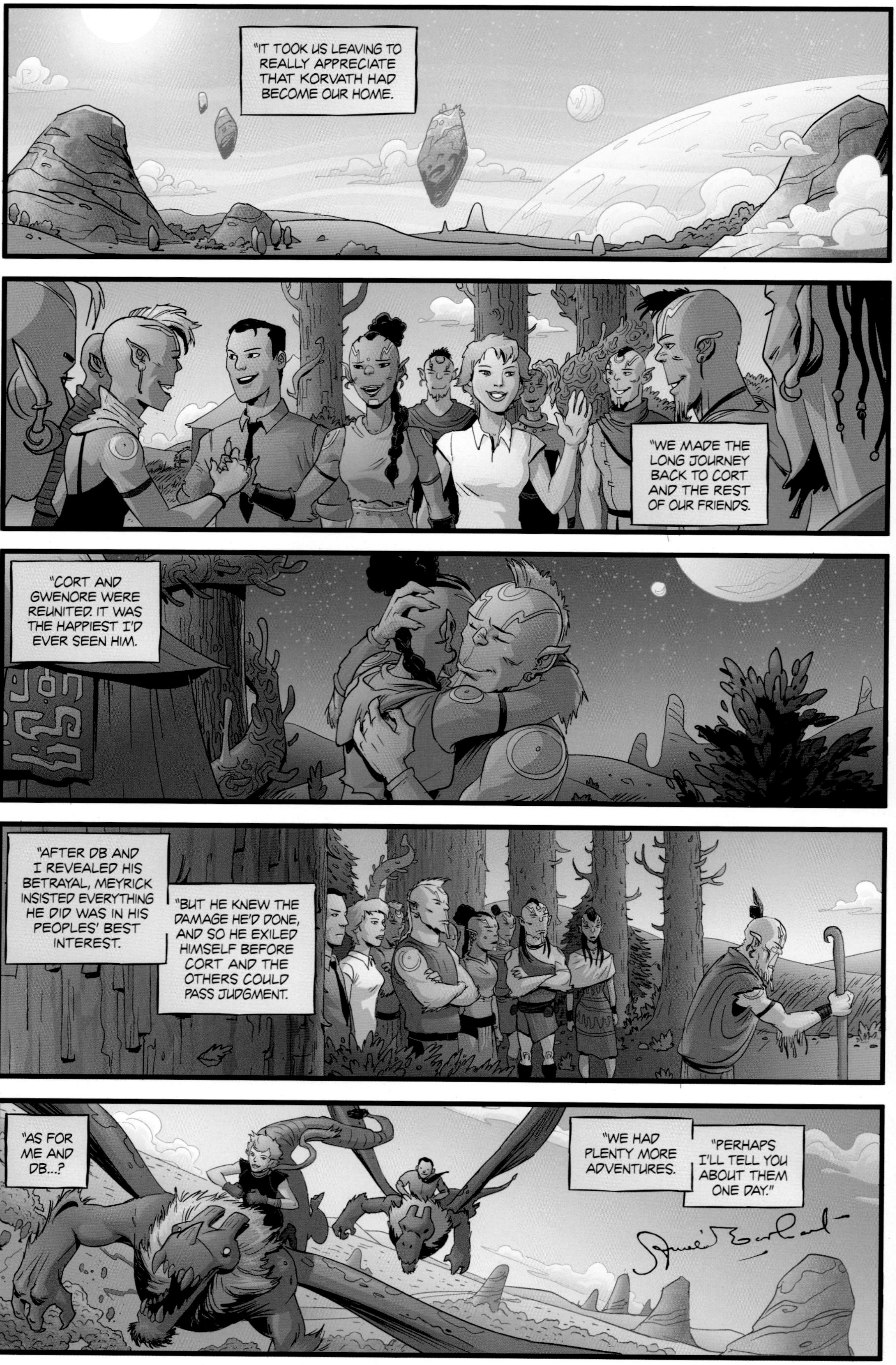
"IT TOOK US LEAVING TO REALLY APPRECIATE THAT KORVATH HAD BECOME OUR HOME.
"WE MADE THE LONG JOURNEY BACK TO CORT AND THE REST OF OUR FRIENDS.
"CORT AND GWENORE WERE REUNITED. IT WAS THE HAPPIEST I'D EVER SEEN HIM.
"AFTER DB AND I REVEALED HIS BETRAYAL, MEYRICK INSISTED EVERYTHING HE DID WAS IN HIS PEOPLES' BEST INTEREST.
"BUT HE KNEW THE DAMAGE HE'D DONE, AND SO HE EXILED HIMSELF BEFORE CORT AND THE OTHERS COULD PASS JUDGMENT.
"AS FOR ME AND DB...?
"WE HAD PLENTY MORE ADVENTURES.
"PERHAPS I'LL TELL YOU ABOUT THEM ONE DAY."

BEHIND THE SCENES

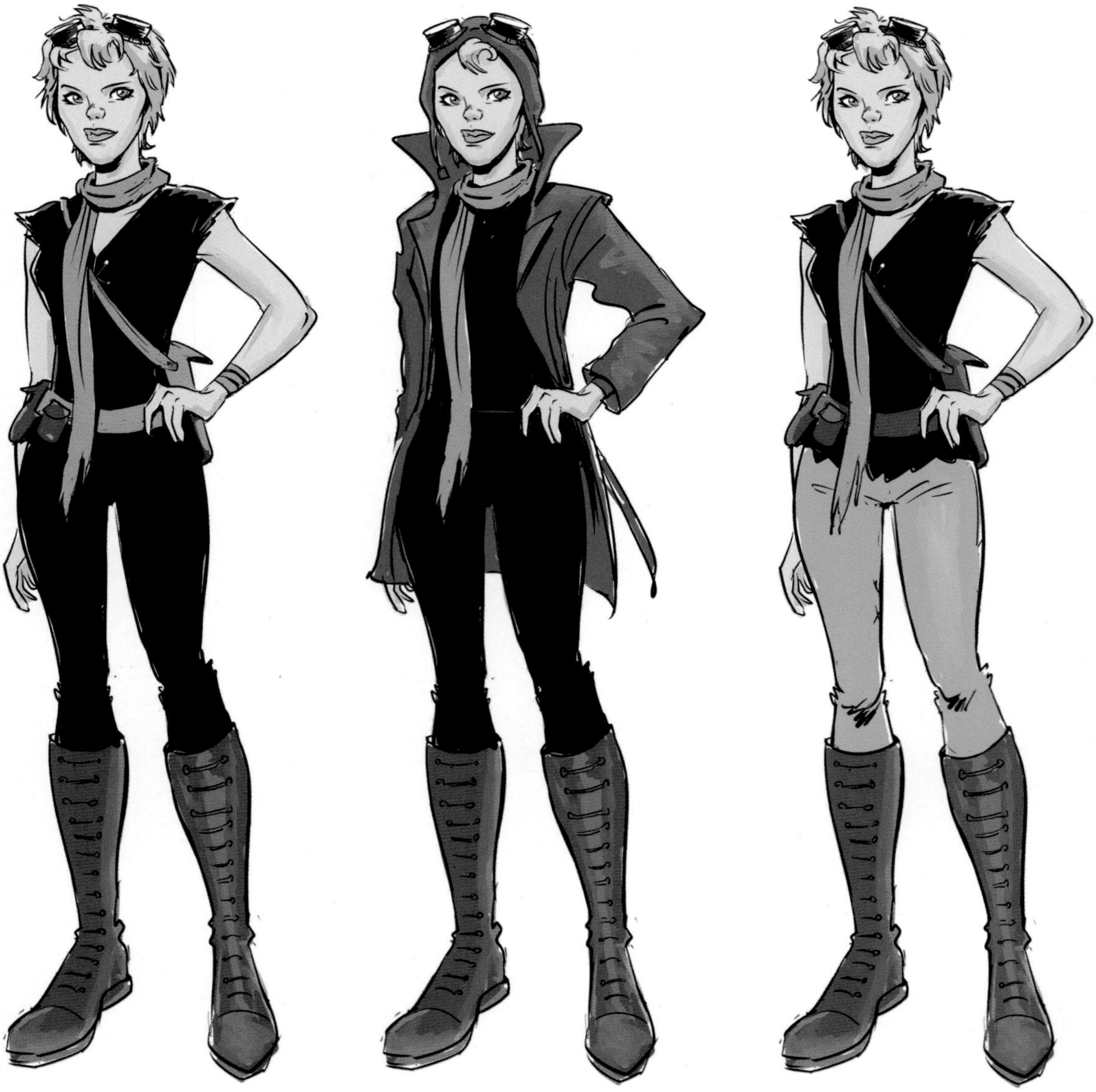

Amelia outfit ideas

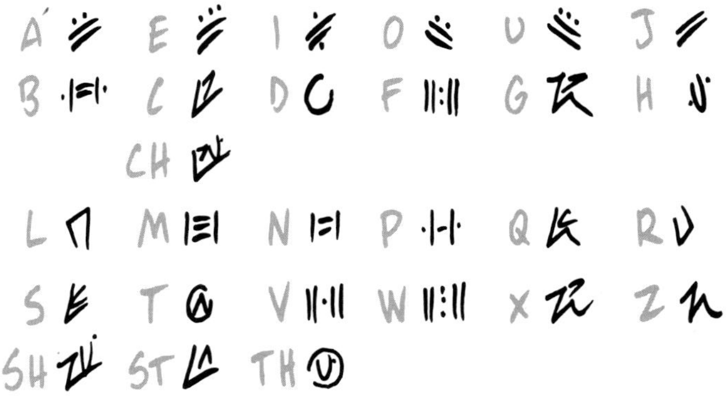
A E I O U J Y
B C D F G H K
CH
L M N P Q R
S T V W X Z
SH ST TH

Alien language key by Thomas Mauer

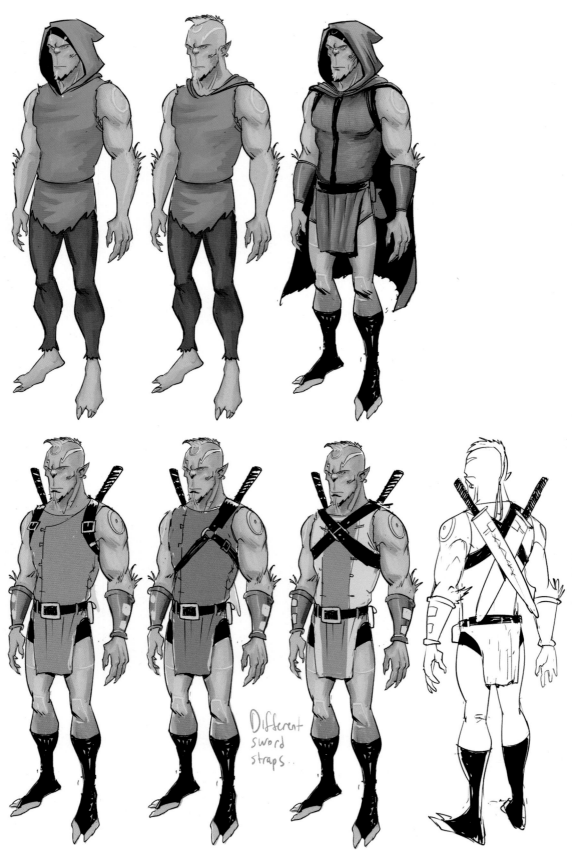

Different sword straps...

Cort outfit ideas

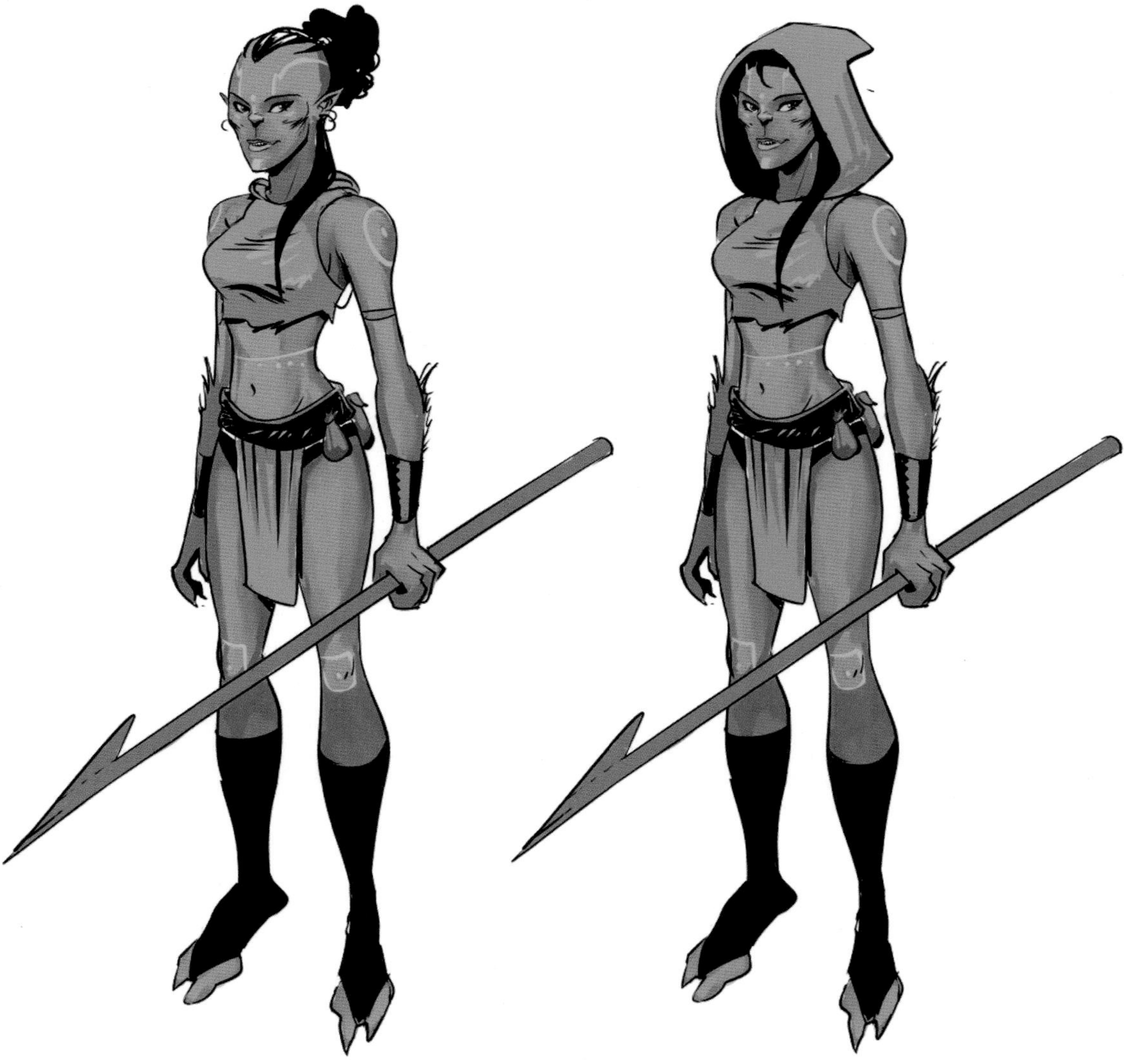

Gwenore character sketches

DB outfit ideas

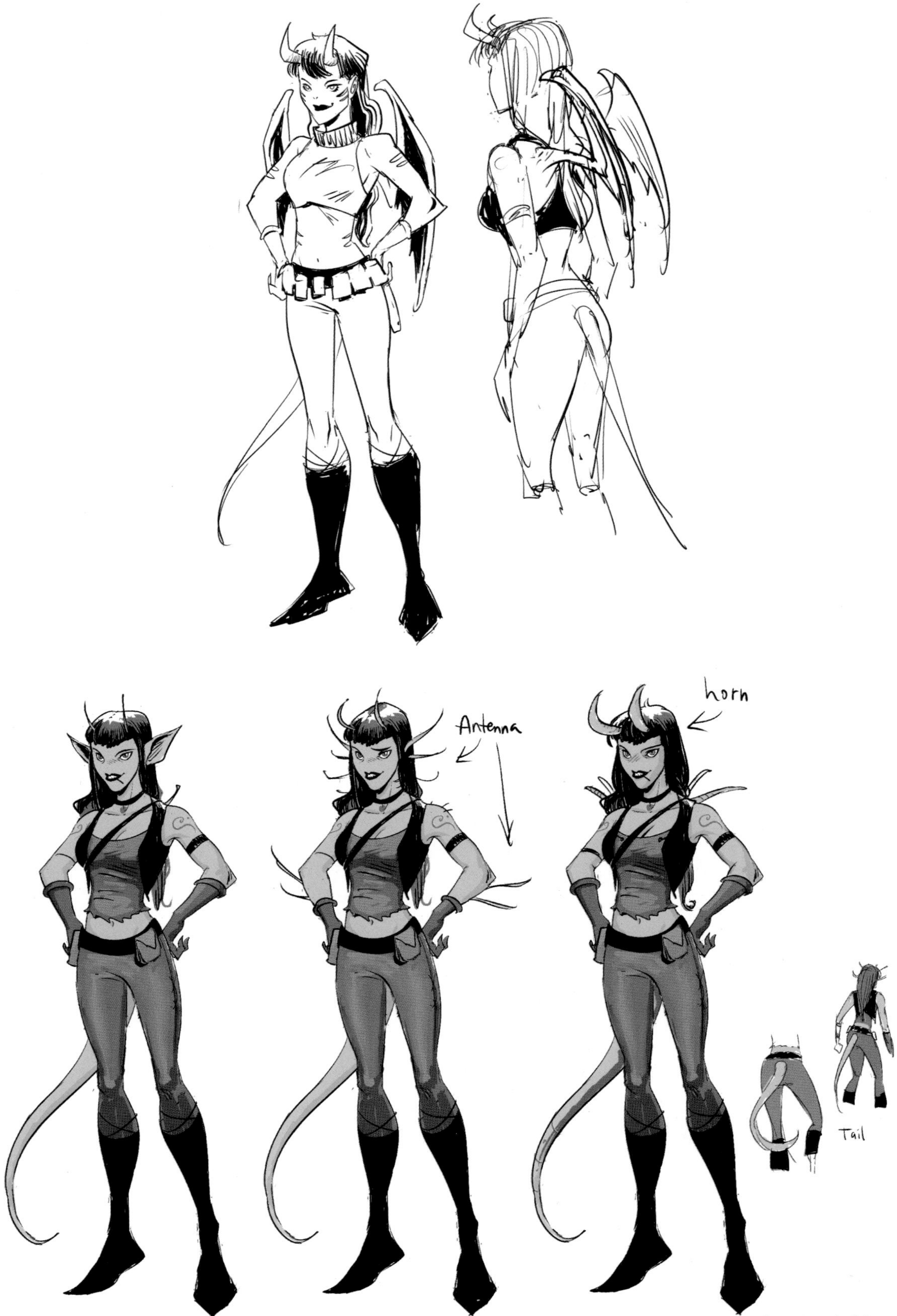
Antenna
horn
Tail

Ravenna character sketches

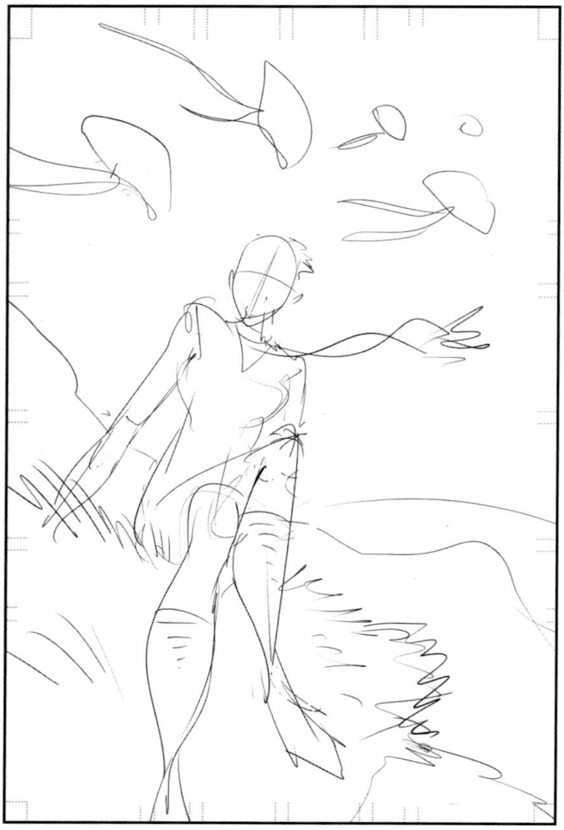

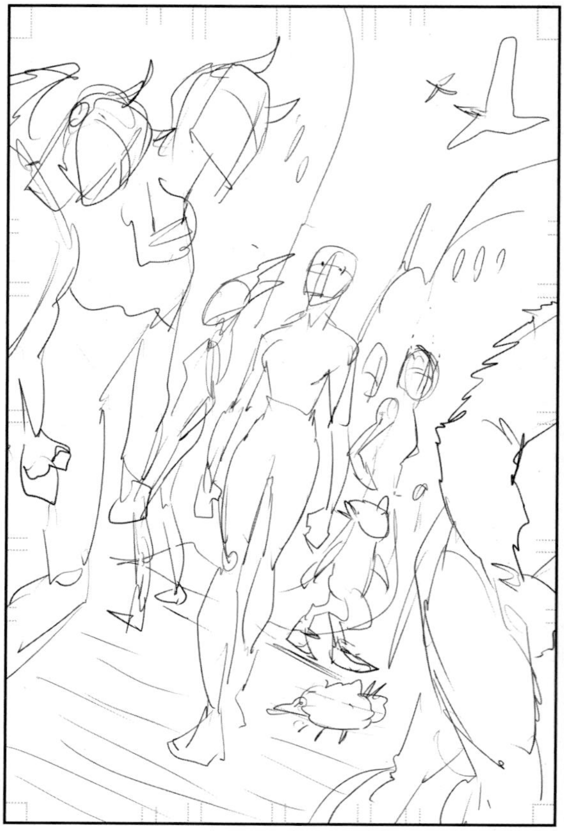

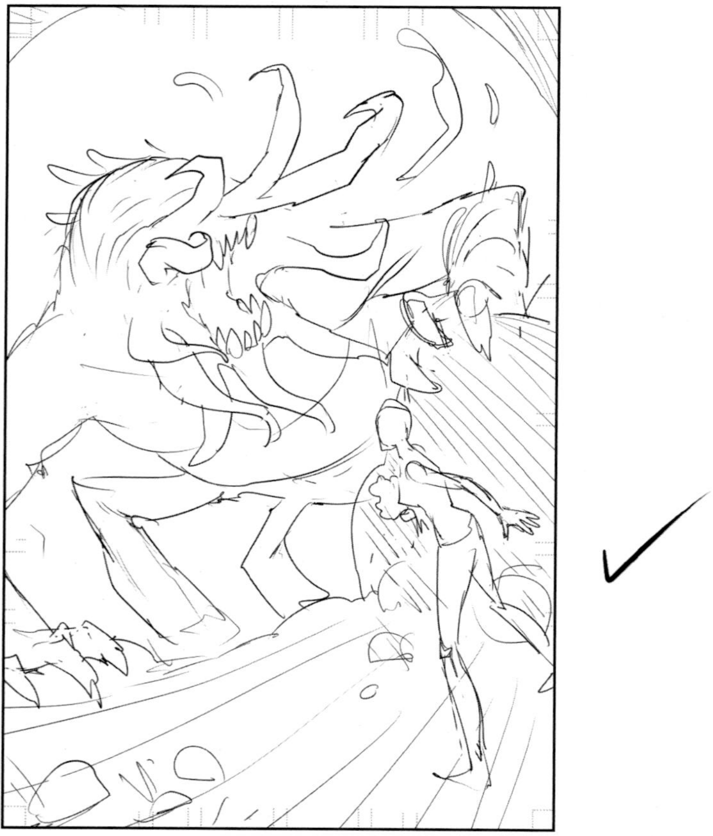

Sumeyye's Cover Concepts for Issue 5 & Inks of the Final Cover (opposite)

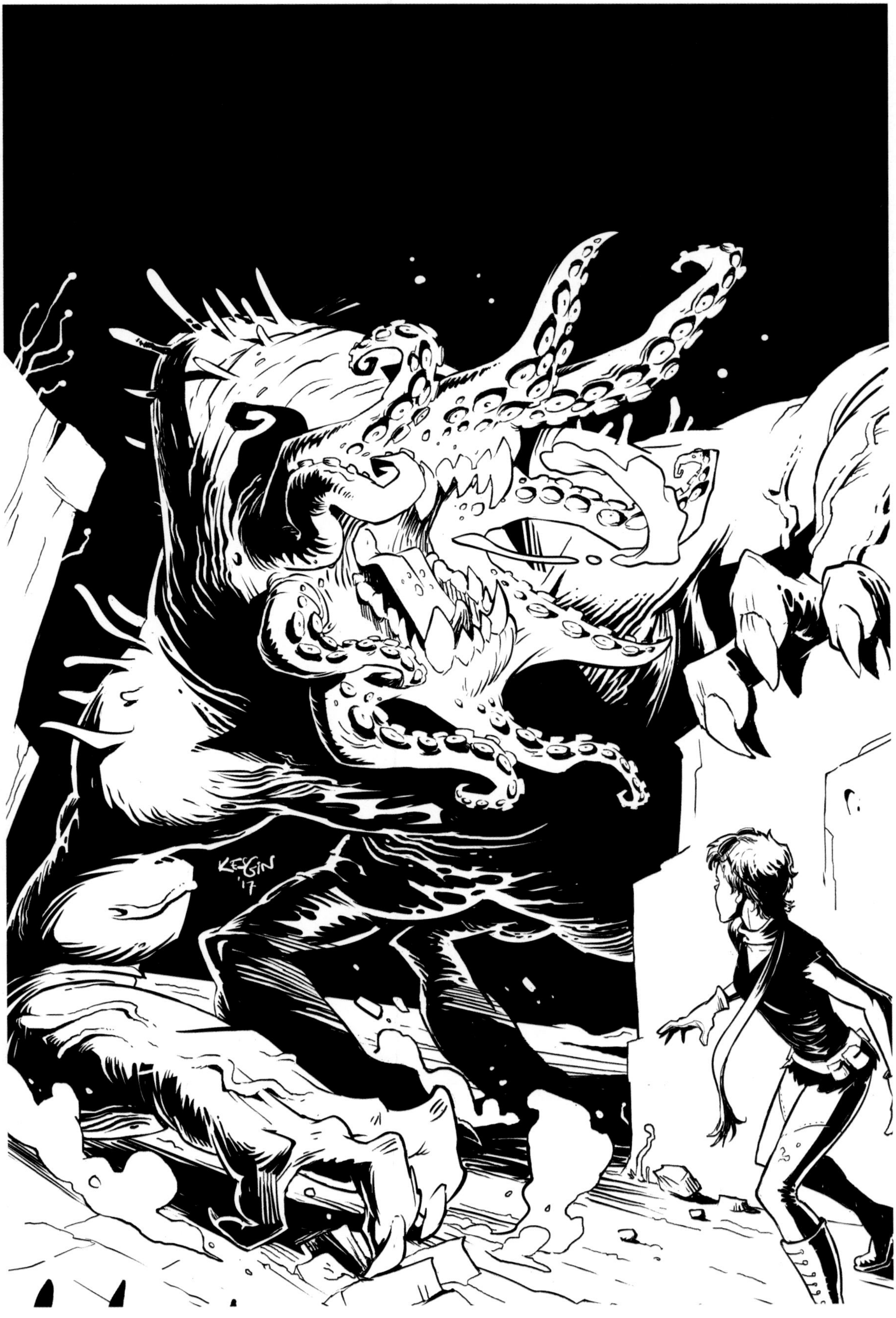

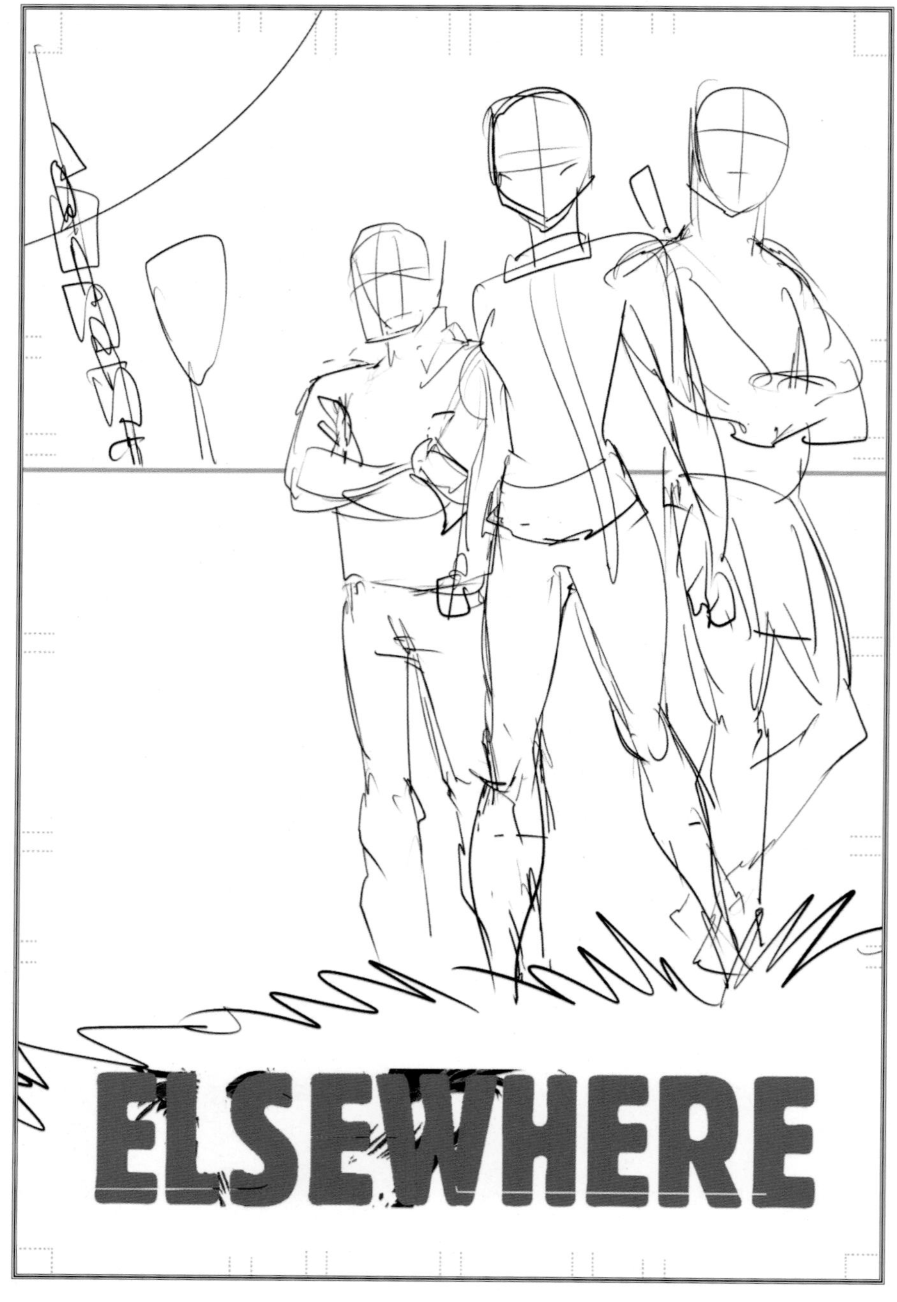
ELSEWHERE

Volume 2 Cover Sketch & Inks (opposite)

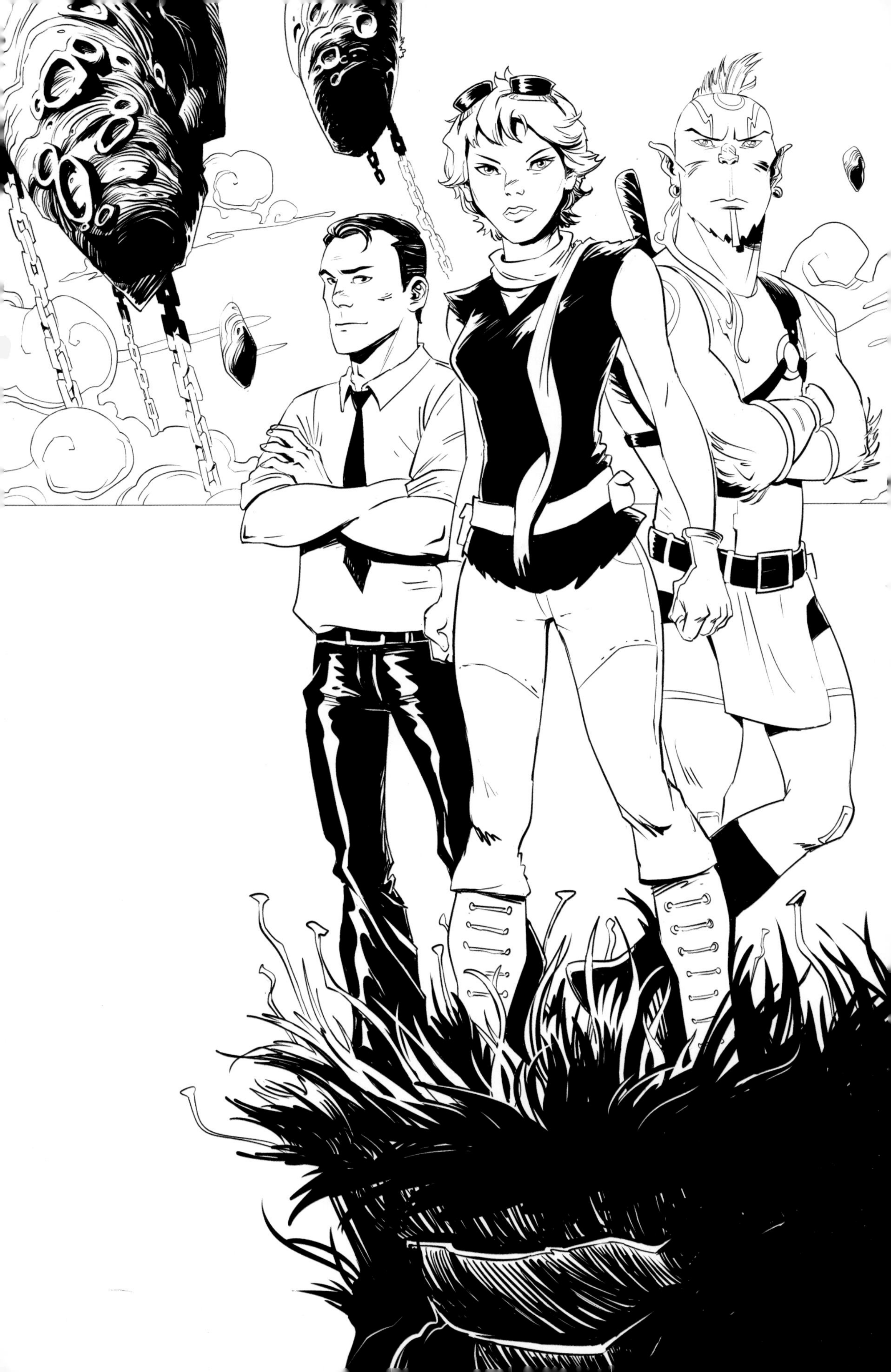

From script to final colors:
Issue 5 page 1

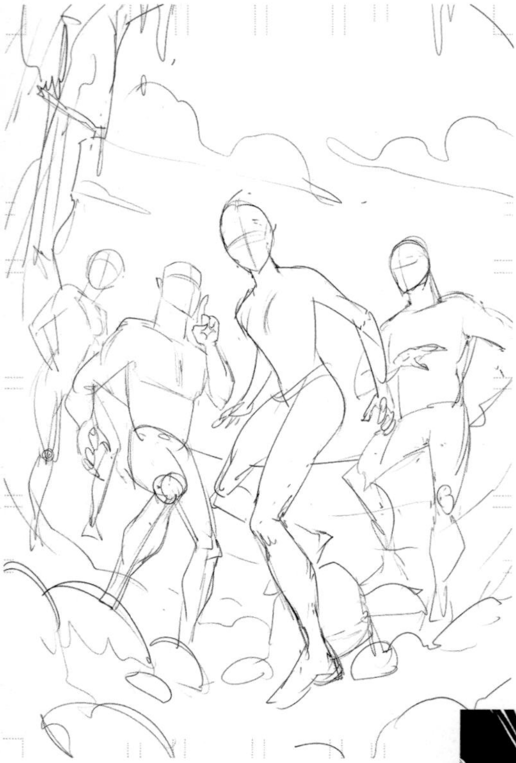

PAGE 1, Splash

We're in a cave, as Amelia, Cort, and three other rebels enter. It's dark. Amelia's leading the way with Cort right behind her. They're all wearing scarves or bandanas around their noses and mouths.

CORT / whisper: Quiet.

CORT / whisper: Don't make a sound.

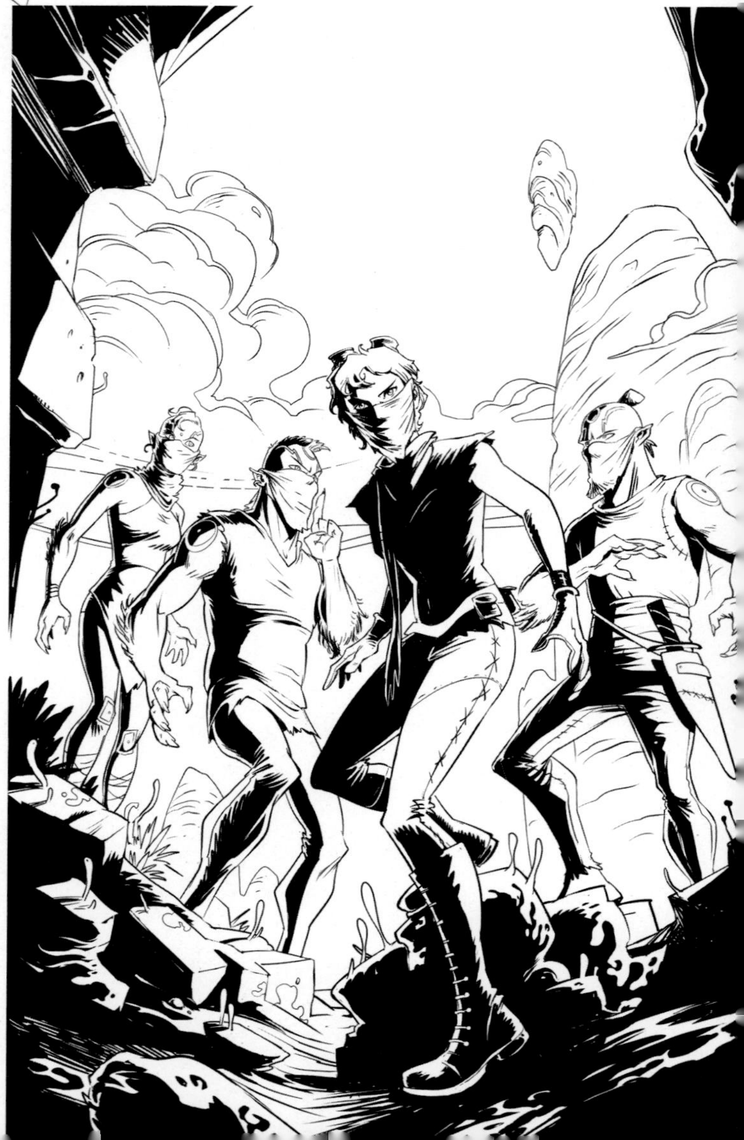

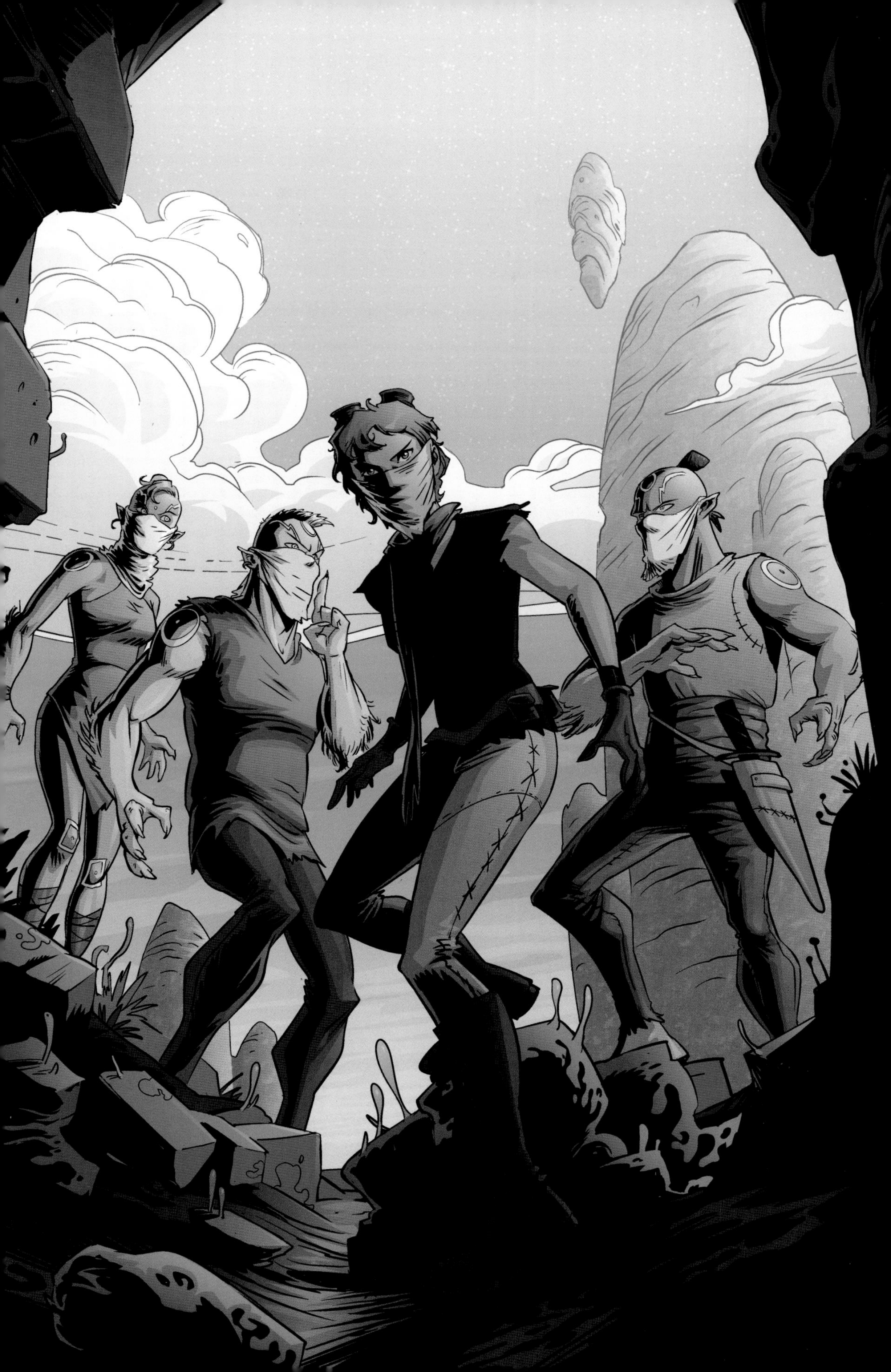

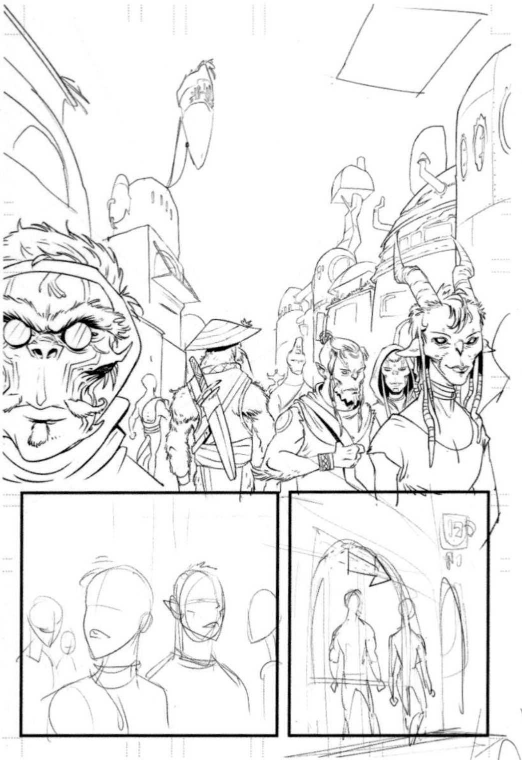

From script to final colors:
Issue 5 page 13

PAGE 13, Panel One

Cut to a daytime establishing shot of a bustling town. It's still within the same aesthetic as we've seen so far, but it features a variety of different races, all with their own customs and appearances. This town is much bigger than the rebel camp. This is in an entirely different region of this world — far outside Lord Kragen's grasp.

NO COPY

PAGE 13, Panel Two

Cort and Amelia walk through the town. Amelia is amazed at all the different sights.

AMELIA: This place is amazing. I had no idea it was here.

CORT: We're far from Lord Kragen's grasp. He has no influence here in TOORBUTU.

AMELIA: If that's the case, why do your people stay where they are? Why not come here?

PAGE 13, Panel Three

Closer in on them, as they walk and talk. They're outside a tavern.

CORT: Because my people were there first. That land belongs to US. Not Lord Kragen.

AMELIA: I understand.
AMELIA: So why are we here, exactly?

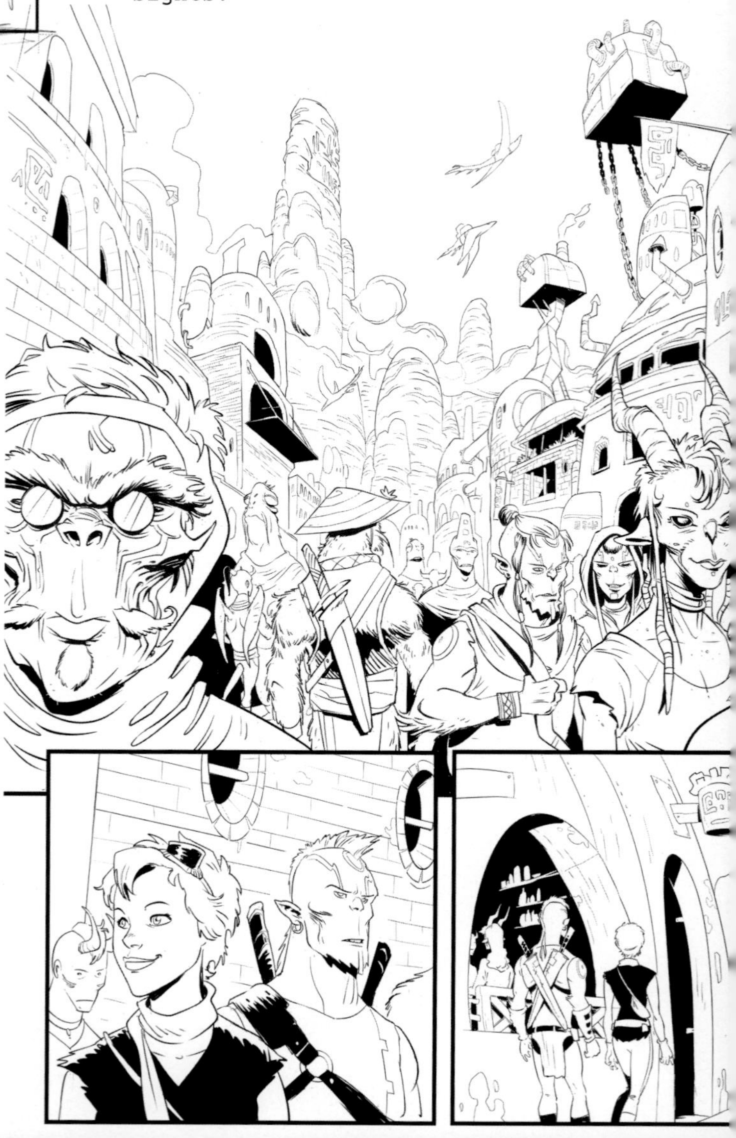

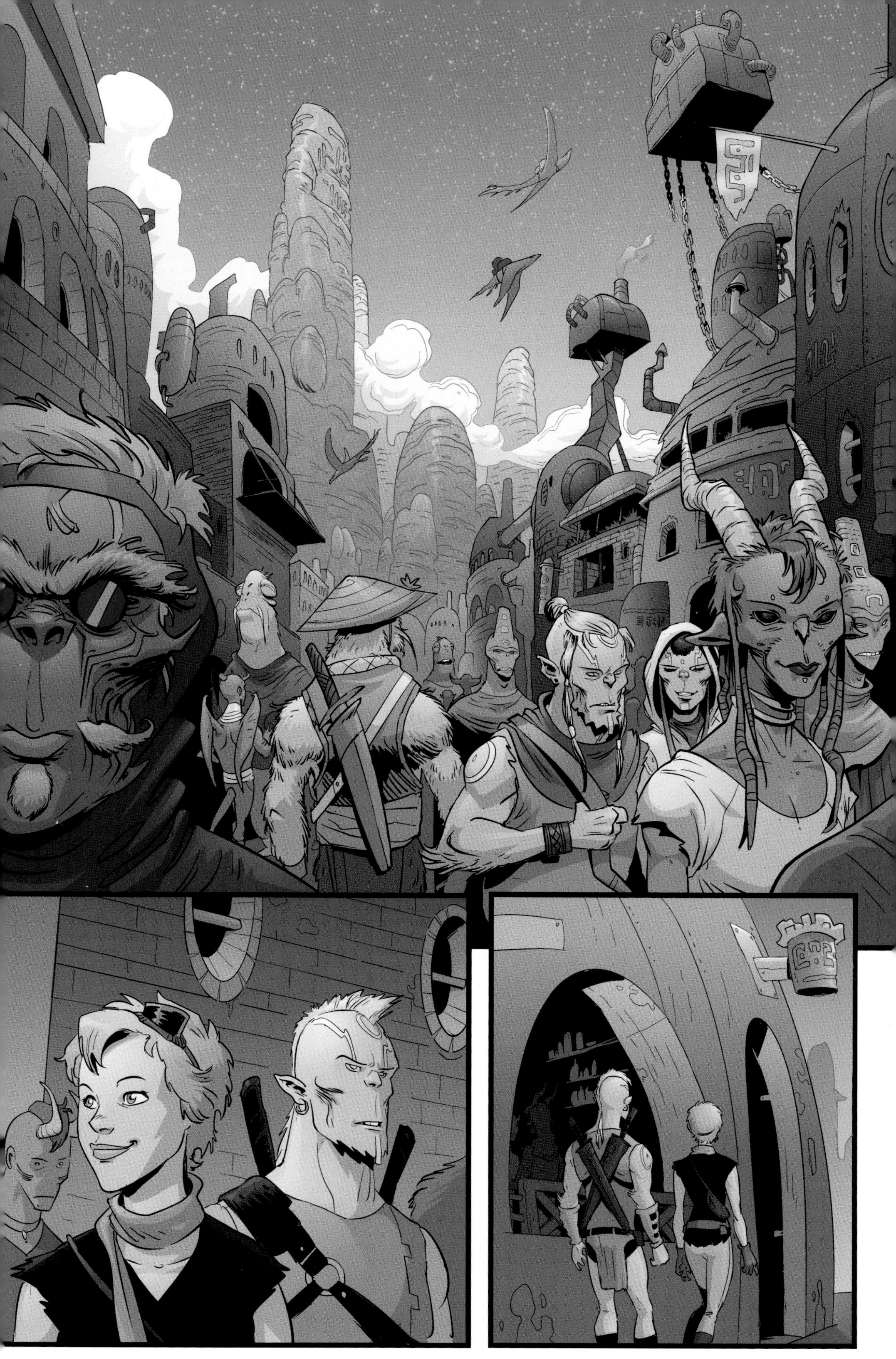

From script to final colors:
Issue 7 page 1

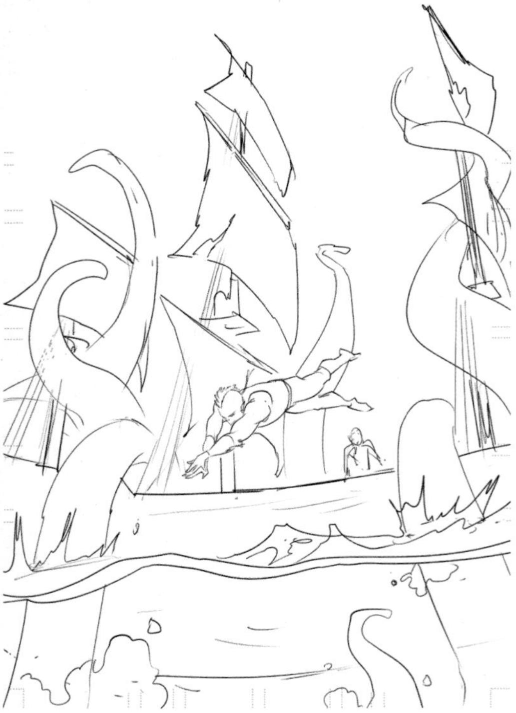

PAGE 1, Splash

Picking up moments after last issue, this is a big, splash page image of Cort, diving off the ship (which is still under attack from the sea creature), his two swords strapped to his back.

CORT / burst: AMELIA!!

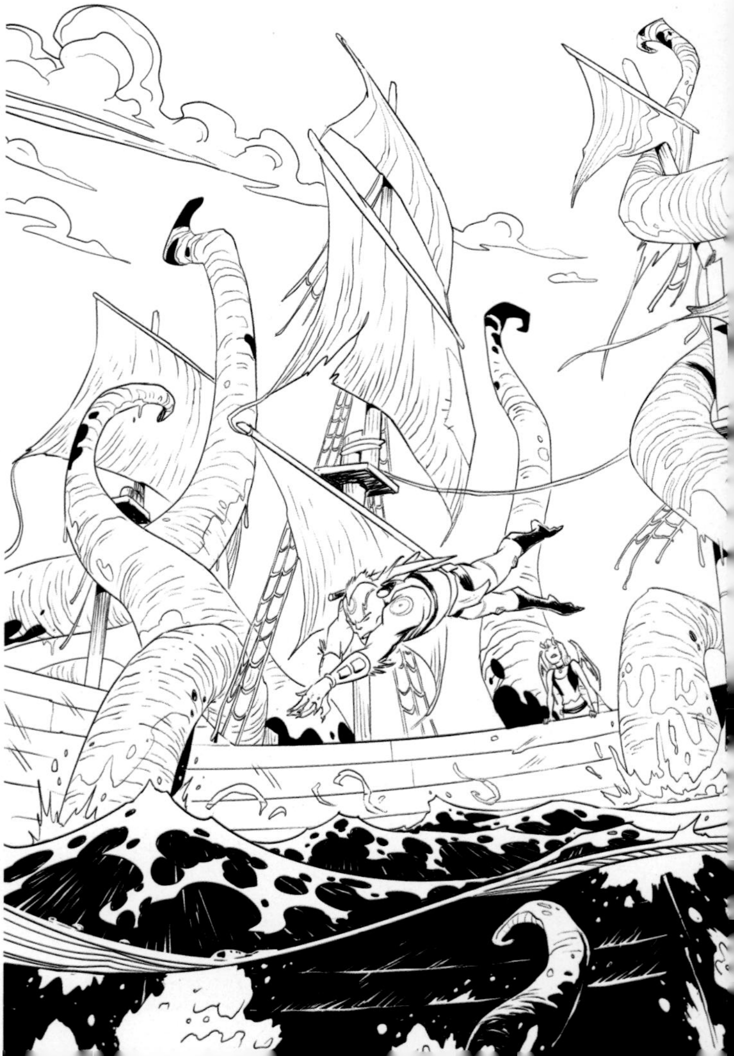

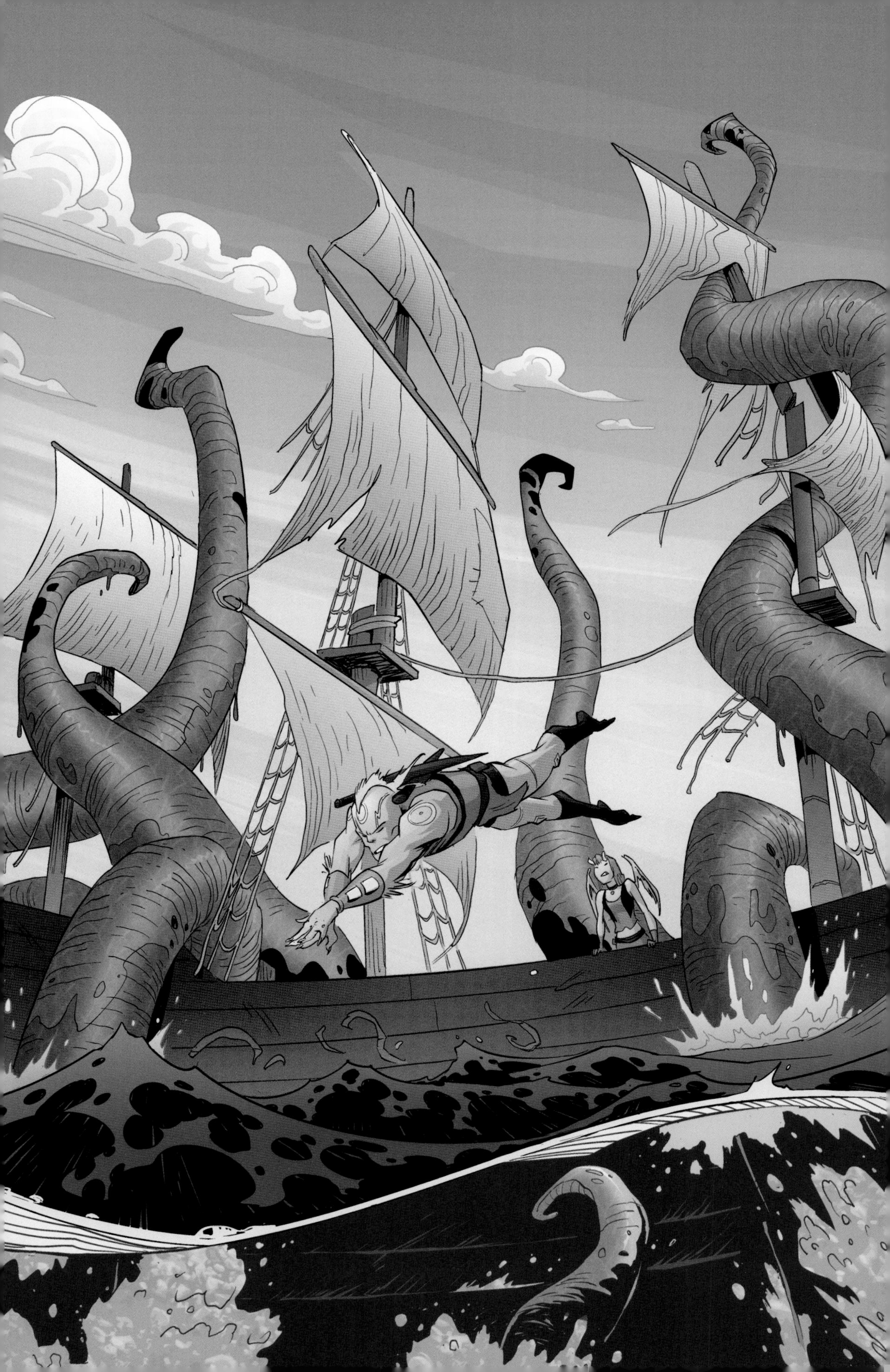

Creature concept sketch by Sumeyye Kesgin

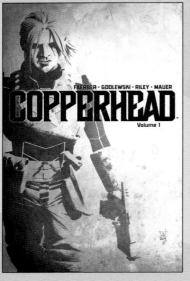
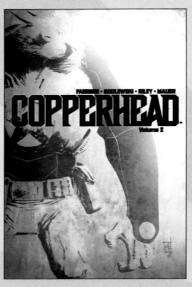
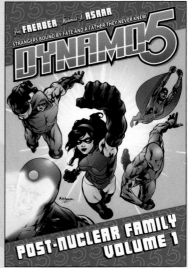
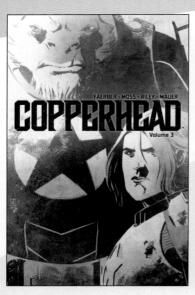
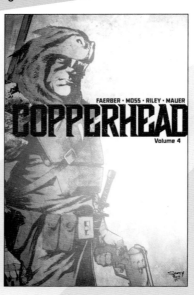

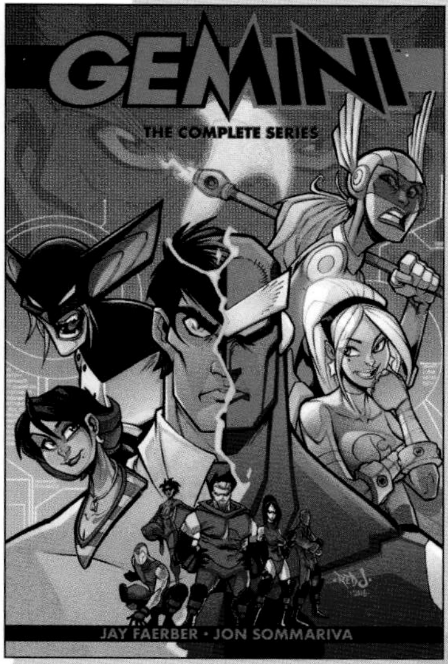
GEMINI
THE COMPLETE SERIES
JAY FAERBER • JON SOMMARIVA

GEMINI: THE COMPLETE SERIES

by Jay Faerber & Jon Sommariva

"I can't come up with a single reason why you shouldn't be getting this book. It's fast, light, and entertaining as hell."

–Comics Bulletin

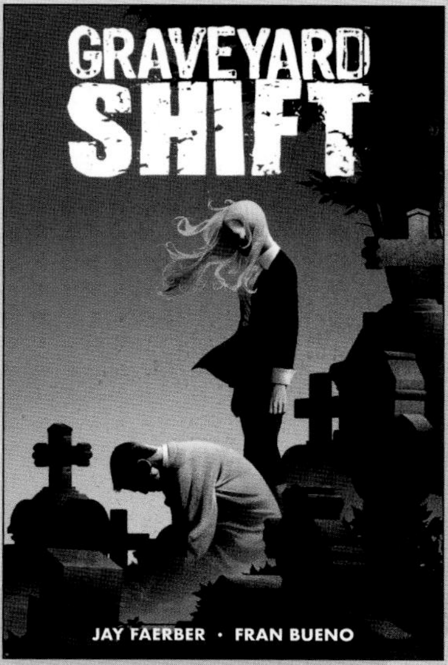
GRAVEYARD SHIFT
JAY FAERBER • FRAN BUENO

GRAVEYARD SHIFT

by Jay Faerber & Fran Bueno

"If you like your vampire crime thrillers with pulse pounding action and fantastic noir-ish art then Graveyard Shift is the title for you."

–Geeks With Wives

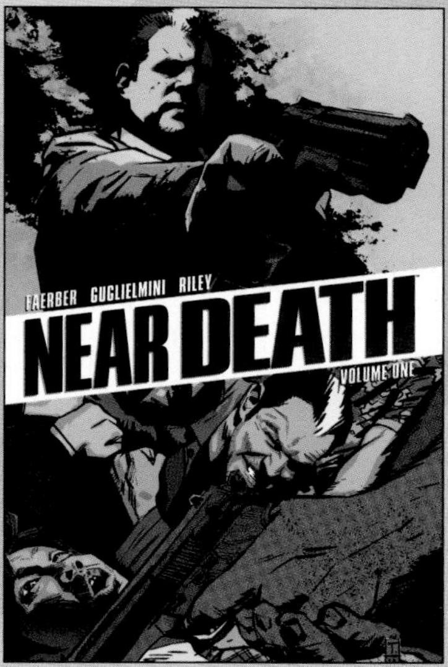
FAERBER GUGLIELMINI RILEY
NEAR DEATH
VOLUME ONE

NEAR DEATH, VOL. 1-2

by Jay Faerber, Simone Guglielmini, & Ron Riley

"A great twist on the hitman genre that I wish I'd thought of."

–Ed Brubaker

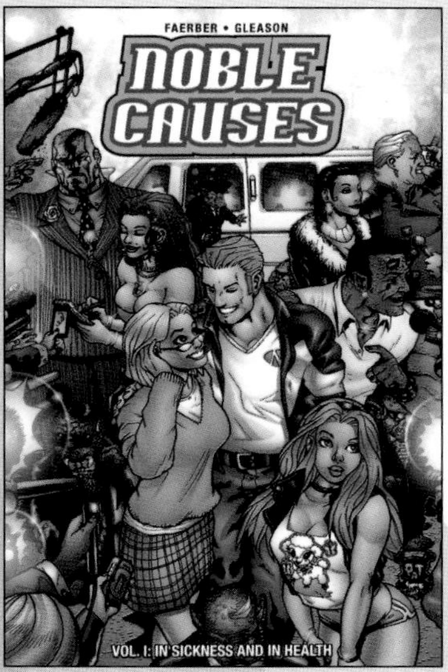
FAERBER • GLEASON
NOBLE CAUSES
VOL. I: IN SICKNESS AND IN HEALTH

NOBLE CAUSES, VOL. 1-10

by Jay Faerber & Patrick Gleason

NOBLE CAUSES: ARCHIVES, VOL. 1-2

by Jay Faerber, et al

"Noble Causes has such a great premise that I actually pay MONEY for it."

–Mark Millar

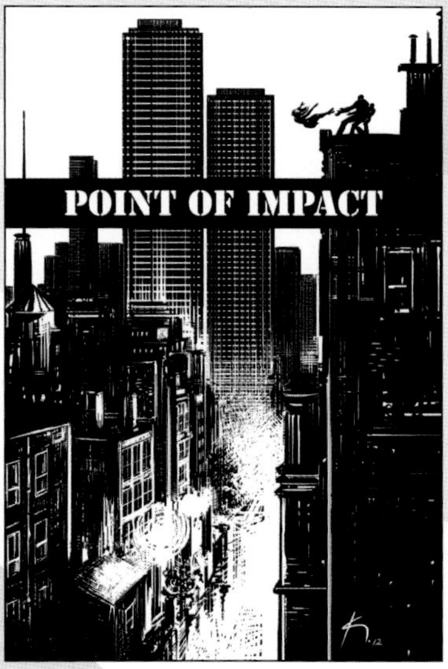
POINT OF IMPACT

POINT OF IMPACT

by Jay Faerber & Koray Kuranel

"Hits the ground running and never loses speed."

–The Onion A.V. Club

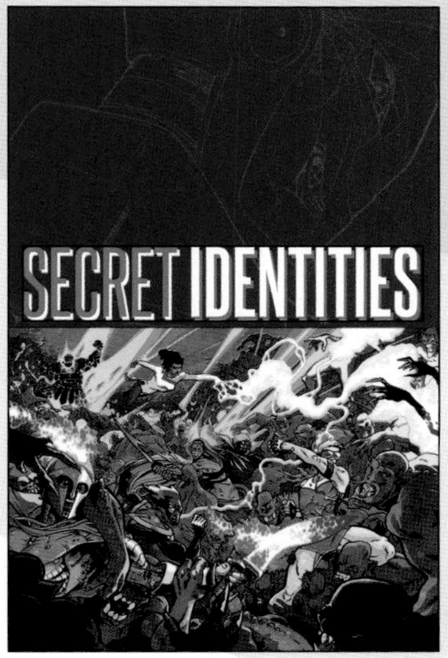
SECRET IDENTITIES

SECRET IDENTITIES, VOL. 1

by Jay Faerber, Brian Joines, Ilias Kyriazis, & Ron Riley

"Secret Identities brings everything a new comic should: action, adventure, intrigue, visually exciting characters and a story that moves. *** ."**

–CBR

ABOUT THE CREATORS

Jay Faerber was born in Harvey's Lake, PA and got his start at Marvel and DC Comics in the late 1990s, where he worked on such series as *The Titans*, *New Warriors*, and *Generation X*. In 2001, he launched NOBLE CAUSES, his first creator-owned series, at Image Comics, which has gone on to garner much critical acclaim. Since then, Faerber has carved out a niche for himself, co-creating DYNAMO 5, NEAR DEATH, POINT OF IMPACT, SECRET IDENTITIES, GRAVEYARD SHIFT, ELSEWHERE, and COPPERHEAD. He also writes for television, most recently on the CBS series ZOO. He lives in Burbank, with his wife, son, dog, and cat. He really loves the Pacific Northwest and 80s television. You can follow him on Twitter @JayFaerber.

Sumeyye Kesgin is a freelance comic artist who lives in the chaotic city of Istanbul. She has worked on Turkey-based comics projects and Top Cow Productions' RISE OF THE MAGI and SEPTEMBER MOURNING. She loves cycling and has an army of stray cats. Her skills do not include writing her own bio. You can find her on Twitter @sumeyyekesgin1 and Instagram @kesgin1.

Ron Riley started off colouring Robert Kirkman's TECH JACKET (which is still kicking butt at Image Comics with an all new creative team), then soon after joined the creative team of Mr. Faerber's then-relaunched NOBLE CAUSES. Ron has been Jay's frequent colouring collaborator ever since, most recently on COPPERHEAD. Ron's also been the colour artist on numerous other titles, like *Rob Zombie's Spookshow International*, BOOM! Studio's *Hero Squared* and *Talent*, among others. Don't follow him on Twitter @thatronriley...unless you're one hip cat.

Thomas Mauer has lent his lettering and design talent to Harvey and Eisner Award nominated and winning titles including Image's POPGUN anthologies and Dark Horse Comics' *The Guns of Shadow Valley*. Among his recent work are Black Mask Studios' 4 KIDS WALK INTO A BANK, BOOM! Studio's *Namesake*, Image Comics' COPPERHEAD, CRUDE, THE BEAUTY, and THE REALM, as well as Devil's Due's *Lark's Killer*, and the World Food Programme's *Living Level-3* series. You can follow him on Twitter @thomasmauer.

Frank Pittarese has been in the comics industry for over 25 years. He's been an editor at DC and Marvel Comics, where he worked on such titles as *Superboy* and *Generation X* (written at the time by Jay Faerber himself), and was also an editor and writer at *Nickelodeon Magazine*, overseeing the adventures of *SpongeBob SquarePants*. He's currently developing new projects for Inner Station, a soon-to-launch comic book publisher. Frank lives in Brooklyn, NY, with his husband and the latest in an ongoing series of hamsters.

5